WINDS OF TIME

WINDS OF TIME

•

Mary A. Benton

AVALON BOOKS
NEW YORK

Published by Avalon Books,
an imprint of Thomas Bouregy & Co., Inc.
160 Madison Avenue, New York, NY 10016

Library of Congress Cataloging-in-Publication Data

Benton, Mary A., 1938–
    Winds of time / Mary A. Benton.
        p. cm.
    ISBN 978-0-8034-7720-9
    1. Veterans—Fiction.   2. Women ranchers—Fiction.
3. Texas—History—1846–1950—Fiction.   I. Title.
    PS3602.E6975W56 2011
    813'.6—dc22   2010031116

PRINTED IN THE UNITED STATES OF AMERICA
ON ACID-FREE PAPER
BY HADDON CRAFTSMEN, BLOOMSBURG, PENNSYLVANIA

For my family—
thank you for all your support and for being
there in the "crunch" times.

Acknowledgments

Thanks go to the Visalia Writers Critique Group and The Exeter Writers Group for their patience, help, and encouragement. Their support and friendship is what keeps me writing.

Chapter One

The only emotion Jed McCabe felt as he tossed the last rock on his brother's grave was anger. He looked at the blood-smeared boulder where Johnny's head struck when his horse fell, then shifted his gaze to the rolling mid-Texas plains. Bile seared his gut. He grabbed the reins of his brother's light-colored sorrel and then mounted his own horse. His sister, Kate, was out there, and he would find her.

Rays of sunlight pressed down on Jed's shoulders. A slip of a shadow skittered across the sand in front of him. He glanced upward into the early spring sky and saw the circling source of the shadow. Settling the brim of his hat against the wind, his heels bit sharply against the belly of the large black stallion. The horse grunted, tossed his head, and moved forward with a strong gait. Jed never looked back, wishing only to put distance between him and the brother who would rather dance, whistle, and gamble than settle down with a good woman.

He pushed the horses hard for the rest of the day, alternating between riding his horse, Big Blue, and his brother's, Little Jesse. Both horses, Thoroughbreds, were gifts from their mother. It was her belief that the powerful horses would help ensure her sons' safe return from the civil strife that was tearing the nation apart. The horses had proved their worth but did nothing to safeguard their family at home.

Grit and sand, whipped up by the wind, pelted his face and hands. He pulled on worn, leather gloves and wrapped a bandanna over his face. The horses lay their ears back and turned their heads away from the flying silt.

As nightfall approached, Jed saw a scattered stand of cottonwoods several miles off the trail. He urged the horses in that direction. The cottonwoods grew at the edge of a wash, where a small pool of water seeped against the far side of the otherwise dry gully. The trees sheltered enough buffalo grass to satisfy the horses' hunger and, after watering them, he tethered them under the sparse foliage. After gathering an armful of dried roots and branches, Jed built a small fire in the bottom of the shallow wash and settled down to a meal of boiled coffee and jerked venison.

The fire's warmth radiated against his face and warmed the fabric of his trousers. The flames licked at the darkness, sending smoke and sparks floating upward. Jed watched as the embers disappeared into the night air. His thoughts flashed to the war and then turned to the dangers of a fire after nightfall. He stood and quickly banked sand against the lively fire, cutting back the blaze and drifting sparks. He sat back against his saddle, cradling a cup of coffee in one hand. The war was past, and this wasn't Tennessee.

He concentrated on the dying embers that were turning into blackened charcoal. The anger threatened to turn to grief as he thought of Johnny and what had brought them to this unforgiving land.

It had been warm the morning he and Johnny left with the 19th Tennessee Cavalry. The crops had been laid by, and Mother assured them that the harvesting would be taken care of with the help of their neighbor, Phillip Ramsey. Eleven-year-old Kate was crying, and Johnny wanted her to laugh. He picked her up and whirled her in the air, singing and doing a two-step jig. Kate's tears soon turned into laughter, and Jed remembered that even his own wife, Matilda, had wiped her tears and smiled.

Jed shook his head, trying to fling the painful memories from his mind. In the five years he and his brother were away, his family and his home were destroyed. When they returned, once-friendly neighbors turned hardened faces to them and accused him and Johnny of being traitors. In brittle words they told them their mother was dead and that Kate had gone with the Ramsey family to Texas.

He stood, his jaw clenched, and tossed the remainder of the coffee into the fire. Kate held the answers to the questions that plagued him, and he was anxious to keep riding. Sleep was never a welcome respite, only an inconvenience. But the horses needed the rest, and he wouldn't abuse them.

Jed circled the fire, kicking dirt and sand over the remaining coals. A tightening sensation in his chest sent him to his knees. He rocked forward, his face grating against the sand. He thought of the whiskey Johnny had bought in Fort Smith. It had helped relieve the pain.

He pushed himself up and retrieved the bottle from Johnny's saddlebag. The fiery liquid coursed down his throat, sending warmth through his body. He returned to the smoldering fire and settled back against the saddle. After another swallow, he felt the tension in his chest ease.

Morning sunlight covered the tops of the gently rolling hills, eating at the dark shadows still lurking in the deep washes and arroyos. Jed fought through a haze of memories as he struggled to place his surroundings. He thought he heard voices, but couldn't make out the words. Someone laughed, and then came the words, "Hey, señor. You sleep like the dead."

Jed forced himself to lie still. Mentally he tried to focus on the location of his gun. Was it still in his holster, or had he shoved it under his saddle? He eased his hand toward his holster and felt a sharp pain against his forearm. He opened his eyes and saw a scuffed, worn boot bearing down on his arm. Slowly he turned his head and looked into the muzzle of a Colt Dragoon.

A swarthy face and a large mustache backed up the engraved, silver-plated revolver. "The gringo is alive. Shall we rejoice?"

The face laughed, and Jed heard the laughter echo around him. Several men on horseback lined the edge of the wash, their faces steeped in dark shadows under their wide sombreros.

The man whose boot was pinning Jed's arm removed his foot and motioned with his pistol for Jed to stand.

Rubbing his arm, Jed moved to a standing position.

"Do you travel alone, señor?"

Jed kept his expression stony, refusing to answer.

The bandit laughed. "The gringo has lost his voice." The man stooped and raked Jed's Colt Navy from under his saddle and, after examining it, tossed it to one of the men on horseback. He picked up the half-empty whiskey bottle and held it up to the other men. "The *Americano* has a weakness. No?"

A frown creased Jed's brow. *Not a weakness*, he thought. *A mistake that might cost me my life.*

Two riders dismounted and began saddling Jed's horses.

Jed gritted his teeth and took a step toward them. The man holding the gun slammed the barrel against the side of Jed's head. Jed staggered back, dropping to the ground as his legs buckled under him.

"Don't be a fool, hombre. Next time, I will pull the trigger."

The man continued to kick through Jed's belongings, picking up and emptying his and Johnny's saddlebags. Johnny's gun fell from his saddlebag, and one of the men picked it up and stuck it into his waistband.

"Your pockets, señor. Turn them out."

Jed hesitated. Danged if he would hand everything over— the cussed thief could take it off his dead carcass. Then Jed reconsidered. He slowly stood and emptied his pockets of coins, tobacco, and his daddy's watch. He held the watch for a moment before dropping it into the sand. Johnny was sixteen when their father died. Since that time, Johnny had proudly carried the watch with him. Yesterday Jed had taken it as a remembrance, not only of his father, but also of Johnny.

Jed felt a trickle of blood work its way down the side of his face, then saw the drops as they fell into the sand next to where the watch lay.

The outlaw scooped up the watch and pocketed it. The

other two riders gathered the reins of Jed's horses and then mounted their own.

Jed's mind raced. If he were going to make a move, he would have to do it now. He tensed his muscles as he prepared to rush the bandit who was still on the ground.

The man who had claimed his gun spoke to the man who had pistol-whipped him.

"Do we kill the gringo now, Sanchez, or let the buzzards have fresh meat?"

Sanchez squinted into the distance and then back at Jed's bloodied head. A smile broke over his face. "The hombre's no threat to us. He is without a weapon, and by the looks of him, the buzzards won't have long to wait for their dinner."

Jed's mind teetered between taking action and waiting.

One of the thieves pulled his pistol from its holster and aimed it at the canteens that lay in the sand. The pistol bucked as he shot into the remnants of Jed and Johnny's war years. Laughing, the man fired several more times, sending the canteens skipping across the bottom of the wash.

The bandit called Sanchez mounted and then joined with the men as they hooted and spurred their horses away in a swirl of dust, Jed's prized Thoroughbreds in tow.

Jed wiped the blood from his chin and exhaled. He wondered what his chances would have been if he had rushed the desperado.

Cursing silently, Jed sifted through the sandy wash as he collected the few belongings that had been left. His hand brushed across something heavy. Uncovering it, Jed saw that it was his bowie knife. He glanced down to where it had been sheathed at his hip. The edge of the scabbard flapped open, the stitching torn loose. It must have fallen out during the night. He picked it up and wiped it clean. "Now the hombre has a weapon," he muttered.

Jed repacked his worn saddlebag and then closed his eyes as a wave of dizziness washed over him. Lowering himself to the ground, he waited a moment before pulling off his left boot. Running his fingers under the innersole, he lifted it, exposing a layer of bills. Not Confederate currency, but Union bills. Money Johnny had won playing poker with overconfident riverboat captains along the Mississippi.

He pulled the money out and removed several bills before replacing the rest. With slow, careful steps, he moved to the small seepage of water at the edge of the wash. Kneeling, he cupped the water in his hands and drank until he was satisfied, and then drank some more.

Jed threw the worn saddlebag over his shoulder and shifted his gaze to the gently rolling landscape. He didn't like what he saw. The hills stretched before him, sunbaked and dotted with clumps of grayish-green vegetation. The land had swallowed Kate and taken Johnny, and now his horses and guns were gone. Kate had traveled over this hostile land, and he would find her—and the outlaw was wrong. He was a threat to them. But in which order he would proceed, he wasn't sure.

A soft breeze riffled the sleeve of his jacket, reminding him that he was alone in this unfamiliar land. His chest tightened as gusts of wind picked up grit and flung it against his pant legs. He ducked his head and pulled his sweat-stained hat low across his eyes. The well-traveled wagon trail he and Johnny had been following was the stage route. He reasoned that a stage or freight wagon should happen along at some point in time.

Scattered clumps of mesquite dotted the landscape. Prickly pear and sparse tufts of bluestem grew next to the protective outcroppings of shale and rocks. Loose silt blew in curling rivulets across the ground, swirling around the rocks and vegetation. His thoughts drifted to his home in Tennessee, and then to the sickening reality that it was no longer his home. His home and family, ripped from him by circumstances and powers beyond his control. His shoulders tightened as the memories and pain of loss tore at him once more.

As the afternoon wore on, the sound of his boots grating on the coarse sand became a cadence to which he instinctively marched. The smells and images of the farm in Tennessee crept back into his thoughts. The odor of the soil, dank and soft with its black richness as it rolled from the plowshares, lay steeped in his memories. The mental image of Matilda floated in front of him, her hair blowing free as she brought him his midday meal, and the cool shade of a hickory tree where they sat and ate heartily of the freshly baked bread and smoked sausages.

The feel of Matilda's hand in his was as real as if she were walking beside him, her light brown hair spilling across her shoulders and her dark eyes dancing with merriment. Shortly after leaving, he received a letter from her saying she was with child. He ached to return to her, but as the battles raged through mosquito-infested swamps and blood-soaked fields, he became unsure which way was home. Then the letter came from his mother stating that Matilda had died in childbirth. The urgent need to return home was gone, his grief buried along with the countless bodies in hurried, shallow graves. The fact that neither he nor Johnny received any more letters from their mother was lost in the horrors and duties of war.

Jed's boot caught the edge of a rock and he stumbled, breaking the haze of memories. The sun was dipping westward, and he thought he heard a rumbling noise. He straightened and turned his gaze eastward. In the distance, a tower of dust roiled upward. He wondered if it was a wagon or one of the dust devils that skipped ghostlike across the shimmering horizon. He waited, straining his eyes at the swirling, dark cloud. The deep, pounding sound drew nearer, and he could make out a team and wagon. The driver shouted at the team and pulled them to a stop. Dust drifted upward, dispersing in the hot winds and revealing two more teams and freight wagons.

A man with an unkempt beard stared at him from the driver's box of the first wagon. The other two wagons pulled up behind the first, the mules stomping their hooves and swinging their heads in a jangle of harnesses.

The driver looked at Jed, wariness evident in his eyes. "Lose yer horse?" he asked.

"You might say that," Jed answered. "Got any water a fellow could borrow?"

The man unfastened a canteen from the wagon and tossed it down.

Jed caught it and drank deeply. As he handed the canteen back, he asked, "Mind if I hitch a ride with you?"

The man nodded to the far side of the wagon seat. "Climb up and light," he invited.

After Jed had seated himself, the man flipped the reins and sent the team forward. "I'm guessing yer horse went down on you, or you met up with Sanchez's bunch," he said, turning to Jed.

Jed leaned forward, resting both elbows on his knees. "I reckon it was the Sanchez bunch. At least that's what one was called."

"Danged outlaws, the whole lot of 'em," the man mumbled.

"How far are we to the next town?" Jed asked.

"That'd be Mission Bridge," the man answered, spitting a stream of tobacco juice to the side.

"Is there a sheriff there?"

The muleskinner let out a loud guffaw. "Ain't no lawman there. Whatever you lost is gone. Won't do you any good to worry 'bout it none. Got yer hide, so be thankful." The man looked at Jed with sunfaded eyes. "Name's Griffin," he said. "Those two eatin' our dust are McLeath and Rowden. We been haulin' freight through this territory fer nigh on five years. Only had one run-in with Sanchez. Me and him come to an un-nurstandin' right quicklike. He got away with two crates of my finest whiskey, and I reduced his pack of thieves by five. He ain't bothered me none since."

Griffin lifted his hat and scratched at his thick, matted hair. "Mighty dangerous fer a lone rider out in these here parts." He glanced at Jed. "You didn't lose any of yer people to Sanchez, didjuh?"

Jed shook his head. "I buried my brother two days ago. The edge of a wash gave way under his horse, and he hit his head on a rock when he tried to throw himself clear."

"Heck of a way to go," Griffin mumbled, shaking his head.

Jed turned and stared at the dry, rolling plains. Going quick, he thought, was better than going slow from maggot-infested wounds.

"So, what brought you and yer brother to this backside of Hades? I know it cain't be the scenery."

Jed cleared his throat and introduced himself. "We were looking for my younger sister, Kate. She left our farm in Tennessee with a family by the name of Ramsey. She's the only living kin we have left. We traced them as far as Fort Smith. A fellow there remembered them passing through. Remembered Kate in particular on account of her eyes."

Jed rested his back against the freight boxes and rubbed the back of his neck. "Her eyes are green with golden specks. They're almond shaped and sometimes, in the right light, her eyes can turn color and flash like sunlight off a frozen pond. Unnerves most folks."

"Huh," Griffin grunted. "Now I'm not sayin' I seen yer sister, mind you. But I did hear tell of a family passin' through this area with a group of homesteaders. Folks said they had a young gal with them who had eyes like a cat."

Jed leaned forward and looked at Griffin. "When was that?"

"Best I kin remember, was 'bout three years ago."

"Do you know where she was seen?"

"Right here in Mission Bridge." Griffin hawked and spit a wad of tobacco into the sage brush. "Yer right 'bout her eyes. I have a sweet señora waiting for me in Mission Bridge. She tolt me of her. Even crossed herself whilst tellin' it."

"Did she say if she heard where they might have been going?"

"Nah. Didn't ask. Had other things on my mind at the time."

It was well after dark before they reached the small settlement. Music and laughter floated from the lone cantina in the square. Climbing from the wagon, Jed thanked Griffin for his help and walked stiffly toward the soft glow of light spilling out from the noisy establishment.

The door to the cantina stood open, and he approached it cautiously. He watched for a moment as a stout Mexican woman dressed in brightly colored clothing danced with a young, skinny cowboy. In one corner a piano tinkled, played by a thin man with a drooping mustache.

A number of men were leaning against a low bar. A heavily mustached Anglo stood behind the bar, splashing whiskey into glasses. A couple of the men turned to look at Jed as he stepped into the dimly lit and smoke-filled room, then turned their attention back to the dancers, calling out encouragement to the young wrangler.

Jed dropped his saddlebag next to the bar and spoke to the Anglo. "Have anything to eat?" he asked.

"Be one dollar," the man grunted, not moving a muscle.

Jed took a bill from his pocket and laid it on the counter. "I'll also need a place to sleep."

The man chewed on his bottom lip for a moment. "Don't see many Union bills in this part of the country," he said, his gaze taking in Jed's rough appearance. "Traveling through?"

"Maybe," Jed answered.

The man hesitated for a moment and then turned and disappeared into a dark doorway behind the bar. Moments later he returned with a bowl filled with steaming beans, a stack of tortillas balanced on top.

"Shed out back has straw to bed down on," he said, shoving the bowl in front of Jed. "Whoever gets to them first, it's theirs. Need anything to wash that down with?"

Jed shook his head. He didn't plan on repeating that mistake. He picked up a spoon and his saddlebag and selected a table near the wall, where he could observe the men at the bar and the open door. Sitting, he dipped the utensil into the dark liquid, the spicy aroma making his eyes water.

Two of the men who had been watching the dancers shuffled out of the establishment. Jed glanced at them as they filed by. Something about them looked familiar . . . the sombreros. But most of the men in the saloon wore sombreros. What was it about those particular men? Jed studied on it as he spooned the beans into his mouth. The spoon froze in midair as the image of the first fellow who had walked out registered—his size, the heavy mustache and worn boots, but most of all, the Colt Dragoon swinging low on his hip. Jed braced himself against the back of his chair.

"That was Sanchez," he muttered. He rose out of his chair, his hand sliding to his knife. Had they recognized him? More than likely they had and would be waiting for him outside. To chance taking down two armed men with only a knife was foolish. He would bide his time.

From outside the open doorway, the sound of quiet laughter floated in. A horse snorted and the rattle of bridles echoed inside the cantina. Hooves thudded against the ground as the unseen horses cantered away into the night.

The shed offered as sleeping quarters doubled as the roosting place for several dozen chickens and two guinea hens. Piles of straw were heaped on the earthen floor. Across one corner, poles for the roosting fowl were embedded into the adobe walls. Jed's late entrance set the flock to quarreling among themselves as they shifted their positions along the roost.

Making clucking noises with his tongue, Jed tried to quiet the disgruntled hens. *If Sanchez wants to pay a late-night visit,* Jed thought, *those nervous guineas might save my hide.*

He placed the lantern the proprietor had loaned him on the dirt floor and turned the wick low. Kicking some of the dusty straw against the wall near the door, he settled in. The odor of chicken droppings stung his nostrils and brought back memories of places where he had slept during the war.

The skinny cowboy from the cantina stumbled in. The chickens again shifted, emitting deep stuttering noises. Jed heard a startled squawk as one was pushed from its roost.

The young man weaved his way to a pile of straw and sprawled on it. Moments later, the soft puffing sounds of deep slumber filled the shed. It was a comforting sound, and despite Jed's wariness, he drifted into a light sleep.

Chapter Two

The shrill crowing of a red- and gold-colored rooster woke Jed. He jerked upright, his hand searching for his gun. Early dawn had crept into the shed, pushing the murky shadows into the far corners. It took a moment for Jed to digest the fact that he didn't have a gun. He coughed and rubbed his eyes with the heels of his hands, wincing when the pain in his head brought back more memories.

A buzzing noise coming from the pile of straw where the cowboy slept erupted into a snort. The young man mumbled incoherently and lifted a tousled head from the mound of hay.

"Morning," Jed offered.

The cowboy stared at him with sleep-glazed eyes. Dingy blond hair fell across his forehead, and the early light caught the golden promise of facial hair. He nodded, worked his tongue against the roof of his mouth several times, and then uttered something resembling "Morning."

Jed glanced away. The boy reminded him too much of the way Johnny awoke in the mornings—hungover and not the least bit sorry about it.

The young wrangler struggled to his feet, shook himself like a loose-skinned pup, and then tucked in his shirttail.

"Ida Mae is going to skin my hide and hang it out for the buzzards if I don't get my sorry behind on the trail." His voice was soft, almost as though he were talking to himself.

Jed figured that the boy's sister or sister-in-law must be a real starched bonnet.

Gingerly, Jed touched the side of his head. It felt scabbed

over. That was good. His mouth was dry, and he allowed that not only would a drink of water help, but also a place to wash up. He stood and brushed the dust and straw from his clothing and reflected on what his next move should be. He had long ago accepted the reality that his life would never be the same without Matilda. Now he would have to do the same with Johnny. It would be hard without Johnny, but there was still Kate. He would find her and find out the details of Matilda's and his mother's death.

With the money tucked in his boot he could purchase what he needed, but that would eat into the savings—savings he and Johnny had agreed would be used to buy new land and make a home for Kate. A young girl needed a proper home.

Jed thought about the bandit, Sanchez. His bunch had been in the cantina last night, which meant they felt comfortable there. It was a good bet that they had a place within a day's ride. He needed somewhere to stay until the time was right to take back what was his. Jed turned his attention to the young man.

"Do you work on a ranch nearby?" he asked.

"Yeah," the boy grunted.

"Could they use another hand?"

The young man glanced at him. "You right sure you know whose outfit you're asking to join up with?"

"Can't say as I do, but work is work. What kind of an outfit is it?"

"A cattle ranch, the Bar-DI. I'm sure Ida Mae could use more help, but you'll have to wait for your pay. Beans and a bed are about all she's offering right now."

"Sounds like beans and a bed are a fair offer. Maybe I'll ride out with you, and see if she'll take me on."

"You right sure?" The boy seemed puzzled that Jed would be willing to work without the promise of pay.

"Yep," Jed replied. "At the moment, though, I'm shy a couple of horses. Would they have an extra mount a man might use?"

The boy grinned. "Oh, we've got that all right. You best be a good rider, though. Some of those nags she calls horses can be mighty temperamental."

Jed stretched, twisting at the tightness in his shoulders. He had never considered himself a cowboy, but he was no stranger to horses. "Can't say I'm not that way myself at times." He grinned at the boy and settled his hat on his head.

"You can ride out with me," the boy said. "Ida Mae sent me to town for supplies and feed. I have a wagon over at the livery. Just need to load the stuff I bought yesterday. By the way, my name's Kyle. Kyle Landry."

Jed met the young man's outstretched hand with a firm grip. "Jed McCabe," he offered.

"We can get some coffee from the cantina before we leave," Kyle said. "It'll take a while to get out to the ranch."

Jed paid for his and the young man's breakfast. The smoked sausage, scrambled eggs, and spicy red beans were a welcome treat. It had been a long while since he'd allowed himself anything but boiled coffee, jerky, and hardtack. The meal lifted his spirits, and he thought that maybe he shouldn't keep denying himself. A body's future was never a sure thing.

After they finished, Jed helped Kyle load the feed and supplies into the buckboard. Within the hour, they were headed out of town.

The trail they took followed a meandering river that wound through low rolling hills. Scrub oak, willows, and cottonwoods lined the banks, and small wildlife darted in and out of its tangled growth. Kyle remained quiet, seemingly lost in his own thoughts. Jed was grateful. He wasn't one for polite talk, but after several hours of staring at the passing scenery, curiosity got the better of him.

"Does the outfit you work for lay along this river?" he asked.

"Somewhat," Kyle answered. "The ranch's headquarters are about a mile away from it. Can't build too close. When it rains, the river floods."

"You called your boss Ida Mae. Are you kin?"

"No. That's what she told me to call her. Her rightful name

is Ida Mae Greeley, but everyone hereabouts calls her Ida Mae."

Kyle turned to Jed with a serious expression. "Don't go expecting some old lady who's gonna pat you on your head and tell you what a nice fellow you are. Ida Mae can be ornery. She works hard and expects everyone around her to work hard. You slack off any, she won't hold back any from rowing you up salt river."

Kyle was quiet a moment, his gaze straying across the distant hills. "I reckon that's why she's always short on help," he continued in a reflective mood. "Most men won't stand for a woman to boss 'em around, much less call 'em names. The smart ones leave. The dumb ones stay, and the really stupid ones think they're gonna marry her. I guess I fall in with the dumb ones."

Jed surmised that the woman who ran the ranch was ill-tempered and wondered what circumstances brought the boy to the ranch.

"This Ida Mae, is she a spinster or a widow?"

"A widow. Her husband was killed. She doesn't like to talk about it, so I don't ask."

As they came over a low knoll, Jed saw several buildings nestled among some scrub oaks. An adobe ranch house lay against the base of a small rise. Cattle grazed on the hills above it. A low-beamed barn and several outbuildings were built below it toward the river. Corrals connected to the barn held six or seven horses. At the sight of the wagon, the horses tossed their heads and whistled, stirring up dust as they milled about in the enclosure.

"I reckon you can see for yourself if you want to stay," Kyle said. "I see Ida Mae out by the barn."

Jed took a deep breath. He had dealt with strong-willed women before, his mother being one. He envisioned a woman like her—firm, but fair. After his father's death, his mother took over the business portion of the farm. He and Johnny had taken care of the fields, working long hours to keep up with the tilling and planting. Here would be no different.

Kyle guided the team next to the hitching rail that fronted the walled garden surrounding the long adobe ranch house. The tiled roofline of the main building extended beyond the outer walls of the structure, creating covered verandas around its perimeter. Jed could see a neatly tended vegetable garden nestled to one side of the home. A scarred and heavily timbered gate guarded the portal to this unlikely oasis. A red rose bush bloomed at one corner of the gate and offered visitors a welcoming scent.

The figure standing by the corrals walked toward them. Jed found himself staring. Ida Mae didn't appear to be like any woman he had ever met before. He guessed her age to be close to his. Tall and slender, she wore a pair of men's trousers and a man's work shirt. Auburn hair was pulled back into a single thick braid. A soft, broad-brimmed hat rode low on her forehead. A pistol was strapped around her waist. She held a coiled lariat in one hand, and as she walked, she tapped it gently against her leg.

When she drew nearer, Jed saw a woman who carried pride like some men carry walking sticks and gold watches. Burnished freckles covered her high cheekbones, and her full lips were compressed into a tight line.

"Who have you brought back with you this time, Kyle?" A frown creased her forehead and her voice was low, almost throaty.

Jed felt the hair on his arms prickle. Something about the woman unnerved him. He suddenly pictured himself walking back to town.

"This here is Jed McCabe," Kyle said. "He's looking for a job. Seeing as how you sent the last rowdy packing, I thought you might be able to use another hand."

"If he's not any better than the last piece of cow pie you brought in, then I won't need him either."

Jed's eyebrows rose slightly. Already the woman was getting on his bad side. "Excuse me, ma'am," he cut in sharply as he swung down from the wagon. He turned to face her, his hand instinctively sweeping his sweat-stained hat from his head. "I came here because your man said you could use some help. If you don't, I understand and I can head back to town. But I'm not a piece of cow pie, and to my recollection, never was."

The woman's hazel-colored eyes narrowed as she studied him. "Fair enough," she responded slowly. "I suppose I can give you a chance to show your grit." She lifted the coil of rope in her hand and gestured toward the wagon.

"I see you don't have a horse tied to the back of the wagon. Are you afoot?"

"My horses were stolen."

"Is that why you're here, thinking you can pick up a free mount?"

Jed's scowl deepened. "No, ma'am. I need work and a place to stay. If you can spare me some time away from my job, I plan on retrieving my horses and some other property that was taken from me."

"And just how much time do you think that will take?"

"I won't short you in my work, ma'am. You'll get your money's worth out of me."

The woman snorted softly. "Didn't Kyle tell you? There isn't any pay until the cattle are sold. Can't even promise you how much it'll be."

Jed looked at the ground, scraped a ridge of dirt up with the edge of his boot sole, and then glanced up at her. "I'm here. Don't fancy walking back to town today. If you'll have me, I'll stay."

Her eyes flashed, and Jed felt his face grow hot as her gaze swept the length of his body. The war had forced him to endure grief, defeat, and the accusations of being a traitor. But to be appraised as though he were a piece of horseflesh rankled him. His mind flickered back to the slave auctions he had witnessed before the war and the feeling of similarity was not lost on him.

She lifted her chin and her cool gaze locked with his. "Kyle will show you to the bunkhouse," she said, her voice abrupt. "The hands make their morning meals. I cook the evening meal. Work days start an hour before sunup."

She turned away and strode toward the ranch house. "You can start now by helping Kyle carry in those supplies," she said, the words drifting over her shoulder.

Sweat trickled from Jed's underarms as he watched Ida Mae's retreat. He'd met battle-scarred Army captains with more warmth and compassion than this woman exhibited. He would have to agree with Kyle's assessment of her.

Chapter Three

Ida Mae was well aware of McCabe's consternation. The anger in his eyes had smoldered like pools of hot lava just before she turned away, and she knew his gaze was now flailing her backside as she walked toward the house. She climbed the steps leading to the covered veranda and quashed the guilty smile that threatened to expose her. It wasn't that she enjoyed humiliating new hands; it was simply necessary.

After removing her dusty boots, Ida Mae placed them carefully against the wall. Covertly, she glanced toward the wagon as she pushed open the heavy door.

The faint scent of cooking spices, mixed with the earthy odor of adobe, permeated the home's interior. The thick walls and shuttered windows blocked the sun's harsh glare, keeping the wind at bay and the house cool. The precise placement of the heavy furniture reassured her sense of order. Instinctively she stooped and straightened an errant rug that slightly lay askew.

In stocking feet she padded across the adobe brick flooring and into the kitchen area. Stepping close to a window, she quietly cracked one of the shutters open. Concealed by the heavy wood, Ida Mae observed the new hand.

There had been plenty of men with the Mexican fever who had passed through the area. Some, like McCabe, without a horse or even a change of clothes. Men who were broken by the war, homeless, with inner wounds held private behind grim faces. Unable to cope, they had fled south of the border, hoping for a better life. But they were drifters, she told herself, the lot

19

of them. They were all running from something. He would be no different.

She hesitated before turning away. There was something about him that intrigued her. Perhaps it was the way he stood, his back straight, his grayish green eyes defiant. She moved away from the window and began filling a bowl with dried butter beans. From the corner of her eye, she watched him as he came through the open doorway carrying one of the large wooden crates. The side of his face was covered with abrasions and his jaw was swollen. He sported at least several days' growth of beard. Hair the color of flint clung to his scalp where his hat had rested. Her gaze brushed across his broad shoulders and took in his long muscular arms straining against the crate. She had always considered herself tall, but McCabe stood at least six inches above her.

"Ma'am, where would you like me to put these provisions?" His voice was soft, the vowels accentuated by a slow, gentle drawl.

"Set it on the table, McCabe. And next time, remove your boots before you come into my house."

His brow pinched together. He placed the crate on the table and then turned to face her. Light from the open shutter caught the glint in his eyes. "No offense to you, ma'am, or to your home, but I'll keep my boots on."

"Not if you intend to eat at my table, you won't."

"Been doing my own cooking for quite a spell now, so I reckon I can make do with what's out in the bunkhouse."

His impudence surprised her. Most new hands couldn't do enough to please her. Ida Mae watched in stony silence as he turned and strode out through the open doorway.

Kyle passed by him, staggering barefoot with another box of supplies. "This is all you ordered for here, Ida Mae. I'll take the rest out to the bunkhouse."

Her body stiffened, and she glanced sharply at him. "No. I want all the supplies brought inside. I'll ration out what Cotton will need for the bunkhouse."

"But . . ."

"You heard me, Kyle. All the food is to be stored in the house."

His shoulders slumped. "Yes'm," he mumbled as he started to retreat.

"Hold up a minute, Kyle," Ida Mae said. "I want to know where you came across this McCabe fellow. Was he drinking in the cantina?"

Kyle shook his head. "No ma'am. He came into the cantina while I was, uh, eating, but he didn't drink anything. Best to my recollection he only had something to eat. I met him this morning in the shed where we both bedded down."

"Did he say where he was from, or where he was headed?"

"Nope. I didn't ask. Figured he'd tell me if he wanted me to know."

Ida Mae stared at him for a moment. "Kyle, you need to be more careful about the men you bring to the ranch. One of these days you're liable to drag home someone who might kill us all in our sleep."

Kyle ducked his head and suppressed a grin. "Ida Mae, I think I'd know if a man was a killer. This feller, Jed, he's not a killer."

"I didn't say he was," Ida Mae retorted sharply. "I'm just cautioning you."

"Yes'm." A slow smile caught the corner of Kyle's mouth, and he struggled to contain it as he hurried out the door.

Ida Mae turned back to the butter beans and began pouring dippers of water over them. Kyle could smirk all he wanted, she thought. The country was full of men who had killed for as little as a few coins, and some for even less.

Moving into a dark alcove, Ida Mae picked up a cloth-covered bowl and returned to the kitchen. After dumping flour into the bubbling contents, she stirred the sour-smelling mixture. A tantalizing aroma filled the room and wafted out the open window. Finished with working the dough, she covered it with a piece of cloth and set it aside.

Her thoughts turned to McCabe and the flash of defiance in his eyes when she called him on his boots. *He's proud and stubborn,* she thought, *and definitely a man with problems.* He said his guns and horses were taken from him. She wondered if it had been Sanchez.

By the looks of his face, he must have put up a good fight. The fact that he was determined to retrieve them set well with her. A man needed to be willing to fight for what was his. The Bar-DI could use men like that.

If McCabe proved out, he would be an asset to the ranch. But if he refused to follow orders, she would send him on his way—just like the last upstart who disobeyed her.

Stepping out onto the veranda, Ida Mae pulled the door closed behind her. For a moment she sat on a small bench by the door, looking toward the river. It was quiet and peaceful now, but it hadn't always been so. Her mind pulled up the misty images of swirling dust and charging horses racing across the serene setting in front of her. She lowered her head and closed her eyes. The sounds of gunshots and bloodcurdling screams filled her head . . . screams that she knew were hers. Shaking her head, she forced the memory from her mind.

Taking a deep breath, she opened her eyes and shoved her feet into her boots. It served no purpose to dwell on the past. A body must always push forward.

Ida Mae stood and walked to a small shed that was next to the garden. Several tools were placed neatly against one side of the building. She selected a hatchet and then walked across the yard to a small wooden picket lean-to.

Normally, she would have waited until it was Sunday, but there were times when the aroma of a slow-roasting chicken and sourdough bread were called for.

Chapter Four

Jed eased down on the bunk that Kyle had indicated would
be his. He wondered what he had let himself in for as he studied the raw adobe walls and narrow window of the bunkhouse.
Slender poles supported the roof. Sticks of various sizes criss-
crossed the poles and were topped with a thick layer of sod
and grass. He saw a broken shutter hanging precariously by
one leather hinge across the lone window. In the corner a small
potbellied stove made popping and hissing noises. Wooden
crates stacked nearby held coffee, beans, and an assortment of
canned goods. Cooking utensils hung from pegs placed in the
adobe wall. As near as he could tell, the main house was in
good repair, but the bunkhouse could do with some fixing up.

Kyle stood at a scarred wooden table, slicing a slab of salt
pork. His face was flushed, and Jed could hear him muttering.

"I see two bunks are being used," Jed observed. "Is there
another hand working here?"

Kyle nodded, his lank hair falling across his eyes. "The
foreman, Cotton. He's been working here from the get-go.
Came to work here right after Ida Mae and her husband first
came. Ida Mae and her husband were from the East and her
husband didn't have any notion a'tall on how to run a cattle
ranch. Cotton, he knows everything there is to know about cattle. But like I say, Ida Mae doesn't like to talk about the past."

"Your boss lady seems a little . . . set in her ways," Jed said
quietly.

Kyle shifted his weight onto one foot and glanced up at Jed.

"Ida Mae's not a mean-spirited person, mind you. But there are times I wish she wasn't so all-fired ornery."

Jed leaned back and rested his shoulders against the wall. "What brought you to these parts, Kyle? How did you end up here?"

Kyle's mouth twisted. He laid his knife aside and sat on a stool next to the table. He absently wiped his hands on a dingy towel. "My folks and my sister and I were traveling with a wagon train headed to California. We were out of Fort Smith going on a week or more when the fever hit us. My sister, Trudy, died within two days. Ma, the day after. Pa and I buried them along with about six others from the train. After a few days on the trail, Pa refused to move on . . . wanted to go back to Ma's gravesite. I figured he was down with grief and maybe a few days' rest would bring him around. I told the wagon master we would catch up with them. He didn't like leaving us, but the rest of the train wanted to keep moving." Kyle glanced out through the open doorway. He took a deep breath.

"I was wrong about Pa. He just wasted away, right in front of me. Finally, he refused to eat."

Kyle turned to the stove. Opening the lid, he stirred the fire with a metal poker and then added a few sticks. He stared at the flames for a moment before replacing the cover. He didn't look at Jed when he continued. "One night, Pa just died in his sleep. I drove on into Mission Bridge and Father De La Cruz at the mission saw to it he had a proper burial."

He shifted his gaze to Jed. "Ida Mae was in town the day he was buried and offered me a job. I figured the wagon train was too far ahead for me to catch up . . . and I didn't have the gumption to try, so I took her up on it. Been here ever since."

"How long has that been?"

Kyle took a deep breath and shook his head slowly. "Seems forever, but I reckon it's been close to three years now."

Jed leaned forward, his features tense. "You wouldn't recollect a family by the name of Ramsey traveling with that train, would you?"

Kyle's brow wrinkled, and he scratched the back of his neck. "I'm not for sure, but the name seems a little familiar. They kin of yours?"

"One of my kin may have been traveling with them, my sister. They took her in after my wife and mother died. When my brother and I came back after the war, our farm was wiped out. Nothing left of the house but a few charred timbers. Our team, wagons, and tools . . . everything was gone. Even the land wasn't ours anymore. Some of the people around there wanted us gone too. Called us traitors for fighting for the South."

Jed stood and walked to the open doorway. He stared into the distance and then continued in a quiet voice. "One neighbor did tell us the Ramseys left several years before, right after our Ma died, and they took Kate in. Said Ramsey told him he had heard my brother and I were killed at Franklin. I guess Ramsey thought that gave him the right to strip the farm clean and take everything for himself."

He turned back to Kyle. "We traced them as far as Fort Smith. A fellow there remembered them. Told us they were with a wagon train that had taken the stage route into Texas. That's why my brother and I came this way. We were trying to find our sister, Kate."

A surprised expression spread over Kyle's face. "Kate, you say?"

Jed's body jerked. "You know her?"

Kyle shook his head slightly. "Not so much me, but my sister, Trudy. She and Trudy would walk alongside the wagons, singing and picking flowers. Kate didn't get to do it very often. She always had to help with . . . well, what I thought were her younger brothers and sisters. But looking back now, I always did wonder why most of the young'uns had dark hair 'cept for Kate. She sure had pretty blond hair." Kyle smiled, his eyes turning soft. "And her eyes. That's why I remember her, those slanting green eyes. They could turn dark as a mossy pond one minute, and the next, flash like a newly lit fire."

Jed suddenly felt impatient with Kyle. "Did Kate say where the Ramseys were headed?" The words tumbled out, making his voice sound harsh.

Kyle squinted and drew his shoulders up. "Can't say for sure. Everybody was heading for different places. Some were planning on homesteading here in Texas; others planned on settling in California."

The loud squawks of several chickens broke the quiet afternoon air. Both Kyle and Jed stepped to the doorway and peered out.

Ida Mae was coming out of the lean-to. In one hand she held a young rooster by his feet and in the other a short hatchet. They both watched as she walked to a tree stump and splayed the rooster's head and neck across it. With a quick chop, the head separated and she threw the bird to the ground. The headless chicken attempted to run and then spun out of control as it beat its wings against the ground, pumping the last of its blood into the dry dirt.

"Hot dang!" Kyle exclaimed. "Looks like we're gonna have chicken for supper."

Jed turned back to the room, his back stiff. "I was under the impression that beans and a bed would be about all I could expect out here. Does the boss lady usually cook up chicken for new hands?"

Kyle snickered. "I s'pect she has her reasons."

"I'm sure she does," Jed asserted. "But I believe they'll be wasted. I'll go ahead and have that salt pork you're working on." He pulled an iron skillet from the wall and placed it on the small stove. "After I eat, I'll ride out and try to get a feel for the place. Is there any particular horse I can use?"

Kyle had turned quiet. "Yeah, Star. She's the bay mare with the white markings on her forehead. She's a solid mount. A bit barn sour, but there's not a horse out there that doesn't have a fault of some kind. Are you sure about that chicken?"

Two draft horses and six saddle mounts circled the corral, their eyes rolling as they jostled each other for positions against the rails. With a rope halter in his hand, Jed stood in the center of the pen while he tried to figure out which one was Star. Kyle was right, Jed concluded, they were a sorry-looking bunch.

Jed stepped in front of a bay mare with a white blaze on her forehead and hedged her against the pole fence. Gripping his fingers into her mane, he forced her head down as he slipped the halter over her head. After leading the mare out of the pen, he tethered her to a post and threw a saddle across her back. The mare shied, attempting to nip him when he tightened the cinch. Jed thought of the horses Sanchez had taken from him. Both stood at sixteen and a half hands and were sired from champion Thoroughbreds out of Virginia. He wondered if Sanchez knew the worth of the horses he had taken.

Jed exchanged the halter for a bridle with a snaffle-bit and curb-chain. After he mounted, the mare seemed to sense Jed's authority and settled down as they rode away from the ranch buildings. Her pace began to slow down the further they rode and soon she attempted to turn back. Jed cursed, pulled a tight rein, and buried his heel into her side. She dropped her head and pitched. Jed forced her head up, his grip rough as he yanked the bit hard against her mouth. The mare backed in circles, and Jed released the pressure on the reins.

"Whoa, now," Jed's voice was firm. He kept repeating the command, keeping the tone of his voice even.

The mare soon shook herself and bobbed her head. Jed gave the reins some slack, and the mare hesitantly obeyed the touch of the rein and the nudge of his knee and heel.

He was anxious to explore this high desert landscape. Kyle had told him that the foreman, Cotton, was more than likely checking on livestock north of the ranch's headquarters. He headed in that direction and wondered how much land the ranch encompassed or if the cattle roamed on the free range he had heard so much about.

Jed followed the crest of a rolling hill, his gaze automatically turning westward. He felt an urge to turn the mare in that direction and keep riding. Kyle's news about Kate had been good to hear. That meant he was on the right trail, just a couple of years too late. Someone could travel a far piece and a lot could happen in that time. How much more time could he afford to lose before he continued with his search? He had to find Kate. He wanted to know the details of Matilda's death.

The mare was a good mount. She had the strength to carry a rider for long distances; she just lacked the discipline. The further the mare traveled away from anything familiar, the less temperamental she would be.

The boss lady was a bigger puzzle to him. The woman's tongue could slice rawhide. He'd never met a woman quite like her, except maybe for Granny Mavis, who lived down in one of the hollers. Rumor had it she was a witch—and she could've been, allowing the colorful words she used. Jed nudged the horse with his heel. He didn't care to ponder on other folks' problems.

Maybe it would be better if he did move on. He could send this lady, Ida Mae, the money for the mare. If she thought he stole the horse, then be danged with it. It's not like he hadn't taken anything before. War did that to men. Powerful men, whose word and honor were once sacred possessions, were forced to take from others in order to survive.

Rising spurts of dust in the distance caught his attention. Whoever was kicking it up was in a mighty hurry. He pulled Star to a stop and pushed back in the saddle.

A riderless horse topped the small hill in front of him at full gallop, and Jed felt Star shift under him, short-hopping in her eagerness to join in with the runaway horse. Jed gave her free rein, and within a few minutes, the mare drew up next to the galloping animal. Using the mare to hedge the spooked horse into the brush to slow its pace, he was able to grab the reins and bring both animals to a stop.

Jed examined the lathered horse. It bore the brand of the Greeley ranch, and since Cotton was the only hand still out, Jed assumed it belonged to him. The sun was dropping quickly into the horizon, and Jed knew if he were going to backtrack the horse, he would have to hurry.

Pulling on the winded horse's reins, he urged Star into a slow canter while keeping an eye on the spitting hoof marks in the dirt.

The trail was relatively easy, and Jed was able to cover several miles before the sun dropped behind a distant ridge. He pulled the horses up. If the dumped rider was anywhere within shouting distance and was still able to answer, it would be the only way to find him.

Jed yelled Cotton's name and then listened. Only the chirps of birds settling down to roost in the dry mesquite broke the silence. Jed cursed the fact that he didn't have a gun. He pushed the horses on further. Topping another rise, he shouted once more. Across the silent wasteland he heard a dog's bark. Would the hand have had a dog with him? He urged his horse in the direction of the barking. He spotted the dog standing on the edge of a shallow ravine, its fur ruffed up around its neck.

The dog's coat appeared to be the color of aged honey in the dim light. The animal bared its teeth as it worked the edge of the wash, guarding something in the bottom.

"Easy, boy," Jed spoke softly. "You got somebody there?" The runaway gelding lowered its head and snorted at the dog. The recognition between the two animals was evidenced by the dog's tail wagging sporadically while still emitting low growls.

"Anybody hear me!" Jed shouted.

An ominous click sounded in a thicket of mesquite on the far side of the ravine. Jed felt the skin prickle on the back of his neck.

Instantly he rolled from the horse and scrambled for cover. "Hey, friend. Don't shoot! I'm the new hand hereabouts and I think I might have your horse. You hurt?" Jed hunkered down behind a boulder and waited for a response.

"Ain't hurt so bad I can't see you squattin' behind that rock like a frog in a mud hole. Who in blue blazes did'ju say you were?"

"Name's Jed McCabe. Just hired on today with the Greeley outfit."

"Kyle bring you in?"

"Yeah, this morning. You Cotton?" Jed heard the man grunt then crackling noises as brush was pushed aside.

"That's me. Now bring that cussed-fool horse over here and hep me on. I'm not gonna last much longer here."

Jed tied Star to a scrub cedar and led Cotton's horse across the ravine. The dog rushed in between Jed and the man lying in the brush.

"It's all right, Butch," the man said to the dog.

"Your horse throw you?" Jed inquired.

"Ain't no horse alive ever threw me. And the ones that did ain't alive."

Jed took one look at the man's bloodied leg. A belt was cinched tight around his upper thigh. "Did you get gored?" Jed asked, glancing at the man's face.

"No," the man growled. "Now quit yer yappin' and hep me up."

That's just dandy, Jed thought. *The foreman's as bad as the boss lady.* Jed assisted the man to his feet and saw a trickle of blood pool on the man's boot. After helping him mount, Jed retrieved his own horse.

Darkness crept across the rangeland, obscuring the trail and any familiar landmarks. Maybe it was a good thing his horse had an attachment to the barn, Jed thought. If the old cow-puncher lost it, at least the horse knew the way back.

Grunts wheezed past the injured man's lips as he shifted his weight in the saddle, holding his leg free from the stirrup. The old man was in pain, but given Cotton's disposition, Jed thought it best not to badger him with questions.

The dim outline of the barn and the soft glow of light from the main house were in sight when Jed saw Cotton slipping from the saddle. He reined in close and placed a steadying hand on his shoulder. "You right sure you're going to make it back to the ranch, old-timer?"

Cotton grunted and pulled himself upright. He reared back in the saddle and spit to one side. "Don't need to worry 'bout me none. Been ridin' many a year in worse shape and in worse situations."

Jed continued to ride close by. Maybe if he could get the man to talk, it might keep him focused until they made it to the bunkhouse. "Your horse as barn sour as this broomtail I'm riding? She's all fired up on getting back home in a hurry."

"Nope. Gun-shy." The man's words were clipped, and his voice was strained.

Jed raised his eyebrows. "Your leg. That a gunshot wound?"

"Yep."

"Care to talk about it?"

"Nope."

Chapter Five

Dusk wrapped the isolated ranch buildings in a cloak of darkness. The night air was heavy with the scent of sage and cow dung. In the ranch house, Ida Mae fidgeted as she arranged pots on the stove to keep the food warm. The hired men were late for their evening meal. Kyle and Cotton were usually waiting on the back veranda while she finished setting the food out. Where were they?

Ida Mae stared at the pots on the stove and wiped her hands on a small dishcloth. She wondered if the new hand would be willing to remove his boots in order to join them. She pictured his ramrod posture and defiant eyes. It was his eyes that set him apart from the other drifters who had come through. Most of them avoided making eye contact with her, shifting their gaze to the hills or searching the ground for rocks to kick.

McCabe's eyes were slate green, giving them the color of smoke and making them unreadable. She wondered what pain he had suffered to turn his face so hard and unyielding.

Ida Mae shook her head. *He's just another tramp looking for a place to hang his hat. No need to waste time thinking about him. When his belly is full and he has a few dollars in his pocket, he'll be on his way just like the others.*

Impatience gnawed at her, and she walked to the narrow window. The meal was ready to be placed on the table. What was keeping them? Pushing open the shutter, she peered toward the bunkhouse. Light seeped from its lone window. A sudden thump on the veranda signaled a boot being removed

32

and kicked aside. She turned toward the door and waited quietly. The door was pulled open, and Kyle shuffled in.

"Your hat," she reminded him.

Kyle snatched his battered hat from his head and hung it on a peg by the door. "Evening, Miss Ida. Things sure smell good. I'm 'bout as hungry as a lost dog."

"Where's Cotton? Has he come in yet?"

"No, ma'am. Don't rightly know what's keeping him unless he's found a sick cow. Maybe he's trying to bring her in." Kyle looked longingly at the table. "Did you want to wait for him?"

She flung the dishcloth over her shoulder. "The new hand, McCabe. Is he coming?"

She knew the words sounded snappish, and she immediately felt her face grow warm.

Kyle stepped onto a woven rug and rubbed the bottom of his feet against the braided fabric. "I, uh, don't believe so. He had something to eat before saddling up Star. He said he wanted to take a look at the place, but he hasn't came back either. I'm reckoning he met up with Cotton. Might be helping him."

Ida Mae felt her fingers curl into fists. "He saddled Star, rode off, and hasn't come back?" Her voice rose along with the heat in her face.

Kyle dropped his gaze to the floor and inched closer to the table. "I'm sure they'll both show up afore long." He sniffed and glanced at her, easing one hand over the back of a chair.

She stood for a moment, trying to compose herself. Had she been so blind as to hire a horse thief? Only moments ago she had allowed herself to feel some compassion for him, and all the while he was stealing her horse!

She wanted to lash out at someone. She couldn't place the blame on Kyle for bringing McCabe to the ranch. He knew they were short on hands and approaching roundup. He only wanted to help. No, it was she who should have known better and seen through him.

Ida Mae lifted her chin and straightened her shoulders. "I think we shall eat," she said calmly.

Her movements were slow and deliberate as she placed the roasted chicken on the table. There was no need for Kyle to wait for his dinner. If Cotton was wrangling in a sick cow, then he could eat later. Only the devil and his crew knew where McCabe and her horse were.

The thought of being duped by the new hand brought a scowl to her face. Picking up a knife, she hacked at the moist meat, turning it into tattered pieces. She stopped and stared at the shredded chicken. Biting back the harsh words she felt edging toward the tip of her tongue, she finished placing the butter beans and biscuits on the table. This wasn't the first time a new hire had quit. Usually, though, they had worked a few days first—and they hadn't stolen one of her horses.

At least McCabe was a fair judge of horseflesh. Star might be barn sour, but she possessed good stamina and strength. Cost her a good beef cow. Sanchez was a sharp trader. She hadn't asked how he had acquired her; she hadn't really wanted to know. Maybe it was appropriate. Sanchez had taken Star from someone; now McCabe had taken the horse from her. Only now, she was the one taking the loss, and she didn't like it.

The sound of a dog barking cut into Ida Mae's thoughts. She and Kyle exchanged glances.

"That's Butch," Kyle said. "I reckon Cotton and Jed have made it back. You want me to holler them in?"

Ida Mae exhaled loudly, making a puffing sound. "I seriously doubt that Mr. McCabe will be out there." She thought she saw disappointment in Kyle's eyes. He might as well realize now that McCabe was gone and took Star with him.

Kyle stood and walked to the door. Pulling it open he stared into the darkness for a moment and then turned and looked at Ida Mae.

"I think something's wrong with Cotton," he said. He grabbed his boots and pulled them on. With one giant stride he was off the open porch and loping toward the bunkhouse.

Ida Mae walked to the door and glanced out. Jed and Cotton were silhouetted in the light from the bunkhouse doorway. Jed was supporting Cotton as he hobbled into the building.

Her breath caught in her throat as she slipped on soft leather moccasins and hurried after Kyle.

"I ain't no dang cripple," Cotton's quarrelsome voice drifted from the bunkhouse.

Ida Mae smiled in relief. *The old goat can't be hurt too bad; he's as cantankerous as ever.*

She stepped into the doorway and watched as Kyle took Cotton's other arm and helped Jed lower the older man onto his bunk. It was then she saw the blood. Her body tensed, and she instinctively stepped forward as she took a sharp breath.

"How did this happen?" she asked.

Cotton glanced up at her. "Jest a flesh wound, Ida Mae. No need to get yo'self all in a lather."

"I didn't ask the extent of the wound," Ida Mae retorted. "I asked how it happened."

Cotton looked at the floor, his face turning dark. "I tripped and fell. Guess I'm gettin' old."

Ida Mae stepped closer and examined the wound. Straightening, she turned toward Kyle and Jed.

"I'll get some hot water and bandages from the house. In the meantime, remove his boots and trousers." Her gaze took in the small room. "See if you can find a clean blanket to cover him with," she added. She turned to Jed, her eyes questioning. "Did you see this happen?"

"No, ma'am."

She nodded, and then added absently, "You'll need to wash up some before you eat."

Jed's eyes narrowed. "I know when to wash, ma'am, and I've already eaten."

Ida Mae barely heard him as she turned and walked toward the house. Her mind was on Cotton. She had seen gunshot wounds before, and Cotton had definitely been shot. It was clear he didn't want to discuss it in front of the new hand. And McCabe, why was he acting like a proud mule with principles? Well, she'd deal with him later. First, she would tend to Cotton's wound.

After collecting a basin of hot water, towels, and strips of cloth for bandages, Ida Mae walked into the darkened alcove. Pulling a bottle of amber-colored whiskey from a shelf, she tucked it under one arm. On her way back to the bunk-house, she saw Kyle waiting for her in the yard. He was walking in small circles, scraping one sole of his boot against the loose soil.

"Will Cotton be all right?" he asked, as she drew close to him.

"That old buffalo hunter has survived more breaks, scrapes, and cuts than I care to count. I don't think a flesh wound will keep him down long. Go ahead and eat. When you finish, fix Cotton a plate and bring it to him."

Kyle nodded, then turned and walked slowly toward the ranch house.

Ida Mae knew Kyle's concern for Cotton went deeper than that of a co-worker. When she first took Kyle in, he possessed little knowledge of cattle ranching. Under Cotton's tutelage, he had flourished as a ranch hand, subsequently forming a bond with the cranky old man that was closer to a grandfather-grandson relationship. A fleeting sense of panic gripped her as she thought of the many things she relied on Cotton to do. Kyle wasn't the only one who was concerned about Cotton's well-being.

Passing by the barn, she saw Jed unsaddling the horses. The fluid motion of his shoulders and arms as he removed the saddles caused her to stop momentarily. Her throat tightened with the sensation of watching a scene play out from another time.

When Jed turned to toss one of the saddles onto a sawhorse, she noticed his angular frame tense when he met her gaze. Her earlier thoughts on the probability of his taking Star sent a guilty flush through her. She quickly averted her eyes and hurried on toward the bunkhouse. Emotions and feelings that she thought were buried years ago pulled at her. She had watched Dan remove the saddle from his horse in the same manner. It was a simple, masculine move that never failed to catch her attention.

Cotton was still on his bunk, propped up on one elbow. A coarse, green blanket covered his midsection. A shock of white hair fell across his forehead and his thick mustache drooped below the corners of his mouth. Although Cotton's trousers had been removed, he had pulled his boots back on.

Ida Mae suppressed a smile at the sight of his thin, wiry legs protruding from the worn boots. After setting the basin of water on a wooden chair near him, she straightened up and placed her hands on her hips. "For heaven's sake, Cotton. You didn't have to keep your boots on. You're not going to die right away."

"My granddaddy died with his boots on, my daddy died with his boots on, and by hanged I intend to do the same. Ain't takin' no chances."

Laughing softly, she dipped the edge of a towel into the water and began washing the wound. As she wiped away the encrusted dirt, it began to bleed.

"You're lucky," she remarked. "The bullet passed through. If we can keep it open and draining, it should heal without too much of a problem." Uncorking the whiskey bottle, she doused the wound with the stinging liquid.

Cotton flinched. "Tarnation, woman. That's a waste of good liquor. Gimme that bottle. I know a better use for it."

Ida Mae shook her head disapprovingly, but handed him the bottle. She picked up the strips of cloth and began wrapping the wound. "What happened out there?" she asked, glancing up at him.

Cotton took a long swallow of the whiskey and drew the back of his hand across his mouth. "Hard to say. I saw what I thought was the remains of a brandin' fire over in Sandy Gulch. When I got off my horse to take a closer look, someone shot at me from across the ravine. I felt it when it hit me. Went down like a wounded rabbit into some mesquite. Then my cussed horse spooked. If it weren't for the new feller, I might still be tryin' to hobble in."

"Do you have any idea who shot you?"

"Wasn't Apache. I know that fer a fact 'cause I heard only

one rider take off. If it'd been Indians, there would've been a whole passel of 'em, and they would've taken my horse with 'em."

"Do you think Sanchez would . . . ?"

Cotton grunted and shook his head. "I'm not accusin' him. But I'm tellin' you, Ida Mae, if you don't get more firepower on this ranch, not only will Sanchez keep hepin' himself to yer stock, but so will every maverick hunter within a hun'ert miles. You won't have a head left come roundup time."

Ida Mae picked up the towels and basin. She stood a moment, seemingly lost in thought. "I still have Dan's guns in the house. I'll see that the new hire has a sidearm. Maybe a rifle too."

Cotton slid further down on his bunk and rested his shoulders against the wall. "What's the story with the new hand? Seems like a nice feller. Bit talkative. Think he knows how to handle a gun?"

Ida Mae smiled. "I have a feeling he does."

Chapter Six

Jed stepped quietly into the bunkhouse, his mind focused on Ida Mae. Catching sight of her standing in the edge of the lantern's glow from the barn had been unsettling. Her face had been shrouded in shadows, but he sensed she was on the verge of speaking. He wondered if she regretted hiring him.

"Don't come sneakin' in like a chicken-stealin' coyote," Cotton mumbled. "Good way to get shot."

Cotton's gravelly voice caught Jed by surprise. "Sorry, I didn't mean to disturb you."

"Cussin' and hollerin' don't disturb me. Sneakin' does."

Jed scowled. The man carried a cantankerous personality to a new high. "I wasn't sneaking," Jed responded. "I was trying to be considerate."

Cotton was sprawled on his bunk, an outstretched arm slung across his eyes. The green blanket covering his midsection contrasted sharply with the white linen bandages encircling his thigh.

"Looks like the boss lady fixed you up proper," Jed said, trying to make peace.

Cotton grunted. "What did you say yer name was?"

"Jed McCabe."

"What part of the country you from?" Cotton asked, pulling his arm from his eyes and squinting at Jed.

Jed pushed a place clear on his bunk and sat. "Tennessee."

"Since yer here, I'm guessin' you chose the wrong side to fight on."

39

Jed shifted his gaze to the floor. *Depended on which side of the fence you were standing,* he thought, but remained quiet.

"What brings you to the Bar-DI? We ain't exactly on the beaten path."

Jed relaxed somewhat and leaned his shoulders back against the adobe wall. It wasn't his way to talk about his troubles to strangers, but in this wasteland of gullies, washes, and rattlesnakes, privacy was a pitiful reason to remain quiet. Briefly he told Cotton of his search for his sister and of his brother's death.

"The next day this Sanchez fellow robbed me of my horses and guns," he continued. "When I met the boy, Kyle, he mentioned that the ranch he worked on might need help. I figured it might be my only chance to get my horses back."

Cotton shifted his gaze to the ceiling and scratched at the stubble on his jaw. "How determined are you to get yer horses back?"

Jed pulled his boots off and placed them next to his cot. "If I had a good rifle and knew where this Sanchez fellow was, I'd be going after them come first light." He rubbed the side of his swollen head. "I have a feeling the boss lady may be having second thoughts about me."

Cotton turned his head and spit into a tin cup. "It don't matter a mule's left ear what Ida Mae's thoughts are. Right now she needs someone who knows how to handle a gun. She has a house full of rifles and pistols. Come mornin', you'll have yer pick of whatever weapon you want." He turned his gaze back to Jed. "The question is, are you willin' to stay and hep fight?"

Jed turned this over in his mind and wondered what kind of private war he'd stumbled into. "And who, exactly, are we fighting?" he asked quietly.

"Everyone, and no one in particular," Cotton replied, shrugging one shoulder. "Could be Sanchez and his bunch. Could be Apache. Might even be some of yer ex-compatriots lookin' to start their own spread by roundin' up mavericks and slappin' a brand on 'em."

Kyle stumbled in the door, carrying plates of food in each hand. "Take this one," he said, interrupting Cotton and thrusting one of the dishes toward Jed.

"What the . . . ?" Jed was unsure of Kyle's intention. Delicious smells wafted up from the cloth-covered dish, and he felt his stomach rumble.

Kyle continued on to Cotton, placing the other dish next to him on the chair. "Ida Mae said for you to eat up and try to get some rest. She said to tell you she'd be out here in the morning to change the dressing."

Cotton heaved himself upright and forked a piece of roasted chicken into his mouth. He closed his eyes and chewed, clearly savoring the taste.

Kyle snapped the dishcloth at a moth fluttering next to the lamp and dropped his lanky body into a chair next to the table.

Unsure, Jed stood and walked to the table, placing the food next to Kyle.

Kyle shook his head. "No, I've already eaten. That's for you. Ida Mae wants to talk to you in the morning."

Cotton opened one eye and looked at Jed. "Better make up yer mind, boy. If yer stayin', you'd best eat. Might be the only pay you're gonna get."

Jed uncovered the dish. The salt pork he'd eaten earlier had played out. He stared at the food. The smells were tantalizing. He picked up a fork and took a bite. *Round one goes to the witch,* he thought.

Kyle leaned back in his chair and studied Cotton. "Up at the house Ida Mae told me that you thought you saw a firepit down in Sandy Gulch. What made you think it was a branding fire?"

"You know, Kyle, a body could choke to death tryin' to talk and eat at the same time. Why don't you heat up that pot of tar you call coffee and give me a cup? Maybe then I can explain a few things to you and the new hired gun."

Jed frowned and turned to look at Cotton.

"You ate the chicken, McCabe, so I figured yer plannin' on stayin'."

So now he was a hired gun. He didn't care much for the handle, but it wasn't like he hadn't killed another man before. If it was Sanchez he would have to dispose of, then he might be willing to oblige. But the others, what personal quarrel did he have with them? If they were stealing the Greeley stock, was it really his fight? He took another bite. The witch made good chicken, but round two belonged to him. He would gain a gun, maybe even a horse.

"All right," Jed said. "Tell us why you think the firepit was being used for branding."

Cotton swallowed the food in his mouth, rinsing it down with the coffee Kyle handed him. Wiping a dab of gravy from his chin, he cleared his throat.

"I saw a runnin' iron layin' under a bush near it. Looked like it was tossed there in a hurry. I'm reckonin' I surprised the feller who was carryin' it. I believe he ducked across the ravine and hid while I got off my horse to take a look. That's when he took a shot at me. Either he was a bad shot, or he wanted to keep me off his tail until he got himself gone."

"Come morning, maybe we could track him," Kyle offered.

"Maybe," Cotton managed around a mouth full of food. "How 'bout it, McCabe? You any good at trackin'?"

Jed swallowed the last of his meal. "I suppose I can track as well as most. I'm not right sure what we would do with the fellow if we caught up with him. Couldn't prove that he was the one who shot you. And since you're not dead, I don't think we could hand him over to the federal marshals and have him charged with murder. Maybe our time would be better spent getting Ida Mae's brand on those yearlings."

Cotton smiled. "I appreciate yer way of thinkin', McCabe. But it wouldn't hurt none to get a sense of who we're up against— and I can assure you, it ain't Apaches."

Kyle eased forward, his elbows resting on his knees. "How about Thomas Schmidt? You said you didn't trust him or any of that passel from Cradle's Peak."

Jed's eyebrows rose. "Who's Thomas Schmidt?"

Cotton's mouth twisted sourly, and he pitched his empty

plate onto the seat of the chair. "Thomas is a no-good lyin' polecat who's tryin' to sweet talk his way inta Ida Mae's arms. With all his puffed-shirt antics, he's no better than Sanchez. At least Sanchez admits to being a thief. In fact, I'd say he's mighty proud of it."

"Why is that?" Jed asked.

"His family held a large chunk of land when Texas was part of Mexico. After the war, it was divided up amongst the Anglo ranchers and the freebooters. What Sanchez had left wouldn't feed a dozen goats. His excuse fer robbin' and stealin' is that he's only takin' back what's rightly his."

"So he has some type of cattle ranch of his own?" Jed pushed.

"Yeah, if you want to call stealin' from one rancher and sellin' to the other cattle ranchin'. What he doesn't sell or trade here, he drives down to Mexico where some of his family has a large rancho."

"Do you know where Sanchez's place here is?"

"Sorta. Somewhere above Devil's Draw. Never had no call to go up that way. Heard tell you can't get past the sentries. They have guards all over those hills. Only a fool would venture in there. And McCabe, I don't take you fer no fool."

Chapter Seven

Ida Mae held the lamp high as she lifted the lid of the heavy trunk. Inside were her husband's guns, each individually wrapped in blankets. Placing the lamp on a nearby table, she removed one of the rifles, a Springfield carbine. Running her hand over the smooth stock, she laid it gently aside. A small wrapped bundle caught her eye. She knew what it contained. It was Dan's Walker Colt. Since Dan's death, it had remained in the trunk; she preferred her own .32 Smith & Wesson. She stared at the dark material covering the gun. Her hand touched it lightly, lingered a moment, then patted it softly before moving to another bundle.

Pulling the bulky item from among the others, she unfolded the tattered piece of quilt covering it. The barrel of the .44 Remington revolver caught the soft light from the lamp. Coiled next to it was a gun belt and holster. A battered wooden box with a sliding lid held the cartridges. Rummaging down further in the trunk, she found the box containing the cartridges for the rifle. Carrying the guns to the table, she began cleaning them. Her hands trembled slightly. Although things had been quiet since that fateful day, for almost a year afterward she had kept all the guns loaded and hidden about the house, any gun within easy reach at any given moment.

A large portion of the Indian population was now being persuaded to move onto reservations. But renegades, who clung to their old ways, still raided the more remote ranches.

The majority of the Mexican bandits, who had preyed on unsuspecting travelers, were now either dead or behind bars.

44

Sanchez was the only one making life miserable for a few unfortunate folks. She didn't believe he was the one responsible for the theft of her cattle. He had always been courteous in his dealings with her. It had to be the influx of drifters from the East, men who had lost everything during the war and were now looking for a fresh start. Men like Jed McCabe. Her thoughts jarred to a halt. She stopped cleaning the guns and stared at the weapons. Was she arming the very type of man she was trying to defend herself against? Her hands lay quietly on the gun.

She lifted her head and stared at a tapestry hanging on the wall. A wedding gift from an aunt, it depicted an English garden scene. The garden reminded her of her home in Pennsylvania, where she and Dan were married. If they had stayed in Pennsylvania like her father had wished, would Daniel still be alive? Maybe. Probably not. Her oldest brother, Randall, was killed at Shiloh. If they had stayed, Daniel would have been fighting by his side.

Ida Mae sat on the edge of the trunk and rested her elbows on the table. She rubbed her forehead and felt the tension in her face. There was no need to dwell on the past. When Dan told her of his plans to move to Texas and become a cattle rancher, she had come willingly. This was her life now. She would do whatever was necessary to keep the ranch. And if it meant arming a man like Jed, then that was the chance she would have to take.

She picked up the box that held the ammunition for the Springfield. Only three cartridges were left. Tomorrow she would drive into town and purchase more, providing her credit would extend that far. If not, there were other business dealings she needed to take care of, and speaking with Thomas Schmidt was one of them.

Dawn came with shimmering clarity, filling the land with its warm golden rays. Ida Mae loved the smell of early morning dew and took a deep breath as she banged on the bunkhouse door.

Kyle quickly pulled it open while tucking in his shirttail. "Just finishing up with breakfast," he said, his voice brisk.

"I need to change Cotton's bandages. How is he doing?"

"Can speak for myself," Cotton growled. "Don't need no dern translator." Cotton sat on the edge of his bunk, his gnarled hands folded around a cup of hot coffee.

Kyle snatched his hat from the back of a chair and shoved it down on his head. "Reckon you can judge for yourself. There's work to be done and being nursemaid to a snarling old badger isn't one of 'em." With two long strides Kyle cleared the door and headed for the corrals.

Ida Mae's eyes widened. Cotton must be prodding for a fight. She stepped into the small room and placed the basin and bandages on the table. Leveling her gaze on Cotton, she gave him a stern look. "Don't take your anger out on Kyle. He wasn't the one who shot you."

"He needs to get his skinny haunches up and about sooner. Daylight was here, and he was still in bed."

"Perhaps he was waiting for you to wake up. Maybe he thought you might need his help."

"Pshaw! The only time I'll need that young pup's help is to shovel dirt over my sorry hide after I'm dead."

"Maybe that's what he thought he would be doing this morning."

"Well now, aren't you the little sparrow of good cheer?"

"Let's take a look at that leg," Ida Mae said, deliberately changing the subject. She knew that if she kept baiting Cotton she could jolly him out of his sour mood. But Kyle was right: there was too much work to be done. As she cut the dressing away and began cleaning it, she frowned. "It looks a little red," she observed. She finished applying a fresh dressing and stepped back.

"Try to stay off your feet today," Ida Mae said, pushing a wisp of hair from her face. "I'm taking the buckboard into town this morning and I'll check with Father De La Cruz and see if he has anything that might help keep the infection down." She walked to the door and glanced toward the corrals. "Where's McCabe?"

"I loaned him my extra gun and had him ride out early to take a look at that draw. Maybe he can figure out which direction that dang varmint that shot me was headed."

Ida Mae frowned and looked at Cotton. "Since when did you start loaning your gun out?"

"When I found myself talkin' with a feller who had a little sense and knew how to use one."

She opened her mouth to speak and then pressed her lips together tightly. She couldn't deny that she had wanted to be the one to offer a gun to Jed.

She shifted her gaze away from Cotton's piercing eyes. "While I'm in town I plan to ride out to Cradle's Peak," she said, striving to keep the disappointment from her voice. "I plan to ask Thomas if he's interested in buying my cattle. If he'll agree to a fair price, it will save me from having to hire enough men to help with the trail drive into Kansas."

Cotton grunted and hunched one shoulder. "Wouldn't do that if I were you. The trail drives won't start fer another week or two, and you can get top dollar at the railhead." He set his cup down and leaned back against the wall. "In the meantime, we can push all the cattle in close. There's enough feed along the river fer grazin'. When it's time to start the drive, I'll be able to ride. Kyle's old enough now to ride along and hep. It's time fer him to get a little grit in his craw." Cotton paused, pursing his lips. "I don't know about McCabe, though. I think he's fishin' with another line."

"What makes you say that?"

"He wanted to know where Sanchez's place was. I told him he'd be a fool if he tried goin' in there."

"Does he think it was Sanchez who stole his horses?"

"Oh, he knows that."

"Did you tell him the location?"

"Naw, just tossed out a general whereabouts. He doesn't have the least notion where Devil's Draw is."

Ida Mae returned to the table and gathered the basin and soiled bandages. "He must have had some very special horses for him to risk his life to retrieve them."

"I don't think it's the horses that got his dander up. In case you haven't noticed, the man's got a proud problem."

Ida Mae allowed a small grin. "Indeed he does."

Her face turned serious as she walked to the door. "Don't expect me back until tomorrow evening. My plans are to spend the night at Cradle's Peak."

Cotton's face darkened. His eyes were flinty as he glanced up at her. "Ida Mae, I've know'd you since you came here a blushin' bride. Your Dan was a good man. One of the best. I'm sorry for yer loss, but Thomas Schmidt is nothin' but a lyin', sneakin' weasel. And as far as I'm concerned, a woman-izer and a thief."

Ida Mae was silent for a moment before she replied. "Cotton, I haven't asked you for your opinion on how to run my life or with whom it would be proper to socialize. You know very well that Thomas's sister, Gerta, will be at the ranch and she and I enjoy visiting. As business dealings go, I believe Mr. Schmidt will give me a fair deal." She rested the basin against her hip as she continued. "And what do you mean by 'thief'?"

Cotton's mouth twitched, sending his mustache at odd angles with his face. "Jest what I said. I don't trust him, and whether you want my opinion or not, I'm a-givin' it to you. He can promise you the moon, but you'd be hard put to collect on it." He pushed himself to his feet and glowered at her. "Now if you don't mind, I gotta go water my garden."

Ida Mae stepped out of the bunkhouse and walked toward the ranch house. She glanced over her shoulder at the aging cowpuncher hobbling across the dusty barnyard to the wooden privy.

"The old fool will be back in the saddle by tomorrow," she muttered.

It took most of the morning for Ida Mae to drive the team into Mission Bridge. A small settlement, it boasted a general supply store, cantina, livery stable, and the mission. A dozen or more clapboard houses and a few adobe ones clustered on the outskirts of the main square. Construction was underway across the street from the supply store. Men she didn't recognize stood near the new building site. Ida Mae smiled. Mission Bridge was growing. It would be good to have more people here.

After watering the team, she fastened their reins to the hitching bar in front of the livery stable. Meticulously, she brushed the dust from her clothes. She removed her hat and, secured by the string under her chin, it swung against her back. Dipping a large bandanna into the horse trough, she washed her hands and face. When intending to use feminine wiles, she thought, it would be best to at least look feminine.

Unfastening her gun belt, she removed the pistol from the holster and placed it into a large hemp bag that she had brought. Slipping one arm through the looped handles, she straightened her shoulders and looked toward the store. Several cowhands were loitering about and stared unabashedly as she walked up the street to the supply store. The darkness of the interior stopped her momentarily as her eyes adjusted to the diminished light.

"Morning to you, Mrs. Greeley," Joseph Portello's rumbling voice greeted her. He was a large, hairy man, and his bear-sized hands were splayed on the counter. Dark eyes glinted at her from under bushy eyebrows. His face revealed that he thought Ida Mae a fine-looking woman, even dressed in the manly garb she insisted on wearing.

"Good morning to you, Mr. Portello," she responded, and dropping her chin slightly, she smiled. "I've come to pay some on my bill."

"That would be good."

Ida Mae approached the counter and opened the bag, removing a five-dollar gold piece. She slid it across the counter toward him.

"I thank you, ma'am," he said as one massive paw swallowed the coin. "I know times are hard right now, but won't be long afore you'll be sending your herd north. I know you'll be set-tling up the balance when you get your money."

"Oh, very definitely, Mr. Portello." Ida Mae stood quietly for a moment as she looked around the room. Turning slightly, as if preparing to leave, she paused. "By the way, Joseph, would you happen to carry cartridges for a .44 Remington revolver and a Springfield rifle?"

"I surely do, Miss Ida. You need some ammunition?"

"As a matter of fact, yes, Joseph, I do."

The large man chewed on his bottom lip a moment and then stooped and pulled several small boxes from under the counter. "Is this enough for you?"

Ida Mae dropped her chin even lower and smiled sweetly. "Why, yes, Joseph. This will do nicely." She slid the cartridge boxes into her handbag. "If you would add that to the small amount I still owe you, I'll be most appreciative," she said as she turned and strolled out the doorway.

Joseph Portello dug one sausage-sized finger into his left ear and pivoted it slowly. "About as small as my rear end," he growled.

Ida Mae could hear Portello swearing and muttering as she strode up the street toward the mission. She didn't like the role she was forced to play, but she would pay the man what she owed him. And she knew it wasn't a small amount. In fact, she knew the precise amount. She just wasn't sure *when* she would pay it.

As Ida Mae reached the entrance to the mission, she saw Father De La Cruz's housekeeper leaving. Ida Mae inquired as to the whereabouts of the priest. The housekeeper, Señora Gomez, indicated that the father was away, but would return later in the day.

Ida Mae hesitated a moment. "*Gracias,*" she said, "but I cannot wait. I will return tomorrow." She hoped the woman understood. She knew if she left now, she would still have time to reach Cradle's Peak before dark.

* * *

The headquarters of Cradle's Peak lay against a range of dry hills. The ridgetop of the farthest hill sloped into a saddle and then rose into a sharp, overhanging peak. From a distance it appeared the indented hill was hooked to the peak, forming a swinging cradle.

Dust spiraled from Ida Mae's buckboard as she drove her team toward the sprawling ranch house. Several huts, constructed from stone and adobe, were set some distance from the roadway. In the open doorways, Mexican women with cautious children clutching at their skirts stared at Ida Mae's passing wagon with silent eyes.

A young Mexican vaquero, who appeared to be no more than twelve years old, rushed from around the back of the ranch house and stood ready to take care of her team. Drawing the horses up, Ida Mae climbed from the wagon and relinquished the reins to the young boy.

A short, round-faced woman appeared on the veranda. Dressed in a lavender silk dress, her ample bosom was highlighted by the slanting sunlight. Her dark hair was swept up into a bun and fastened with colorful shell combs. Black beads around her neck winked in the fading light.

"How special that you come to our home, Miss Ida. I hope it is not bad news you bring," the woman greeted her with a thick German accent.

"No, Miss Gerta, it's not bad news. Business. Is your brother here?"

"No, he is gone. He will be back this night. Could this business wait until then?"

Ida Mae smiled at the woman. "It can."

"Good," she said, clasping her hands together happily. "We shall enjoy a wonderful meal and then spend much time on the catching up. I shall have Carmen prepare a room for you." Gerta gestured with her arm. "You, Carlos. Bring Miss Ida's things in."

Ida Mae reached for her hemp bag and slung it over her shoulder. Grasping a small satchel, she lifted it from the wagon.

"Thank you, Carlos, but I can manage. If you'll take care of my horses, I shall appreciate it."

The young man lifted his hat and nodded as his dark eyes cut toward the veranda and then back to Ida Mae. Her voice was quiet as she carried her things past him. "Unhitching my horses and feeding them will be all that's necessary."

The boy smiled shyly, white teeth flashing against brown skin. *"Sí,"* he whispered.

"Ahh," Gerta scolded from the porch. "You should let the young man carry your bag. That's what he's paid to do."

Ida Mae smiled at the older woman. "I prefer to carry my own things."

"My dear, some day you will wish for a man to carry your bag, and he will tell you to carry it yourself. Then you have only yourself to blame."

The original adobe home had undergone several additions through the years, and Ida Mae hastened to keep up with the Schmidts' housekeeper, Carmen, as she led her through a maze of hallways. Carmen stopped at a narrow wooden door and pushed it open, motioning for Ida Mae to enter.

The small bedroom was sparsely furnished with a single bed and washstand. Two narrow windows faced west, allowing the setting sun to fill the room with warm, golden light. After freshening up, Ida Mae changed her clothes, donning black Kentucky jeans and a white, long-sleeved silk blouse. Brushing the dust from her boots, she slipped them back on. She stood and eyed herself in the small mirror that hung above the washstand. *Gerta may dress like she's on her way to attend the Governor's Ball,* she thought, *but she doesn't have to worry about feeding a sick calf before she leaves.* Unfastening her braid, she brushed her hair and then twisted it into a bun at the nape of her neck. Her mind turned to the new hand, Jed, and wondered what he thought of her manner of dress, then chastised herself for even thinking of it.

Dining at Cradle's Peak was always a pleasure. The food was plentiful, the setting lavish, and conversation with Gerta a delight. This evening's meal was no exception. Roast duckling, mashed squash with just a touch of honey and cream, boiled potatoes, and bread pudding not only filled Ida Mae, but also left her feeling guilty. She thought of her crew at the ranch and wondered what they were having for their evening meal.

The two women had moved to the parlor and were preparing to sit when voices could be heard on the open veranda.

Gerta glanced toward the arched doorway leading to the front entrance. "That should be Thomas," she said, nodding her head.

Carmen bustled into the foyer and pulled the heavy entrance door open. Boots scraped and a deep voice directed Carmen on where to put items.

"Thomas," Gerta called as she moved toward the foyer. "We have a guest. For business Miss Ida has come."

Thomas stepped into the parlor. Solidly built like his sister, his dark blue eyes sparkled when he saw Ida Mae. He stepped toward her, his arms outstretched. "Frau Greeley, how good to see you." Placing his hands on her shoulders, he leaned forward and kissed her lightly on both cheeks.

As he drew back, Ida Mae noticed the heavy creases in his face. "It's always good to see you too, Thomas," she said, taking in his rumpled clothing. Ida Mae concluded that Thomas had been somewhere all right, but it wasn't out working cattle.

Thomas glanced at Gerta. "Have you fed our guest?"

"But of course."

"Good, good. Then we shall have a glass of wine before we talk your business." Walking to a tall armoire, he opened the dark paneled doors and took a decanter of red port from the shelf. Gerta hurried to his side, and removing three glasses from the chest, held them as Thomas poured. After replacing the decanter, Thomas took two of the glasses from Gerta and handed one to Ida Mae. Raising his glass, he nodded. "To the two most beautiful women in Texas," he said.

"And to my most gracious hosts," Ida Mae replied, raising her glass to both Thomas and Gerta. She smiled as she took a sip of the wine.

"Now sit, sit. Tell me of this business you wish to discuss." Thomas waited until the women were seated before settling into a comfortable chair.

Ida Mae briefly told them about Cotton's injury and her plans to sell her cattle. "I thought I would give you the first option," she said, looking at Thomas over the rim of her glass.

Thomas nodded slowly as he returned her bold gaze. "Your foreman. How bad is he hurt? Did he see who it was who shot him?"

Ida Mae frowned. "No, it was too dark. One of my men left this morning to see if he could track him."

"One of your men? The young, skinny kid?"

Ida Mae shifted uneasily. She hadn't wanted to tell them about Jed. She wasn't sure why. "His name is Kyle," she said defensively.

"I believe you should know, my dear, that I have now just come from Fort Chadwick. It is a very serious matter we have with the Indians again." Thomas rose and paced a few steps. "A rogue band has left their reservation in New Mexico and is plundering the ranches along the Upper Concho. They have burned homes and stolen livestock, and I was told a young woman was taken." He turned and faced Ida Mae, squaring his shoulders and thrusting one hand into his pocket. "I and a group of cattlemen have traveled to the Army post and demanded they give us protection. It is not safe for anyone, much less a young widow with ranch hands who are unable to help with the defense."

A wave of fear gripped Ida Mae. There had been plenty of hands for defense the day Dan was killed.

Suddenly Thomas smiled. "Ahh, you needn't worry, I will buy your cattle and give you a good price." He moved closer to her and, leaning forward, spoke softly. "Perhaps then my other offer you will consider?"

Ida Mae carefully set her wine glass down and folded her hands in her lap. She didn't trust herself holding the glass. Thomas' news had shaken her—and she knew what his other offer was. But for now, she needed to stay focused. "And how much per head will that be?" she asked quietly.

Thomas straightened his back and smiled, but his eyes didn't reflect merriment. "What they sell for in Abilene, I will give to you."

Cotton's words floated across her mind. *He can promise you the moon . . .* "That's very generous of you, Thomas," she said. "But I will need my money when you take possession of my herd."

Schmidt raised one shoulder and threw out his hand. "Ehh, you don't understand business, my dear. Half the cattle could be lost before they reach this Abilene."

"Then perhaps you'd like to pare down your offer?"

A frown creased Thomas' forehead. "I have given you my offer," he said, shaking his head. "I don't wish to profit from you. You are only a woman." He turned to her, his cobalt-blue eyes glistening in the soft glow from the lamp. "You need a man in your life. One who knows how to handle this business."

Ida Mae glanced down at her hands and rubbed one thumb against the other. Slowly she stood, facing him. "Thank you, Thomas. You're right. Your offer is a generous one. But since it's late, and I'm sure you're tired, I will think on it tonight and make my decision in the morning."

Thomas smiled broadly, his eyes sparkling. "You will not regret my handling of your cattle for you." He raised his glass slightly. "And my other proposal . . . it still awaits your answer."

Ida Mae felt the heat rise in her face and turned away. "Another reason I'm here," she said, looking at Gerta, "is that Cotton's wound looked a little red this morning. I was hoping that you would have something that might help."

Gerta had sat quietly, drinking her wine as Thomas and Ida Mae discussed the cattle. Now Gerta nodded absently, pressing her fingertips against her lips. "I have the dried comfrey leaves," she finally said. "A poultice can be made and applied to his wound. That should help to heal."

"Thank you, Gerta. And thank you for the wonderful meal. If you both will excuse me now, I will retire for the evening."

Ida Mae walked stiffly down the hall and to her room. Thomas' words circled in her mind like birds of prey. *You are only a woman. You are only a woman.* She didn't want his pity. She didn't want charity, and she didn't want marriage. At least not now. She wanted only to be dealt with fairly and honestly, and she wasn't sure if Schmidt's offer was either.

Chapter Eight

Jed dismounted and inspected the tracks that he had been following all morning. He first picked them up at the edge of the wash where Cotton had been shot and knew it was the same horse because of its gait. The mount was throwing its right foreleg, causing a slur of dirt to the outside edge of the print. More than once he had lost the tracks but was able to pick them up again when horse and rider crossed over scabbed alkali wallows. Now he was at least six miles east and slightly south of the Greeley ranch headquarters.

Shoving his hat back, Jed shifted his gaze to the surrounding terrain. The tracks were now intermingled with those of other horses. Judging by the depth of the hoof imprints, the horses all carried riders. At least several more riders were in the group, and they were all headed south. That direction took them toward Mission Bridge.

The only range of hills of any size lay west. Cotton had said Sanchez's place was located in the higher mesas above a place called Devil's Draw. That wasn't the direction these riders were headed.

Jed mounted and circled his horse. Mesquite, cactus, and sage dotted the area. Stunted cottonwood trees grew along the edges of the gullies and washes. Riders could easily hide in one of the washes, Jed thought. And a dozen riders were more than he cared to tangle with. He hadn't survived the war by being lucky.

He pulled the horse up and studied the low ranging hills that lay southward. *If it's not Sanchez and his bunch I'm chasing, I don't give a whit about the rest,* Jed thought. *I can deal with a pack of thieving lowlifes anytime. If left alone, that type of thief would become braver and more careless. That's when they could be taken care of. Not out here with only a revolver and a dozen places to be ambushed.* Reining his horse around, Jed started back to the ranch.

The rolling plains were deceptive. They appeared flat when gazing across them, but unexpected ravines and washes criss-crossed the area. A roan-colored cow with one broken horn stood in one of the dry streambeds and watched Jed's approach with wary eyes. Her calf edged cautiously into a brush thicket, its nose lifted, sniffing at the unfamiliar scent of horse and rider. Jed saw the Greeley brand on the cow, but couldn't see one on the calf. Loosening his lariat, he waved it in the air and nudged his horse in behind the cow. The cow snorted, raised her burr-matted tail, and bolted toward the dense brush on the hillside.

Star quickly proved her worth as a cow horse by plunging in between the cow and the thicket, almost unseating Jed with her quickness. Working back and forth with bone-jarring motions, Star cut the rogue cow off and started her toward the ranch's headquarters. The calf let out a dismal bawl and broke from the brush as it raced after its mother. Before long, Jed had rounded up several steers along with more cows and their calves. Star stayed alert and moved quickly whenever any of the cattle turned to make a run for it.

The small herd looked impressive. He reached down and patted Star's shoulder. "Good job, old gal," he said. He smiled. She had proven to be a good horse.

Dust drifted from the cattle's movement and the killdeer with their fake injuries and shrill keening brought a smile to Jed's face. *A fellow could get used to this type of life,* he thought. No wonder the Greeley woman was determined to keep the ranch. But at what cost? As far as he could tell, trying to fit into a man's world had taken her youth and turned it into jaded bitterness. He thought about Schmidt and wondered if Cotton's feelings toward the man were grounded in fact, or prejudice.

Shading his eyes against the slanting sun, Jed reckoned it was getting close to midafternoon. Before he left this morning, Cotton mentioned bringing the cattle in closer to the ranch and grazing them along the river. Over a dozen head were now in the small herd, and Jed hesitated to gather more for fear of losing what he had.

By late evening he had the herd pushed in along the river. After unsaddling Star, he rubbed her down, fed her, and turned her into the corral. As Jed approached the bunkhouse, he saw Cotton leaning against the frame of the open doorway.

"See you was able to gather up a few head," he said, nodding his approval. "What about the bushwhacker? See any sign of him?"

"I followed him for a number of miles. It looked as though he met up with some other riders. Decided not to go any further with it."

"What direction?"

"They were east of here and headed south."

Cotton fingered his mustache. "That comes close to what I figured."

"And that is?"

"What I said. It wasn't Apache, and it wasn't Sanchez."

"So who does that leave? Schmidt?"

"Never said that either," Cotton mumbled as he turned and limped to his cot.

Jed removed his hat and swatted some of the dust from his clothes before entering the bunkhouse. "What've you got out here that I can stir up for us to eat?"

"Already did that," Cotton said. "There's beans on the stove and coffee in the pot. Hep yerself."

After dishing up a bowl of red beans, Jed poured a cup of coffee. Sitting at the table, he glanced around the room. "Where's Kyle?"

Cotton frowned. "Wasn't he hep'n you round up those cattle?"

"Nope. Haven't seen him since I left this morning."

"Huh." Cotton puckered his lower lip and scowled. "I hope that fool kid hasn't gotten himself in a fix."

"If he doesn't come in soon," Jed said between bites, "I'll ride out and see if I can find him." He scraped the last of the beans from his bowl and then settled his back against the chair. He took a slow sip of his coffee. "Has the boss lady been out to change your bandages?" Jed inquired, nodding at Cotton's leg.

"This mornin'," Cotton said, his voice a low growl. "She left after that. Won't be back 'til tomorrow sometime."

Jed blew on his coffee as he mulled over this bit of information. He wondered if Cotton would give him an answer if he were to ask where she went and why. But judging by his surly mood, it was somewhere Cotton didn't approve of, and that would be Cradle's Peak.

Stretching out his long legs, Jed lazily crossed them. He took another sip and glanced at Cotton. "What gave the boss lady the sudden urge to visit Cradle's Peak?"

Cotton's head jerked up and he squinted at Jed. "Yer right smart for a young feller." He shifted his injured leg onto the bunk while easing his weight down on one elbow. "She's got it in her head to sell her cattle to one of the outfits that'll be pushin' a herd north. Doesn't think we have enough hands or large enough remuda to handle a drive on our own."

"Maybe she's right," Jed offered.

"I'll be able to ride by then," Cotton responded. "Five or six hands would be aplenty to handle the amount of cattle we'll be pushin'. Besides, by sellin' them in Abilene, her profits will be more than enough to pay for the extra help."

A chuckle gathered in Jed's throat. "As hard as the boss lady is on help, where do you plan on picking up those extra hands?"

"Come round-up time, there's always drifters' lookin' fer work. As long as they can sit a horse and throw a rope, that's all you need."

Somehow Jed didn't think that Ida Mae would agree with Cotton's philosophy.

The sound of lowing cattle drifted into the bunkhouse. Jed rose and walked to the door. He could see Kyle loping his horse up to the barn. "The boy made it in," Jed said, turning back to

Cotton. "Looks like he was able to bring in more stock. How many head are out there to be rounded up?"

Cotton rubbed his chin thoughtfully. "Not countin' the brood cows, there should be close to three hun'ert head ready for market. But I wouldn't place a nickel bet on it now."

"I've been thinking," Jed said as he settled back into his chair. "If I could get my horses back, that would give us a couple more mounts."

"Cheaper to buy horses than go after yers," Cotton stated. "I'm tellin' you, boy. Don't go thinkin' otherwise."

Jed met Cotton's gaze. "I will go after them. Maybe not today, or tomorrow. But I intend to get them back."

Kyle paused to scrape his boots on the steps of the bunkhouse as Butch bounded past him and into the room at a run. The large dog jumped onto the end of Cotton's bunk and sank down on the soft blankets.

Cotton laughed, and reaching out, rubbed the dog's head. "There you are, you ornery piece of squirrel meat. Thought you'd deserted me."

"He followed me out this morning," Kyle said. "Couldn't get him to stay so I figured what the heck, just let him come."

"How many head did you bring in?" Cotton inquired as he continued to rub Butch's ears.

"Close to a dozen," Kyle said as he spooned beans into a tin plate. "Funny thing, though. One of the cows with the Greeley brand had a calf following her with a different brand." He glanced at Cotton. "Now there's a right puzzle for you."

"So whose brand is it?" Cotton asked, clearly irritated.

Kyle shrugged his shoulders. "Don't know. Never saw it before."

"Well tarnation," Cotton snorted. "Rope the cussed thing and bring it up here where I can take a look at it."

Butch sank lower into the bunk and Kyle squinted one eye shut. "All right," he said softly. "But can I eat first?"

* * *

The roped calf bellowed and bucked as Kyle snubbed it to a corral post. The mother, disgruntled at the mistreatment of her yearling, tossed her head and pawed at the dirt, threatening to charge Kyle and his mount.

Jed followed Cotton as he hobbled to the corrals for a closer look.

"I'll be danged," Cotton muttered. "Not one I recognize either."

"By the way that cow is acting," Jed observed, "I would say it was her calf all right. What do you expect has happened?"

Cotton placed a twist of tobacco between his lower lip and gum. "It means the calf got away from the rustlers and came back to his mama."

"Then I would reckon that the cattle thieves are just that," Jed said. "A pack of no-goods looking to make a quick dollar."

"Don't bet yer hat on it, sonny."

Jed shook his head. "Why are you so all-fired certain that it's the Schmidt fellow behind the rustling?"

"Cause you can't break an egg-suckin' dog, that's why." Cotton shot an arc of tobacco juice into the dirt, turned, and limped back to the bunkhouse.

Kyle freed the calf from the post, and he and Jed watched as the calf ran back to its mother.

"Tell me something, Kyle," Jed asked, stepping closer to him. "Where exactly is Devil's Draw and Sanchez's place?"

Shading his eyes with one hand, Kyle squinted westward. "Not rightly sure, but I know you gotta cross over part of the Circle-M rangeland to get to it. Some of the hands from that outfit say it's located at the edge of the big rock country. There's a trail that follows a ravine up a narrow canyon. At the top is a small valley. That's where Sanchez has his headquarters." He turned and looked at Jed. "Are you thinking about going after your horses?"

Jed nodded slowly.

Chapter Nine

Early-morning sun splashed golden streams of light across the breakfast table. The meal was delicious, but Ida Mae found it difficult to enjoy and laid her fork carefully alongside her plate. She was aware of Thomas' gaze searching her face as he waited for her answer. She slept little through the night, wrestling with conflicting emotions. Thomas' vague offer on her cattle was unacceptable. She needed the money now. Driving the cattle to Abilene with the few hands she had would be near-impossible. She didn't have enough money to buy the supplies it would take to get the cattle to the railhead.

So why am I hedging away from Thomas' offer? Maybe it was a small thing, but it was there. Questions that perhaps amounted to nothing, but nonetheless, were bothersome. Why did Thomas go to Fort Chadwick to complain about the Indians? He said they were raiding along the Upper Concho. That was several hundred miles away.

There were allegations when Dan was killed that it was the Cradle's Peak hands that caused the Indian uprising. It was never proven, and she turned a deaf ear to Cotton when he brought it up. After the attack, Thomas immediately came to her aid, supplying hands and provisions to help her cope with Dan's death. How could she question Thomas' integrity?

"I see you are still hesitant to accept my offer, Frau Greeley," Thomas said. "I understand your reluctance, but you must realize I only want to help. Perhaps I can make the proposition more appealing." Thomas leaned toward her, his dark blue eyes intense. "Would you consider selling me your ranch along

63

with the cattle?" He paused a moment, studying Ida Mae's surprised expression. "I am prepared to give you a very substantial down payment," he continued. "Enough for you to return to your home in the East, if that is what you wish. As soon as the cattle are sold, I will forward the remainder of the money to you."

"Thank you, Thomas. Yes, that does help me to make a decision." Ida Mae fixed a smile on her face, rose from the table, and placed her napkin to the side. "Thank you, Gerta, for having me as your guest," she said, addressing the older woman. Turning to Thomas, who had also risen, she spoke quietly. "I appreciate the help you gave me after Dan's death. I also want to thank you for your offer. However, my ranch isn't for sale. Now, if you will excuse me, I'll retrieve my things and be on my way."

"But . . . but," Thomas blustered. "My dear, if I've offended you, I am deeply regretful. Please, we should talk."

"You didn't offend me, Thomas. You merely made me realize a few things. Dan's dream was for us to live here and build a place for ourselves. I won't sell his legacy. I'll find a way to send my cattle north, and in time I'll see that the ranch does prosper."

"Then I implore you to let me repair the blunders of my mouth by sending you some assistance. I shall have two of my hands report to your ranch in the morning. They will help with the gathering of your cattle."

"That's not necessary."

"I insist. It is at no cost to you. With your foreman injured, you and the skinny kid will not be able to handle such an undertaking."

Thomas took a step toward her and grasped her hand lightly. "My dearest Ida," he said softly. "If only you would reconsider my proposal of marriage. This worry for your ranch would be only a memory. A woman such as yourself should not be burdened with the running of a cattle ranch."

Ida Mae slipped her hand from his grasp. "You're quite mistaken, Thomas. I rather enjoy the trials of managing the ranch. It's the life I have chosen."

"There is much here that would give you fulfillment. Gerta is becoming homesick and wishes to return to the Old Country. I will need someone to run my household. And surely you have given thoughts to having children?"

"Hold on now, Thomas. You need to pull the brake on that wagon," Ida Mae said, the color rising in her cheeks.

Thomas grinned broadly. "Ehh. Neither of us is holding to our youth. We must consider these things."

"I'll consider some of your proposals, Thomas, but others require much more thought."

"Please excuse my brother's manners," Gerta said. "I'm afraid in his effort to court you, he has done the opposite and frightened you away."

"Ehh!" Thomas cut in. "This is a private matter, Gerta. I know how to court a woman."

Gerta shook her head. "Like the kitchen you oversee? If I didn't keep my good eye on Carmen, she would give all the food to her large tribe of relatives."

"Yes, yes, of course. You are an excellent manager, Gerta." Thomas flicked his fingers dismissively. "But I am sure I will be able to handle it."

Gerta frowned and lowered her gaze to the floor. She turned and retrieved a bundle that lay on the buffet. "Here," she said, turning to Ida Mae. "These are the leaves for the medicine. Soak them in boiling water and make a poultice for your foreman. It will help."

"Thank you, Gerta," Ida Mae responded. She felt embarrassed for Gerta and looked at Thomas. "There's no need to send the wranglers, Thomas. My men and I will be able to handle the work."

"No, no. I shall take it as an insult if you do not let me help you."

Dust curls danced across the trail in front of Ida Mae's wagon. Wind plucked at her sleeves, and she felt herself shiver in the changing temperature. Her mind still reeled from the scene that played out at the breakfast table and Thomas' offer. She had no intentions of returning to the East. Both of her parents were dead. Her brother had been killed in the war, and her sister had married poorly. Through exchanges of letters she knew her sister's life was one of hardship. There was no home left for her to return to. This was her home.

Thomas' bold verbalization of marriage in the presence of his sister had caught her by surprise. He had hinted at the prospects of marriage before, but she never took his remarks as serious. Perhaps it was something to think about, but not now.

The offering of the cowhands was different. If she could come up with enough supplies, the extra cowboys might make it possible to push her own cattle north. Then she would be able to pay the hands and have enough left to get through another year. Next year. That was what Dan always said. *Next year it will be better.* Ida Mae felt her chest tighten. She straightened her back and rattled the reins over the backs of the team. She would not allow herself to succumb to the self-defeating game of "if only."

The wind picked up bits of sand and sent it with stinging assaults against her face. She glanced southward over her shoulder and saw clouds piling up on the horizon. The black underbelly of the clouds and the towering white pillows above meant only one thing. A huge thunderstorm would hit before she could make it back to the ranch. Town was still several hours away, the ranch another three. The Circle-M ranch was the closest. Their headquarters wasn't more than an hour away. She slapped the reins harder against the horses' rumps, startling them into a trot. She spotted the turnoff to the Circle-M and pulled the team onto its dim trace. Not counting the open rangeland it claimed, the Circle-M covered over a thousand acres. The ranch lay west of her spread and was managed by a foreman, and depending on the time of year, at least a dozen wranglers. The absentee owners resided in Memphis and only visited the ranch once or twice a year.

Several cowhands spilled out of the bunkhouse at the sound of Ida Mae's wagon. One of them broke from the group and hurried across the yard toward her, his bandy-legged gait criss-crossing in awkward motions as he shifted into a lope.

She could see the ranch's foreman, Cliff Worley, coming from the rear of the main building. Cliff and Cotton had both worked for the Circle-M when she and Dan first arrived in the area. Dan had hired Cotton away from the Circle-M, but the two cowboys had remained close friends. After Dan was killed, Cliff and his crew helped her and Cotton with the spring roundups and branding.

The eager cowboy reached her wagon before the foreman did and, sweeping off his stained hat, gave her a gap-toothed smile. Ida Mae pulled the horses to a halt, and the man grasped one of the team's halters, steadying them. Light drops began to spatter the ground as Ida Mae handed the reins to the grinning cowhand.

Worley lifted his hat a few inches as he approached and then resettled it. "What brings you out our way, Mrs. Greeley? Is something wrong?"

"No. Just needed a place to get out of the storm for a few hours. Hope you don't mind my taking shelter here."

"Nope. You're more than welcome." He glanced toward the bunkhouse and the cowboys who were shuffling toward them. "Boys here haven't had this much excitement since Rooster bet them he could ride a wild hog."

The bowlegged cowpuncher laughed. "Did it too, didn't I, boss? Made myself five dollars."

"Yes, you did, Rooster," Worley said, his voice quiet and laced with patience. Turning to Ida Mae he continued. "Why don't you come on into the ranch house, Mrs. Greeley? Rooster here can take your team on to the barn and see they're taken care of."

Ida Mae grabbed her bag and satchel and handed them to Rooster before climbing from the wagon. Thanking Rooster, she took her bags from him and followed the foreman to the ranch's main building. She heard one of the men call a greeting to her. She turned and waved at them. "Morning, boys," she responded before entering the open door that the thin, older foreman held for her.

"Can I get you some hot coffee?" Cliff had removed his hat and held the curled brim in one callused hand.

"Coffee would be nice if you have some, Cliff. But please don't make it for me. I hope to be on my way as soon as the rain lets up."

Worley shifted his boots on the rug. "You set yourself down, Mrs. Greeley. I got a pot on the stove in my quarters. I'll be right back with it."

Ida Mae noticed how stoop-shouldered Worley had become as she watched him leave the room. She shivered slightly and inhaled the musty air of the room, surmising it had been some time since the house was thoroughly cleaned. Worley more than likely had it cleaned only when he knew the owners would be coming for a visit. She sat down on a coarse camelback sofa and glanced longingly at the cold fireplace. Even though it had been warm before the rain, she felt the chill of the dank room.

Worley returned with a pot of hot coffee and two cracked and chipped mugs. "Sorry 'bout the cups," he said. "Only ones I could find that were clean."

She gratefully accepted the steaming mug of coffee and settled back against the worn sofa. "I don't want to keep you from whatever you were doing," Ida Mae said. "The rain should let up shortly, and then I'll be on my way."

"Twern't doing a thing that couldn't be done later," Worley mumbled as he sat down stiffly on an ornately carved, straight-back chair. His craggy eyebrows forked upward as he glanced at her. "You been over visiting with the Schmidt woman?"

Ida Mae took a slow sip of the coffee. She rested the cup on one knee before answering. "Yes . . . and Thomas."

His faded blue eyes turned inquisitive, and he leaned forward expectantly.

"Thomas told me he just returned from Fort Chadwick. He said that he and some other ranchers had lodged a complaint with the Army about the Indians who've been raiding along the Upper Concho." Ida Mae took another sip and observed her host closely.

Worley frowned and buried his gaze in his cup as he took a long swallow.

"Would you know anything about these raids?" Ida Mae asked quietly.

He lowered his cup and slowly shook his head. "Hadn't heard 'bout it."

"Have any of the ranches west of here complained about the Indians?"

The weather-beaten foreman stared at her for a moment. "No. Do you have reason to believe Schmidt wasn't being honest with you?"

She curled her hands around the warm mug. "The Upper Concho is several hundred miles west of here. If you're not worried, why is he?"

"Didn't say I wasn't worried. Said I hadn't heard of any troubles." He pushed out his lower lip and studied the floor. "A hundred miles isn't that far for a band of Indians, Mrs. Greeley. On horseback, they can travel that far in a couple of days."

Worley shifted his gaze back to Ida Mae. "If they're raiding along the Concho, they'll be taking cattle. Not enough deer left to see them through the winter and the buffalo are all but gone. I would say the ranches west of here might have reason to complain. As far as Schmidt, his spread lays south. He has enough vaqueros working for him that he shouldn't have any trouble."

"Perhaps I overreacted," Ida Mae said with a slight shrug. "But I'm puzzled why I wasn't notified of the problem. Especially after what I endured. And you. You said you hadn't heard anything, and this ranch is west of mine. Doesn't make sense. Then there was Thomas' offer to buy my spread."

Worley stiffened and his chin jutted forward. "Huh?"

Smiling slightly, Ida Mae brushed wind-tousled hair from her forehead. "I approached Mr. Schmidt with the idea of selling my market cattle to him in order to save myself the expense of a trail drive. With Cotton injured, I didn't think I had enough hands to undertake a trail drive on my own. Instead, he offered to buy the ranch."

Both of Worley's eyebrows shot up. "What the heck happened to Cotton?"

"Someone ambushed him. Shot him through the leg. If it hadn't been for my new hand, he might not have made it back to the ranch."

Worley blinked several times as he processed the information. "Now why would someone ambush Cotton? And when did you hire on a new hand?"

Ida Mae took a slow sip of coffee. She regretted letting the information concerning Jed slip out. She had wanted to keep it under wraps for a while longer. But why? Was she ashamed to admit she needed help? Or was she afraid Jed would leave and she would be left to explain once again why a ranch hand had quit?

"We're losing cattle," she said, hoping to head off any more questions about Jed. "Cotton found a running iron and signs of a firepit when he was shot." She lifted her cup and looked at Worley over the rim. "Has this spread lost any cattle?"

"Nope. But I've got a dozen more wranglers than you do to keep an eye on things. It's good you hired someone. You needed more help. Now, about Cotton. How bad is he?"

"Gerta gave me some herbs for a poultice. I'll apply it as soon as I get back. It was a clean wound, and I believe he'll recover without any problems."

Taking a gulp of the hot coffee, Worley's Adam's apple bobbed several times. "Maybe I'll ride back with you to your place. See how the old goat's doing."

A sudden crash of thunder rattled the building and rain hammered on the roof. Worley stood and walked to one of the windows. He used his shirtsleeve to wipe the condensation from the glass and peered out. "You may have to spend the night, Mrs. Greeley. By the looks of this, you won't be able to cross any of the washes between here and your place before tomorrow."

Chapter Ten

"Move those cattle away from the river!" Cotton yelled from the bunkhouse doorway.

Jed and Kyle had taken shelter in the barn from the hail that was now bouncing like popcorn across the muddy yard. Jed glanced at Kyle. "Does he mean now?"

Kyle squinted through the downpour at Cotton, who was waving one hand in a circling, hurry-up motion. "Yeah, I think so."

"I swear," Jed muttered. "Why did we push them in so close to the river if we have to push them right back out?"

"Because that's what cowboys do," Kyle observed as he pulled on his oilskin slicker. "We push 'em here and then we push 'em there. If those cows had any sense, we wouldn't have jobs."

Jed smiled at Kyle's dry humor and, picking up a saddle, threw it across Star's back. As he tightened the cinch, he thought of Ida Mae and wondered if she would attempt to return to the ranch during the storm. If Cotton was worried about the river rising, it stood to reason that it would be dangerous for Ida Mae to cross the washes.

The cattle balked at leaving the shelter provided by the trees and brush that grew along the river. It took most of the afternoon to flush them out and herd them toward the rise in back of the ranch house. The river was already flooding into the brush, and Jed wondered if the herd might try to return.

"Will they stay up there?" he yelled at Kyle.

71

"We'll move 'em over the rise and into the swale on the far side," Kyle shouted back. "When we get 'em there, keep moving around them until they bunch together."

Star was beginning to slip on the muddy slopes when Kyle judged the cattle secure enough to leave. Most had turned their backsides to the driving rain while some continued to mill about, seeking protection within the inner part of the herd.

As Jed rode back to the barn, his thoughts returned to Ida Mae and wondered if he should offer to ride the trail and look for her.

"Tarnation, Jed, that woman can take care of herself. She's a Texas cattle rancher, not one of yer Southern plantation ladies."

Jed's back stiffened. Cotton hadn't known his mother—or Matilda.

"Maybe that's why someone should look for her," Jed replied, his words sharp. "She's stubborn and strong-willed. I can see her trying to bully her way back here, regardless of the dangers involved."

Cotton slowly stirred the pot of beans bubbling on the stove. "She won't. If she's already left Cradle's Peak, she'll hole up at the Circle-M, or town, dependin' on which is closest." He tapped the wooden spoon on the rim of the kettle and glanced at Jed. "She would've had to leave Cradle's Peak afore dawn to been on this side of town when the storm hit."

Cotton limped back to his bunk and listed sideways as he sank down. "Tell you what. If she's not home by early afternoon tomorrow, you can posse up and go look for her."

Jed shook off his oilskin slicker. Maybe Cotton was right. His reasoning sounded logical. *Could be I'm the one who's the greenhorn here. I don't know this country and I don't know the people or their ways.*

"If this rain keeps up," Cotton said, interrupting Jed's thoughts, "you and Kyle need to be out ridin' the washes. Cattle will be caught in sinkholes and mired down. They'll need to be pulled out."

"Could we have some of those beans first?" Kyle asked, eyeing the simmering pot.

It was almost dark when Jed and Kyle managed to make it back to the ranch. With them they brought in a half dozen mud-smeared cattle. Herding them in with the others, Jed observed that the cattle seemed content in their small valley. Feed was ample for a few more days and rain pooling at the low end of the swale provided water.

The yard was shrouded in murky dampness by the time Jed unsaddled Star and turned her out. Butch brushed up against his leg as he walked toward the bunkhouse. He stumbled slightly as the dog crowded against him. "What's the matter, boy?" Jed asked. Butch whined and cut ahead of Jed, impeding his stride. Opening the door to the bunkhouse, Jed waited as the dog crept in on silent paws.

Cotton was lying on his bunk. Jed could see his reddened face, the skin taut and shiny with fever.

Kyle stood by him with a wet towel in one hand and a cup of water in the other. He turned and looked at Jed, worry evident on his young face. "He looked like this when I came in," he said. "I'm trying to get him to drink something. I think his leg is swollen."

Jed moved in closer. "We'll need to take a look at the wound. I don't think it's been cleaned since the boss lady left."

Butch inched in closer and licked Cotton's dangling hand. "Dang-it-all!" Cotton croaked. "I kicked that hound out once. Who let him back in?"

"He's just worried about you," Jed said quietly. "When did you notice the leg swelling?"

"I was fine this morning. It was later this afternoon when it started throbbin' like a dang war drum."

"Kyle, put some water on to boil," Jed directed. "I'll get his britches off and see what I can do."

After removing Cotton's trousers, Jed could see the wound had matted and was no longer draining. He carefully washed his hands with soap and made a lather of suds on a washcloth. He washed the wound, breaking away the crusted scabs that covered the bullet hole. He could hear Cotton taking deep gulps of air and saw his face pulled into a tight grimace. Jed worked gently as he cleaned the wound and rewrapped it with the fresh bandages Ida Mae left.

By the time he finished dressing Cotton's leg, the biscuits Kyle had made were turning a golden brown in the Dutch oven and the reheated beans filled the room with a moist, tantalizing aroma. Kyle fixed Cotton a plate, but he refused to eat and turned his face to the wall.

Kyle looked at Jed, his eyes dark with worry.

"I opened the wound and it's draining now." Jed tried to sound reassuring as he addressed Kyle. "He should feel better come morning."

Jed woke up several times throughout the night. He could hear Kyle turning restlessly in his bunk and Cotton mumbling. As near as Jed could make out, Cotton's mumblings were simply a string of profanity followed by more cusswords.

Up before daybreak, Jed found the makings for slapjacks and had already made a stack when Kyle raised his tousled head. He turned and stared at Cotton's sleeping form, watching the steady rise and fall of the blanket that covered him.

"Is he resting any better?" Kyle asked.

Jed nodded. "I'd say just afore daylight he drifted off to sleep. Either the fever broke, or he plumb wore himself out with all his cussing."

"Great crawdads alive," Kyle said as he threw off his blanket. "I never knew a man who could rattle off as many cusswords as he did and not repeat himself." He picked up his trousers and shoved one leg in. "If I'd had a pencil and some paper, I could've written a book."

Jed chuckled. "Now, who would want to read a book that contained nothing but swearwords?"

"Why, it would be reference material. Some dandy fresh out from the East might want to learn how to talk like a genuine cowboy."

"Dad blame it!" Cotton sputtered. "Don't you two yahoos have anythin' better to do than stand around jawin' about some old dyin' man who's out of his head with fever and don't know horse pee from lemonade, or where he is, or what the Sam Hill is goin' on?"

"Dang," Kyle observed. "I'd say you're feeling a mite saucy this morning."

"No, I don't feel 'saucy' this mornin'," Cotton growled. "But I sure could have some of whatever it is that smells so good."

"Here you go," Jed said as he poured molasses over a stack of hotcakes and placed them on the table.

Cotton pushed himself into a sitting position and slowly stood, bracing himself on the back of a chair. Using the chair as a crutch, he shuffled and thumped to the table.

Jed watched the older man's efforts from the corner of his eye. He knew better than to offer help.

Cotton cut into the flapjacks and surreptitiously slid a piece under the table and into the waiting mouth of Butch. After cleaning his plate, of which Jed figured over half went to Butch, Cotton heaved a contented sigh. "Now I feel a mite better." He belched loudly and eyed Jed and Kyle. "Did you two bring in any cattle yesterday?"

Jed nodded. "Pulled several from Sandy Gulch and found a few more along the river as we came in. We pushed them in with the others on the hill."

Cotton glanced at Kyle. "How 'bout Bitter Creek? Did you check there?"

Pausing while he swallowed a mouthful of hotcakes, Kyle took a swig of coffee. "Didn't have time," he answered. "It was dark when we made it in as it was."

"Then you need to get on it. Run out Cottonwood Canyon too. More cattle have been trapped in there than I care to count."

Jed gathered up the plates and placed them in a tin wash-basin. "What about the boss lady?" he asked.

"If she's not in by the time you get back, then go ahead and look fer her." Cotton rubbed the gray stubble on his chin. "I don't see that bein' necessary, but if it'll make you happy."

The sun was breaking over the horizon and prisms of light sparkled in the heavy dew as Jed and Kyle rode away from the ranch. A few scattered clouds were the only remnants of the storm that had rolled across the plains the previous day.

Kyle adjusted his hat and glanced at Jed. "I've been thinking. No need for both of us to ride to Bitter Creek and Cottonwood together. Why don't you see about the creek, and I'll ride the canyon. Take what you find and bring them in. That should put you back here by late morning. If Ida Mae's not back, then do what Cotton said. Go look for her."

Jed was quiet a moment. It was obvious that Kyle was also uneasy about Ida Mae's overdue return. "I didn't mean to rattle the wagon. Maybe Cotton's right. I don't know the ways of the people here. I know she's a tough lady, but with Sanchez's bunch running loose, anything could happen."

"Ida Mae will shoot first and decide later whether or not she should've." Kyle dipped his head and shot a glance at Jed. "As far as Sanchez, I don't think he would bother her. He likes her. In fact, like every other fool that comes along, he fancies himself marrying her."

Jed shrugged his jacket closer around him. Suddenly the morning seemed colder.

After they split up, Jed followed a small streambed that led up a wash where a trickle of water seeped through the rocks and sand. It was evident by the debris washed up on the banks that the water had rushed through earlier, tearing out vegetation as it rose. Working his horse through the rocks and around a bend, he was startled to see several buzzards suddenly take flight. A closer look revealed a carcass lying embedded in a jumble of rocks. Jed dismounted and examined the animal for a brand. It was a young steer, ready for market, and bearing the Bar-DI brand. Jed shook his head. One less for the trail ride. Remounting, he rode on. Within a few hours he gathered two brood cows and three steers that appeared in good shape. Herding them toward the ranch, his thoughts returned to Ida Mae and the situation he was in.

I'm nothing but a hired gun. Protecting cattle that don't belong to me, a nursemaid to a crotchety old man, and taking orders from a boy still wet behind the ears. Now I'm worried about a witch of a boss lady. What is it about her that gets under my hide? She's not given me any reason to care about her, or the ranch. So why do I?

Satisfied the cattle would stay in the small valley with the others, Jed rode across the rise and down toward the barn and corrals. Even at this distance, he could see that the team wasn't in the corral and the buckboard wasn't in its place under the shed. What did catch his attention were the two saddle horses tied to the corral fence and the two men standing in the yard between the barn and the bunkhouse.

Butch guarded the bunkhouse steps, his tail stiff, hair bristling across the ridge of his back. Jed felt a bit uneasy.

He rode up to the two men, and they shifted their attention from the disgruntled dog to him.

"You fellows looking for someone?" Jed asked.

The taller of the two spoke. "We were sent over here from Cradle's Peak. Our boss told us that the range foreman, Cotton, was injured and the kid who works here needed some help." The man appraised Jed with cold, guarded eyes. "I don't think the old man is hurt that bad. He told us to get our hairy haunches off the ranch."

The shorter of the two men spat a stream of tobacco juice into the dirt. "You don't look like any kid. Who are you?"

Jed dismounted and stepped toward the men. "I'm the new hand here. Name's Jed McCabe." He offered his hand. "You fellows?"

The older and taller of the two men hesitated a moment before taking Jed's hand and shaking it. "I'm Joe and this here is Laredo." Both men were of dark complexion, and the smaller one smirked as he shook Jed's hand.

Jed prided himself on being able to size up a man by his handshake. If his instincts were still on track, he would have to agree with Butch.

"Is Mrs. Greeley still at Cradle's Peak?" Jed inquired.

"Not that I know of," Joe responded. "Schmidt said she left yesterday morning."

"When did you fellows leave Cradle's Peak?"

"This morning, before sunup."

"And you didn't see any sign of her along the way?"

Joe shook his head. "Rain would have washed any tracks out. Could be she stopped by the Circle-M. Maybe she hadn't left there yet when we came by."

Jed rubbed one hand across his jaw. Everyone was of the opinion that Ida Mae had ridden out the storm at the Circle-M. Where was this ranch, and what kind of men ran it? "You fellows sit tight for a spell. I need to have a little talk with the foreman."

Shoving Butch aside with his knee, Jed entered the bunkhouse. Cotton was seated at the table, a half-filled cup of coffee before him. Jed swore softly. Cotton's eyes were round and glassy. His cheeks were flushed, and the distinct smell of whiskey lay heavily in the room.

"What the . . . ?" Jed muttered as he stared at him.

"Those two saddle bums still out there?" Cotton asked.

"They are. Said you ordered them off the ranch."

"Dang right I did. We don't need their kind of help."

"Don't you think that's up to the boss lady?" Jed said quietly.

"I'm still straw boss here, and I ain't havin' a couple of thieves bunkin' with me. A body would never be able to get any sleep for keepin' an eye on his poke."

Jed stood for a moment, trying to decide how to handle the belligerent, slightly tipsy old man. "I'll send them out to Cottonwood Canyon to help Kyle. Maybe it's best if I try locating the boss lady."

"First you send those polecats on their way. If you don't, I will. And I'll make dadgum sure they know I mean it this time."

"All right, old-timer," Jed said, his voice patronizing. "Why don't you let me help you back to your bunk? You've worked yourself into such a froth, you're liable to start having fits anytime now."

"I . . . ah. Dern it, leave me alone." Cotton's hand shook as he waved Jed off. "You take care of things out there. I'm . . . I think I'll just sit here for a while."

Jed stepped out of the bunkhouse and, after shutting Butch in with Cotton, walked over to where the two cowboys were still standing. "Do you fellows know where Cottonwood Canyon is?" he asked.

"Pretty much," the tall cowboy responded. "Why?"

"The kid's bringing in some cattle from there," Jed explained. "You fellows ride out and help him bring them in. When you get back, bunk the night in the tack room. The old man is in a foul mood right now and he doesn't need to get riled any more than he already is. In the meantime, I'll run down to the boss lady and see if we can sort this out."

Jed watched as the two cowhands mounted and rode off toward the low range of hills. Turning Star back into the corral, he selected a fresh mount. He hated to take matters into his own hands, but if it were Ida Mae's plan to use the two cowhands, he'd rather not be on the receiving end of her wrath if he carried out Cotton's instructions. He still needed time. Maybe if he worked long enough, the boss lady would be willing to pay him off with a horse. He was getting a mite partial to Star.

Chapter Eleven

Breakfast at the Circle-M ranch was far different from the lavish spread Ida Mae enjoyed the previous morning at Cradle's Peak. Worley had retrieved two plates of food from the cookhouse, and they were enjoying the meal in the ranch house dining room. Sausage, beans, sourdough biscuits, and black coffee were the offering of the day.

"I'm anxious to get started this morning, Cliff," Ida Mae said, finishing the last of her coffee. "Cotton's wound will need attention, and there's two hands coming from Cradle's Peak who are supposed to help with the roundup. If I'm not there to explain, no telling what Cotton will do with them—or to them."

"Right you are, Mrs. Greeley," Worley said, rising from the table. "I'll have Rooster hitch your team, and I'll get my horse. We should be on our way within the hour."

The sudden noise of pounding hooves and the excited yelps of several dogs caused both of them to freeze.

"Dadburn it, what in tarnation is going on out there," Worley grumbled. He walked to the door and pulled it open, staring across the yard for a moment before stepping out onto the porch. Curiosity prompted Ida Mae to follow him.

A rider was in front of the bunkhouse, circling on horseback. The cowboy gestured widely with one hand and his head twisted to and fro as he searched the grounds for someone. Spotting Worley on the covered porch, the cowhand spurred his horse toward them.

Raking his hat off at the sight of Ida Mae, the rider jumped down from the nervous horse.

"We got troubles, Boss," the wrangler said, his words tumbling out. "It's Indians. A whole passel of 'em. Pete and Bear Face are pinned in at Eagle's Rock. I was down in the draw, and they didn't see me. I got clear of the brush and rode full chisel back here. We gotta do something quick!"

Worley shoved his hat down hard on his head. "Tell the boys to mount up and bring plenty of firepower." Turning to Ida Mae he said, "You stay here, Mrs. Greeley. I'll leave a wrangler to watch the home place. I don't want you to leave until I get back."

Ida Mae could feel the muscles in her body tighten with apprehension. "Yes, of course," she mumbled. She gripped the post supporting the porch's roof and watched as the hands scrambled to catch their horses and saddle up.

Rooster was tightening the cinch on the foreman's horse when Worley emerged from his quarters, carrying a rifle under one arm and buckling on a gun belt. He loped across the yard and slid the rifle into a scabbard. Grabbing the reins from Rooster, he mounted and yelled at his men, "If you have rifles, bring 'em!" His chin jutted forward as he spurred his horse westward. The wranglers followed, some skip-hopping as they tried to mount their already-moving horses.

Ida Mae felt herself tremble and she glanced around, wondering where the wrangler was that Cliff said would be left to guard the ranch. The only hand she could see was Rooster, who was standing on the top rail of the corral, watching the quickly disappearing cowhands.

She gently rubbed the side of her face, trying to put her thoughts in order. The men all rode west; the danger lay in that direction. Rooster was left to guard the ranch's main quarters and, she had to assume, her. That was not a comforting thought. She turned and entered the house. Grabbing her bag, she removed her gun belt and revolver. Automatically checking the cylinder, she slipped shells into the empty chambers.

Belting the holstered gun around her waist, she picked up her things and stepped from the building. Her ranch lay northeast of the Circle-M. It would be in the opposite direction of the disturbance. She had to get back to the ranch, back to her home. Back to where she would be safe.

"Mrs. Greeley," Rooster called when he saw her running across the yard toward him. "You best stay in the ranch house. I'll take care of things out here."

"That's fine, Rooster. You do that. But I'm hitching my team and heading out. I have to return to my ranch."

"No, you can't," Rooster protested as he hopped down from the fence. "The boss said I was to look after you and the ranch buildings."

"And I'm sure you will do a fine job, Rooster. But I'm leaving."

"Uh-uh," Rooster said, shaking his head and planting himself in front of her. "The boss will kill me if I let you go."

"I won't leave him that privilege if you don't get out of my way." Ida Mae elbowed him aside as her hand flew past him, grabbing one of her team's halters from its peg.

Rooster's face paled, and he backed up against the corral fence. "Do . . . do you want me to come with you?"

Ida Mae had already entered the corral and was placing the halter on one of the horses. "No, Worley needs you here to watch the main buildings. The attack might be a ruse to pull everyone from the headquarters and then some of the Indians will ride in and torch the buildings." She led the horse out and adjusted the harness across its back. "But you can help me get the buckboard hitched. That way I can get on my way sooner."

Rooster gathered the other harness and draped it over his shoulder before moving into the corral. His face twisted with uneasiness as he caught the horse and helped Ida Mae hitch the team to the buckboard. "I surely wish you wouldn't leave, Mrs. Greeley," Rooster said.

Ida Mae gathered the reins in one hand and climbed aboard the wagon. "Look at it this way, Rooster," she said, forcing her voice to remain calm. "You have the cook to help you defend this place, but the buildings are mostly made of wood. If they were torched, we would be smoked out like prairie dogs from their holes. If I can get far enough away, I'll be safer out on the trail than here."

Ida Mae didn't wait to hear more of Rooster's protests. The overwhelming feeling of urgency to flee gripped her. The wagon slid in a semicircle as she slapped the reins against the backs of the horses, pushing them into a run.

The thick adobe walls of her own home beckoned her. She thought of the rifles stored in the chest and the boxes of ammunition shoved underneath the wagon seat. It would be enough to defend herself and her property for days. "Curse them all!" she shouted aloud. "I'll sit at the edge of Satan's campfire before I'll let them take anything more from me."

The horses were showing signs of tiring when Ida Mae reached the main trail. She eased them back and glanced over her shoulder once more. The landscape was nearly treeless, so she could see for some distance. Her main concern was the washes she would be crossing. Not only could they still be muddy from the rains, but also hide horses and riders.

She brought the horses down to a walk. It wouldn't be good to have an exhausted team. It might be necessary to make another run. The slower pace of the team made Ida Mae impatient. She cursed herself for not making the trip on horseback.

The trail she was following would cross through a gully in less than a mile. Ida Mae searched the horizon for any sign that would indicate someone might be hiding within the ravine. As she grew nearer, several crows lit in the skeletal branches of a hackberry tree. If there had been someone nearby, the crows would have bypassed their roosting place. She watched her team carefully to see if they picked up the scent of another horse. The team approached the crossing without lifting their heads or flicking their ears. She felt confident that she was alone in the vast rolling landscape. The bottom of the ravine was still muddy, and the wagon's back wheels sucked down into the sand. The horses halted for a moment.

"Haw! Get on!" Ida Mae yelled, slapping the reins hard against their hindquarters. The horses lunged forward and she heard a popping noise, but the wagon pulled free and the horses scrambled up the other side of the wash. She felt it best not to stop the team to examine the wagon. If anything had broken, there wasn't much she could do about it. If the wagon became disabled, she could always ride one of the horses.

Another five miles rolled past, and she approached a gully that swept its way through the heavy chaparral and crossed the trail not more than five hundred yards ahead of her. She let the team walk slowly while she studied the landscape.

She angled the wagon into the ravine and pulled the team to a stop. The bottom appeared dry, but that could be deceiving. It would be disastrous for the horses to suddenly lunge with the wagon. If the axle or wagon tongue had splintered, a sudden strain on the wood could cause it to break. The horses needed to keep an even pull on the wagon.

She urged the team forward and watched as the front wheels of the buckboard rolled into the sand at the bottom of the ravine. She smiled with relief. The sand wasn't as deep as she feared, and the wheels rolled through without any difficulty. As the team began to climb up and out of the ravine, the mare slipped on the incline and fell to her knees. The dark gelding paired with her snorted and shied away, fighting the drag against his harness. Anxious, Ida Mae stood in the driver's box, striving to control the panicked gelding.

"Whoa now! Easy," she shouted. The mare struggled to gain her footing and then fell again, rolling to her side and sliding back toward the wagon. The gelding reared and turned back toward the bottom of the ravine. A loud cracking sound filled the air. Ida Mae suddenly felt herself jerked forward, her hands wrapped in the reins. Realizing what was happening, she attempted to release her grip. It was too late. As she was pulled out and over the front of the wagon, her legs scraped against the edge of the driver's box. She fell downward on the broken wagon tongue, knocking the wind from her.

The frightened mare regained her feet and plunged after the

gelding, popping the kingpin and ripping the tongue from the axle. Ida Mae clung to the splintered beam with one hand while trying desperately to untangle her other from the reins. After a short distance, she shook her hand free and rolled from the wooden beam as it continued to be dragged through the rocks and brush lining the bottom of the wash.

The sounds of the horses racing up the wash echoed against the earthen banks as the team tried to rid themselves of the snakelike demon chasing them.

Ida Mae made an effort to get to her feet, but a searing pain engulfed her midsection and she gasped for air. She eased her body down and lay in the damp sand. Dazed, she found it difficult to concentrate. Help was what she needed. In order for that to happen, she would have to return to the wagon. Any riders passing by couldn't see this far up the wash.

Her gun belt was still fastened around her waist, but her revolver was missing. "It must be somewhere between here and the wagon," she whispered.

The sun had mysteriously changed positions when she once again tried to push herself up from the ground. She clenched her teeth and managed to get one knee under her. Crossing her arms tightly around her lower ribcage, she rose to her feet. Taking small gulps of air, she started the difficult trek back to the wagon.

The buckboard was within sight when she felt herself sway. The pain shot up the side of her neck, and her right arm throbbed. Rather than fall, she sank down on her knees to rest. It was becoming clear to her that she had either broken or cracked a rib. She thought of the wranglers' ribs she had bound after they had been thrown from wild broncos they were breaking. She knew she needed to improvise some type of support for herself.

A glint from the corner of her eye caught her attention. It was the barrel of her pistol protruding from the sand. Inch by inch she moved toward it on her knees, then carefully reached down with one hand and pulled it from the sand. Shaking off the soil, she examined it and then slipped it back into her holster. Once more she pushed herself to a standing position, and with small, measured steps, walked the remaining distance to the wagon. She lowered her body to the ground and sat with her back against the front wheel. How long would it be before someone passed this way?

Ida Mae tried to calculate what time of the day it was and concluded that the sun had definitely shifted to the western horizon. If she started walking now, she might be able to make it to town before dark.

Using the wheel as leverage, she pushed herself upright and reached for her canteen. She drank sparingly. It might be a long walk. Retrieving her bag, she removed the blouse she had worn for dinner at Cradle's Peak. Slowly, she twisted the long sleeves into a ropelike bandage. Unbuttoning her shirt, she pulled the bottom free from her trousers. Grunts wheezed past her lips as she wound the twisted blouse tightly around her ribs.

The effort exhausted her. She leaned against the wheel, closed her eyes, and sucked in small breaths of air.

A jingling sound floated down into the wash. She listened and thought she heard voices. Jingling meant bridles. Indians used thongs fastened to their horses' lower jaws. It must be the two hands Thomas insisted on sending. Clutching the loosened shirt with one hand close to her bosom and her other hand on her revolver, she fixed her gaze on the rim of the ravine.

Two riders materialized as though from thin air. Sunlight reflected from the silver conchos attached to the horses' bridles. Large sombreros silhouetted against the clear blue sky and leather botas fastened below their knees distinguished them as hard-riding vaqueros.

"*Dios mio,*" the larger of the two men exclaimed, as they pulled their mounts to a stop. They sat on their horses for a moment, staring at Ida Mae. The smaller rider shifted his gaze to the horizon and turned his head back and forth as if searching the low, rolling sand hills. The one who had uttered the oath spoke quietly to his partner and then nudged his mount down into the ravine.

Ida Mae thought she recognized the heavily mustached

rider who was approaching her. The tall, dark horse he was riding edged into the bottom of the ravine. The silver-lined saddle and bridle reflected the afternoon sun in glints of light. The horse and its riding gear didn't look like a mount a wrangler would be riding. "Are you one of the hands from Cradle's Peak?" she asked.

The man flashed a wide smile, his teeth gleaming against dark skin. "No, señora."

A chill went through Ida Mae. Tightening her grip on the butt of her revolver, she pulled it free and eased it up under her loosened shirt. She remembered now. His name was Gonzales and he rode with Sanchez. His reputation was one of ruthlessness.

He stepped from his horse, the smile never leaving his face as he dropped the reins to the ground and approached her. "The proud Señora Greeley needs help, no?"

Ida Mae forced air into her bruised lungs. "Yes, I do need some help. Would you be kind enough to ride back to the Circle-M and notify them of my accident? Someone will come and assist me to my ranch."

The man laughed. "That is not necessary. They are busy men and have no time to rescue foolish women." He moved closer. "My amigo and I will help you, señora. Come, I will assist you onto the back of my horse."

Instinctively, Ida Mae stepped back from him. "I would prefer you notify either the Circle-M, or Mr. Schmidt at Cradle's Peak. They'll see to my needs."

The man's smile faded and his eyes narrowed into fine slits. "Our help is not good enough for you?"

"It's not that I don't appreciate your offer," she said, her voice even, "but with my injuries, I would be more comfortable riding in a wagon."

A smile flitted across the man's face as he surveyed the damaged wagon. "We cannot leave you here alone. One of us would have to stay. And with so many desperadoes about . . ." He raised one hand, palm upward. "You see our *problema*, no?"

"I'm not afraid to stay here by myself. If you're worried

about your own hide, then I suggest you both leave together and send help whenever you reach your destination."

"But our destination isn't to either one of your neighbors' ranches."

"I guessed that much," Ida Mae snapped. "Perhaps when you return to your snakehole, you will inform Sanchez."

A low chortle came from the bandit's lips. "That would make Señor Sanchez happy to know you wished for him to rescue you. Perhaps too happy."

"What do you mean?" Ida Mae asked, frowning.

"My friend boasts how someday he will marry the desirable Mrs. Greeley." Gonzales' top lip lifted in a sneer and he laughed. "Señor Sanchez found a woman much like you wandering the desert. She had escaped from the Indians. Her beauty was such that he desired her for a wife. But he changed his mind. The woman has the eyes of *la gata* and the tongue of *la bruja*. His only desire now is for a handsome reward from her family."

The man's smile disappeared, and his face turned hard. "I wager Señor Sanchez would pay *mucho dinero* for knowledge of the unfortunate Widow Greeley's accident and her whereabouts so he could play the hero and ride to her rescue."

Ida Mae's finger curled tightly around the trigger. "I'm not in need of Mr. Sanchez's help. There are plenty of people who are willing to come to my aid. Now I suggest you and your partner move on. I can take care of myself."

Gonzales shook his head. "I have always known Americano women were foolish, but not this foolish. Your rescuers can only save you if they know where you are." He stepped toward her and grasped her shoulder.

The pain in her side struck like a blacksmith's hammer. She gritted her teeth, and with a small prayer that the barrel wasn't clogged with sand, she pulled the trigger.

Chapter Twelve

The Spanish mustang that Jed rode was barrel-chested with a short coupling and stocky legs. This made the mare's gait choppy and jarring, but she was rugged and would be able to go for hours at the steady pace Jed set for her.

After several hours of riding, he crossed two washes and was now approaching the small town of Mission Bridge. Neither wash had shown signs of being crossed by a wagon. If Ida Mae was lodged somewhere in town, he wondered where it would be.

Kyle mentioned the padre at the mission had taken him in when his father died. Maybe he would try there. Tying the black-and-white speckled horse to the hitching post, he removed his hat and entered the large adobe structure. The coolness and serenity of the church surprised him. Clean tile flooring and whitewashed walls gave it a tranquil atmosphere. A figure dressed in a coarsely spun brown robe approached him.

"May I be of help to you, señor?"

"I'm looking for a lady. A Mrs. Greeley. Would you know if she spent the night here?"

The elderly man shook his head. "No, señor, no one spent the night. I'm Father De La Cruz. Is Mrs. Greeley missing?"

"I'm not sure." Jed hesitated before continuing. "Do you know Mrs. Greeley?"

"Yes. Mrs. Greeley is a well known and respected woman of this area."

89

"Would you have any knowledge if Mrs. Greeley spent the night elsewhere in town?"

"Yes, I would have known. As you can see, we are not a large settlement." The padre smiled. "I can assure you, Mrs. Greeley would have sought refuge here from the storm, if this is what you're asking."

Jed nodded. "Yes, that's what I needed to know. Could you tell me how to get to the Circle-M ranch? Her foreman seems to think she may have spent the night there."

"Of course. Continue west across the river and follow the stage route. Turn south on the first wagon trail you see. It will not only take you by the Circle-M, but also to Cradle's Peak."

"Thank you, Padre. Mrs. Greeley was visiting the Schmidt ranch and was due back yesterday. We're concerned that she's not yet returned."

"Mrs. Greeley seeks the companionship of Mr. Schmidt's sister, Gerta," the priest said. "Unfortunately, there aren't many women in our area, and as it is with women everywhere, they seek the company and friendship of other women. Perhaps she stayed longer than she originally planned."

"Perhaps," Jed agreed. Thanking the priest, he returned to his horse. He held the mustang down to a walk as he left the town and crossed the river. He continued at the same pace until he saw a wagon trail that turned south. Impatience grated at his nerves. The padre was probably right. He was wasting his time.

He nudged the mustang into a canter. After several miles, Jed saw a wash snaking across the road ahead of him. He pulled the mare up and checked the bottom. Horses had crossed, but no wheel tracks. Satisfied that Ida Mae hadn't come this way after the storm, he urged the horse out of the gully. At the top of the ravine, Jed saw a small pinprick of light flash in the distance. It seemed to originate from the road he was on. Something moved and another glint of sunlight flickered in the distance. Jed kicked the mustang into a full lope. That something was a horse. The light must have come from a bridle. A horse with a bridle meant a rider.

A crack of gunfire echoed across the deserted landscape. Jed pulled his horse into a sliding halt.

Thundering blazes! Was someone killing a varmint, or another someone? The sound of the gunshot caused the mustang to become agitated. She shifted sideways, shaking her head and rattling the bit.

"Easy girl, easy," Jed spoke to the horse, urging her forward. With only Cotton's pistol, he would have to get closer to the situation than he would have liked. As he drew nearer, he saw he was approaching another wash. The horse he'd seen was across the cut and standing in some mesquite. Silver conchos on the bridle glinted in the sunlight. He pulled the mare up when he realized the rider wasn't visible.

Looping the reins in the low-growing shrubs, Jed pulled Cotton's gun from the holster and thumbed a shell into firing position. Using the cover of the mesquite that grew along the wash, he worked his way through to the rim. He could hear voices . . . loud voices. A man was yelling in Spanish.

Jed dropped to the ground and peered over the edge of the ravine. Tension fanned his senses as he took in the sight before him.

Ida Mae lay crumpled against the wheel of the buckboard, a gun held steady in her hand. The body of a man lay sprawled at her feet. A horse stood on the far side of the wagon, and the man who was doing all the swearing stood halfway down into the ravine. One of his hands rested on the butt of his holstered gun. He was looking at Ida Mae and gesturing with the other toward the man lying in the sand.

Jed waited for the man to take a breath and then said calmly, "Get your hand off your gun."

Startled, the man glanced up at Jed.

"Take your hand off your gun and turn around," Jed repeated.

Anger flared in the man's eyes as he slowly raised his hand off his gun handle.

"Good. You understand English." Jed looked at the man more closely. Something about him looked familiar. "Now turn around slowly," he continued. "One wrong move, and you'll join your partner in the mud."

The man held his shoulders back and his spine stiff as he turned.

"Are there any more?" Jed called to Ida Mae.

"I'm not sure, but I don't think so," Ida Mae said, her voice weak.

Jed slid on his heels down the embankment, crossed the bottom of the ravine, and approached the bandit from behind. Carefully, he reached forward and pulled the man's gun from the holster. There was something about the gun. Its weight, its feel. Like shaking an old friend's hand, it felt comfortable. He glanced down at the revolver. It was a blue Navy Colt. He ran his thumb across a chipped place in the grip. The place where a bullet had nicked his hand and glanced off the handle in the battle at Stone River.

A movement caught Jed's eye as the bandit whirled, a knife held high in his hand. His face was contorted as he lunged downward at Jed. Dropping to one knee, Jed twisted away from the flashing knife and squeezed off a shot.

The man grunted and fell forward, sliding down the embankment and next to the sprawled body of his partner.

Jed scrambled to his feet, his gun ready, his breathing quick and shallow. He saw the knife lying near the man's boot where he had dropped it. As Jed kicked the knife away, the man rolled to his side and pushed himself into a sitting position.

Grabbing his right arm, his face twisted with agony. A bright red stain spread through his khaki-colored shirt.

"Give me another reason to finish you," Jed gritted between clenched teeth. He approached the man. "Pull off your boots," he demanded.

The bandit looked at Jed with flat, sullen eyes.

The hammer rose on the pistol as Jed slowly put pressure on the trigger.

"Si, señor," the man said quickly and began removing his boots. A small derringer tumbled out and into the sand. The bandit's gaze quickly shifted to Jed and back again to the pistol.

Jed swiftly raked sand into the man's face with the edge of his boot and then kicked the derringer away. He circled the man warily. "Now your shirt."

It took a while for the man to unbutton his shirt. Jed waited, cursing himself for not checking the man more closely for weapons before being distracted by the discovery of his gun. Satisfied that the desperado didn't carry any more weapons, he stepped next to the body lying in the streambed. Pulling the dead man's gun from its holster, he tossed it against the embankment. Checking the motionless body, he removed a knife from beneath one of his botas.

He approached Ida Mae. "Did they hurt you?"

"Not as bad as I did that one," she answered quietly.

Jed dropped down on his heels next to Ida Mae. The side of her face was scraped raw and smeared with blood. With one hand she gripped the pistol and with the other she clutched at her shirt, pulling it tightly around her midriff. He could see the top of the twisted blouse that bound her ribs. It was obvious that Ida Mae's injuries were more than she was willing to admit.

Jed quickly retrieved Ida Mae's canteen while pulling the bandanna from around his neck. He poured water over the cloth and knelt next to her, pressing the wet fabric to her face.

She glanced at him, a surprised look on her face. "I . . . I'm all right. It's just a scrape."

Jed shook his head. "How badly are you hurt?"

"I believe some of my ribs may be cracked," she said, wincing as she tried to sit up straighter.

"Try not to move around too much," Jed advised. He looked at the bandit and the broken wagon. "Where's the team?" he asked, surprised he hadn't noticed their absence before.

"Probably somewhere in Mexico by now."

"Were there more highwaymen than these two?"

"No. Those two churn-headed horses managed to cause this disaster all on their own."

A scrabbling sound brought Jed's attention back to the desperado who was attempting to remove his belt.

Jed stood. "Can you keep your gun on this scoundrel while I take a look-see around?"

Ida Mae nodded as she pushed herself up on one knee.

Jed circled the man, giving Ida Mae a clear shot if the need arose. He holstered his gun, and with deft motions, finished pulling the man's belt from his trousers. Placing the belt above the wound, he wrapped it around the man's upper arm, checking the bleeding.

The wounded man remained silent as he stared at Jed.

"Why did you do that?" Ida Mae asked. "Why didn't you shoot him?"

Jed backed away from the man and shifted his gaze to Ida Mae. "Why didn't you?"

He held Ida Mae's gaze for a long moment and then turned his attention to the tall dark-colored horse standing attentively on the far side of the wagon. He had to take a double look as recognition bolted through him. It was Big Blue. His horse. The one Sanchez had taken. First his gun, now his horse. Could the horse at the top of the ravine be Little Jesse?

"Hold on another minute, sweetheart," he called to Ida Mae. "I need to check on something." He scrambled up the side of the wash. One look told him what he wanted to know. The rangy dun wasn't Johnny's. After searching the riding gear to make sure there weren't any hidden weapons, he gathered the horse's reins and led him down into the ravine next to the body. Rolling the dead man over, Jed studied him. His heavy mustache reminded him of Sanchez, but this man was of a larger stature. Jed took the man's arm and pulled him up and over his shoulder. With one hand on the man's chest, he heaved the body across the saddle. Untying a lariat fastened to the saddle, he lashed the body to the horse.

"Okay, hombre. You're next," he said, motioning to the wounded bandit.

The man struggled to his feet and looked toward Big Blue.

Jed shook his head and pointed to the back of the cantle behind the body. "Here's where you're going to ride, and you'll be heading back the way you came." Jed moved away from the horse, allowing the bandit to mount. He walked behind the dun as it struggled up the embankment under the weight of the two men. He stood for a moment watching, as the wounded Mexican leaned over the body and urged the horse forward.

Jed stepped into the sagebrush and continued to observe the rider for another few minutes. The bandit kept to the roadway for a while, then veered off and headed northwest. Jed wondered if he had done right by letting the bandit go free.

He turned back to the gully and hurried to the bottom, where he retrieved his Navy Colt and the confiscated weapons. Walking to Big Blue, he collected the reins and led the horse back to Ida Mae.

She stood facing him, her pistol now lying on the seat of the buckboard. Her face was pinched as she supported herself against the wheel.

"Since when have we become so familiar with each other that you feel you can call me sweetheart?" she demanded.

Jed frowned. "Sorry, ma'am. I got carried away. I . . . uh, this gun here, it was the one that Sanchez took from me. When I realized this horse was my mine, I got to thinking that the other horse on top of the wash might be my brother's. It wasn't."

Ida Mae blinked several times. "Well, I must say that is an amazing coincidence. But I still can't believe you let him ride out of here after he tried to kill you."

"Let's just say I owed him one," Jed said quietly.

"Why would you think you owed him anything after what he took from you?"

He glanced at her, a ghost of a smile on his lips. "He was the one who suggested to Sanchez that they not kill me, but leave me for the buzzards."

Jed turned to his horse. The large black horse nickered softly. Running his hand down Big Blue's jawline, Jed cupped his whiskered chin gently in his palm. He had always carried a treat for him. He wished he had one now, even a handful of parched corn would have been reward enough, but he had nothing. He turned to Ida Mae. "We'll see if you can ride this fellow back to the ranch. Your wagon will need some work before it can be moved."

"What about the team? I can't afford to replace those horses. And what about the ammunition I have in the wagon?"

"We'll take the cartridges with us. I'll take you as far as the mission, then come back and look for the horses. I don't want to leave you here while I ride thirty miles looking for horses that could be anywhere."

Ida Mae turned to Big Blue and raised her hand to the pommel. She gasped as she attempted to pull herself up.

"Best you get on him another way," Jed said. "Let me help you into the wagon, and then you can step onto him from there."

Jed placed one arm around her waist and the other in back of her knees, easing her back into a cradling position. He picked her up and held her against his body. The lightness of her weight surprised him. For some reason he had envisioned her as being much heavier, all muscle and bone. It had been a long while since he had held a woman, and he felt a warm, pleasing sensation course through his body.

"Are we going to stand here all day?" Ida Mae asked, her voice cutting into his thoughts.

Now he remembered why he imagined her heavier. It was her mouth.

After lifting her into the wagon, he pulled himself up after her and then assisted her onto the back of the horse. He quickly retrieved the ammunition from beneath the wagon seat and began sliding the boxes into the saddlebags.

"I don't mean to hurry you, ma'am," he said, "but that highway bandit left the trail and was headed northwest. He might be planning on circling back on us."

"I don't think so," Ida Mae said, gripping the saddle horn. "Sanchez's place is in that direction. He probably wants to get there as soon as possible. But if he thinks he will rile Sanchez up because of the man I shot, he'll be in for a surprise."

"Why do you say that?" Jed inquired as he gathered the reins and began leading the horse out of the wash.

"The man's name was Gonzales. I heard rumor that he wanted to push Sanchez out. Said Sanchez was getting soft in his old age and wanted to settle down with a family."

Jed thought of what Kyle had told him about Sanchez and wondered if it was true.

After Jed climbed out of the wash leading Big Blue, he turned and searched the horizon around them. Across the gully and toward the south he saw a small dust cloud moving close to the ground. He handed the reins to Ida Mae and retrieved the mustang from the brush. With a short hop, he mounted and glanced once more at the moving forms in the distance.

"Someone's coming," he said. "They look like they're in a powerful hurry."

Ida Mae turned and looked in the direction Jed indicated. "They're not Indians," she said quietly. "Indians wouldn't be coming up the trail."

"I give all due respect to your knowledge of the Indians and their habits, ma'am, but I'd feel a mite better if you moved up the trail. If for some reason this bunch is unfriendly, kick that stallion in the ribs and haul ashes into town. That horse can outrun anything hereabouts."

Ida Mae continued to stare at the fast-approaching riders.

"Ma'am . . ."

She shook her head. "That's Cliff Worley from the Circle-M. Several of his men are with him."

Jed eased his pistol out and rested it against his thigh. He hoped she was right. He watched as the riders swarmed to a stop at the opposite side of the ravine, their revolvers pulled and pointed directly at him.

Ida Mae urged Big Blue back toward the wash. "It's okay, Cliff," she called. "I'm all right."

The rider Jed assumed was Worley sent his horse down into the ravine and then charged up the near bank in front of them.

Pulling his horse to a stop, Worley stared at them. He frowned when he saw Ida Ma's blood-encrusted face.

"I was afraid something like this would happen," he said. His voice held an accusatory note as he continued. "Why didn't you stay put like I told you to?" He glanced at Jed and bobbed his chin in Jed's direction. "Who's this feller?"

"He's the new hand I told you about, Jed McCabe."

The two men nodded at each other, and Worley turned his attention back to Ida Mae. "What happened? How bad are you hurt?"

"I'm all right. A few bruised ribs. The wagon tongue busted out, and the team ran off across all creation with it clacking at their heels."

"I was seeing Mrs. Greeley to the mission," Jed put in. "I'll come back and look for the horses after I get her settled."

"No need fer that, McCabe. The boys and me will round them up. We'll take the wagon back to the Circle-M. I have a fellow who's a good wheelwright. He'll have a new tongue in it afore you know it."

"That's good of you, Cliff," Ida Mae murmured.

Worley shifted his weight in the saddle. "There's one heckuva lot of blood at the bottom of that ravine," he said slowly. "That all come from you?"

She shook her head and told him briefly about her encounter with the two bandits and Gonzales' intentions to kidnap her.

"You killed him?" Worley's voice was tinged with disbelief.

"If Mr. McCabe hadn't arrived when he did, I would have been forced to kill the other one too."

Worley glanced at Jed. "Should've let her do it."

"What happened with the Indians that had your men pinned down?" Ida Mae asked.

Worley squinted as he shifted his gaze between his men and Ida Mae. "Peculiar thing. When we got out there, the Indians had pulled foot. Bear Face said it wasn't much of a fight. None of 'em could shoot straight, and when he and Pete started laying down lead, they scattered like dandelion fluff in a tornado. We tracked them for a while and then I got to thinking you'd do jest what you did, so I called it off and headed back to the ranch."

"I'm sorry to cause such a bother," Ida Mae said, "but I saw no sense in sitting there waiting. You had your troubles to tend to, and I figured I could be home by early afternoon."

Worley nodded. "I always did reckon you to be the most hardheaded woman west of the Mississippi." He gathered his reins in one hand and glanced at Jed. "Best you be on your way. Mrs. Greeley needs her injuries looked at. Father De La Cruz's housekeeper is good at fixing up people who's been hurt. I'd suggest you look her up. And McCabe—take good care of Mrs. Greeley. She's a special lady in these parts."

Chapter Thirteen

Big Blue stepped out ahead of the shaggy mustang, slipping into his easy mile-eating stride. Ida Mae balanced enough of her weight in the stirrups to keep her body from swaying with the motion of the horse, but not enough to put a strain on her ribs. She shivered and clenched her teeth to keep them from chattering. The image of Gonzales' body lying in the ravine was stuck in her mind. Revulsion roiled in her stomach and she was afraid she might be sick. She couldn't let McCabe see her like this. She had to remain strong.

Ida Mae glanced back to see Jed goad the sturdy mustang into a trot in order to keep pace. The shorter horse's jarring gait was forcing Jed to keep his weight in the stirrups. Despite her pain, she smiled inwardly. She'd ridden that horse before. She knew what a pounding he was taking.

The events of the morning began reeling through her mind and Ida Mae mentally squashed them, switching her thoughts to the horse she was riding. She was savvy enough about horses to appreciate the bloodlines this one carried. If the other horse that Sanchez had taken from McCabe were of the same conformation and disposition as this one, no wonder he had been so determined to retrieve them.

Jed referred to Big Blue as a stallion. Could this beautiful, easy-gaited horse truly be a stallion? Unaltered male horses were notorious for their unstable behavior. Jed had either great faith in this horse or in her riding ability. She hoped it was the horse. Her riding proficiency had suffered greatly in the past few hours.

The journey into town was quiet. Ida Mae could see a stage in the distance leaving the small settlement, a dust cloud already forming behind it.

She was keenly aware of Jed's constant vigilance as they rode past the mesquite and sage lining the trail. Before today she would have been annoyed with any man who saw her as weak and in need of protection. Now she was thankful for Jed's cautious behavior, and rather than irking her, she found it comforting.

The day the ranch was raided and Dan was killed, she'd picked up a rifle and fired at the attackers. She didn't know if she'd hit anyone, but her need to fight back had been overwhelming. After Dan's death, all she could think about was tracking down those responsible and killing them.

Gonzales was the first man she had knowingly killed. It wasn't the gratifying experience she had envisioned.

"Ma'am?" Jed's voice cut into her thoughts. "Could you rein in old Blue a mite? This piebald is about to beat me to death."

Ida Mae pulled the large horse up. She smiled weakly. "I appreciate your letting me ride your horse, McCabe. I certainly can understand your anger at his being taken. I don't believe I've ridden a finer animal."

Jed shot her a quick glance. "Thank you, ma'am."

"The horse that Sanchez still has, is his disposition as even as this one's?"

"Little Jesse is a mare, and no, she's full of fire and cannonballs." Jed pushed back in his saddle and remained quiet as a wagon full of freight rumbled over the bridge and down the main stage route. His voice was soft as he continued. "They're both Thoroughbreds. Johnny and I . . . we planned to use them as breeding stock as soon as we found a place we liked." He shook his head slightly. "But like most things, it didn't work out that way."

Ida Mae nudged Big Blue forward. "I'm sorry that I failed to ask before, but what happened to your brother? Was he killed in the war?"

Jed swung his horse in beside her. "No, on the trail outside of Mission Bridge. It happened just before Sanchez hit me. Jesse is as surefooted as any horse around. We had stopped on the side of a wash and the bank gave way. They both went down hard. Johnny managed to throw himself clear, but his head hit a rock." Jed was quiet as he checked the horizon. "The shame was that he'd never gotten more than a few bramble scratches during the war. And then to end up . . ."

Ida Mae shifted her gaze to Jed's face. His lips were drawn tight and a muscle in his cheek flexed. Sorrow and bitterness pooled together, making his smoky green eyes seem darker.

"Dan and I left our home in the East hoping to escape the discord prior to the war," Ida Mae said. "Little did we realize that out here we would face a different kind of battle. I still became a widow, just like so many of the women back home."

Jed held her gaze. "You're still alive, ma'am, and have a place to live. My wife and unborn baby didn't survive. Neither did my mother. Some so-called neighbors helped themselves to all our farm tools and goods, and then took our kid sister with them when they headed out west. My brother and I were looking for her when the accident happened."

Ida Mae remained quiet. The hardness in his voice shook her. They both had suffered losses, except the death of his brother was recent and his grief still raw. She searched for words to express her sympathy, but the only words she could think of seemed inadequate. She shoved the damper closed on the spark of emotion she felt. No need to become maudlin about it. Nobody should dwell on the past. One must always push forward.

"I'll ask if I can rest a bit at the mission and wash up before we continue on to the ranch," Ida Mae said abruptly.

"Do you need any help? I mean, help to get down off Big Blue and into the mission?" Jed asked.

Ida Mae turned to look at him. Was he actually blushing? "The mission has several local women who help clean and cook. I'm sure one of them can help me. But, yes, I will need help down from this walking mountain."

Ida Mae edged the horse in next to the hitching rail in front of the church and waited while Jed dismounted and tied the mustang. She kicked her right boot free from the stirrup and attempted to lift herself from the saddle. The pain was like hot lightning around her midsection. Involuntarily, she gasped.

Jed stepped quickly to her side and, placing his hands around her hips, assisted her from the saddle. She felt the hard muscles of his torso as he supported her against him and lowered her to the ground.

For what seemed to be an indeterminate length of time, he kept his arms around her, bracing her. Blackness threatened to engulf her and her feet tingled with numbness. She grabbed at Jed's arm, hoping to steady herself, but felt her knees give way.

When she awoke she was lying on a narrow bed in a room that was shrouded in dark fog. For an instant she wondered if she were dead. An attempt to sit up sent reminders of her injuries. She felt the touch of someone taking her hand and a gentle restraint against her shoulder. The black cobwebs floating around her were disgusting, and she wished she had a broom to sweep them away. Murky figures hovered nearby. Words were whispered. Words she didn't understand. Then a man's voice.

"I think she's coming out of it."

Slowly the dark fog lifted, and the figures appeared more clearly. Father De La Cruz stood at the foot of the bed where she lay. A plump Mexican woman with sparkling eyes and a smooth brown complexion was applying a warm cloth to the side of her face. She turned to see where the voice had come from. Jed was kneeling by her side, his face intent, his brow pinched with concern.

"What happened?" she whispered.

"You fainted," Jed replied.

"I never faint," she protested.

"Then you did a pretty good job of faking it, sweetheart."

"I'm not your sweetheart," she said between clenched teeth.

"Well, the padre here thinks you are, and it's probably best we let him think that way for now."

Ida Mae closed her eyes for a moment. "Why?" she whispered.

"Because he might not think it proper for me to be here holding your hand while Señora Gomez undresses you," he whispered back.

Her eyes flew open. The warmth of his hand covering hers felt searing hot. "She's what?" she demanded, snatching her hand away and struggling to sit upright.

"I figured that would bring you out of it," he said, a small grin on his face.

"Mrs. Greeley, please don't fling about so," the elderly priest admonished. "Señora Gomez will assist you with a bath and clean your injuries. I suggest you spend the night here. You can resume your journey in the morning."

Jed spoke softly. "If I were you, I'd take Father De La Cruz up on his offer."

"I have a ranch to tend," Ida Mae protested. "Then there's Cotton. His wound may have become inflamed. The poultice Gerta gave me is in my bag. He may need it."

"I changed Cotton's dressing last night, and this morning he was up and about. As a matter of fact, I would say he was back to his old self."

Jed stood and studied her face. "Two wranglers showed up at the ranch this morning. Said they were from Cradle's Peak. Did you arrange for them to be there?"

"I told Thomas it wasn't necessary, but he insisted," she replied. "Did Cotton throw a fit?"

"You could say that. But everything is taken care of now." Jed rubbed the back of his neck. "I know a place I can stay for the night, and I'll be back in the morning. With an early start, we should get to the ranch afore noon."

Jed and Father De La Cruz left, and the pleasant housekeeper helped Ida Mae bathe. The woman then gently rubbed Ida Mae's side with a tincture of juniper. Using strips of fresh muslin, she wrapped Ida Mae's ribs.

Satisfied that the bandages were firmly in place, the woman stood back and frowned.

"Is something wrong?" Ida Mae asked. "Do you wish to ask me something?"

The woman shook her head and, gesturing with one hand, spoke in heavily accented English. "Father De La Cruz. He wishes you to share the evening meal with him."

Ida Mae was quiet a moment before she spoke. "Tell Father De La Cruz that I will consider it an honor. And Señora Gomez, gracias for your help. It was greatly appreciated."

The woman smiled and nodded as she disappeared through the doorway.

Ida Mae tried to find a comfortable position on the cot. She was tired, but it was difficult to rest lying down. She thought of the food. It would be good to have something hot to eat. Her mind drifted to Jed. He said he knew of a place to stay. That would be the adobe shed in back of the cantina where most of the cowboys slept when they were in town. Would he have enough money to purchase a hot meal?

She didn't know how long she had been dozing when Señora Gomez gently shook her awake. "Come." She motioned with one hand. "The meal is ready."

The matronly woman helped Ida Mae up from the cot. The bandages helped, but the pain still bent her forward, clutching her side. She walked slowly, taking small steps as she followed the woman down a long hallway.

Stopping at a low, arched doorway, the housekeeper motioned for Ida Mae to enter. The room was small and the padre was standing at a narrow window, gazing out into a darkened courtyard. He turned to her and indicated for her to be seated.

"Are you feeling better?" he asked.

"Yes, thanks to your wonderful housekeeper. I believe my injuries aren't as severe as I first thought."

The padre smiled. "Tell me again tomorrow how you feel. I believe the answer will be different."

Ida Mae eased down onto the chair. She winced as she slid her feet under the table. "Perhaps you may be right, Father," she said.

The housekeeper brought steaming bowls of lentil soup. Hard-crusted bread resting on a breadboard was placed in the center of the table. Ida Mae sat silently as the elderly priest stood behind his chair. He made the sign of the cross and bowed his head for a moment as he murmured a blessing before taking his seat.

"I'm grateful for this chance to speak with you, Father," Ida Mae said as she picked up her spoon. "When I was being accosted, my assailant mentioned that the outlaw named Sanchez found a white woman lost in the desert. She had escaped from the Indians." She sampled a taste of the soup. "I was wondering if you had heard of a woman in the area being taken by the Indians?"

The padre leaned over his soup, clearly relishing the thick broth. He laid his spoon aside and began slicing the crusty bread. "I'm not aware of the story," he said, his attention focused on cutting the bread evenly. "But I can ask. Several of the region's native people work on the grounds. Perhaps they know something."

"Thank you, Father. I'm concerned for her well-being. The outlaw, Sanchez, thinks he should have a reward for finding her. The desperadoes think she is somewhat of a witch, and I'm afraid some harm may come to her."

The padre separated the bread and handed her a piece. His expression was puzzled. "Why would they think her a witch?"

"I'm not sure. Something about her eyes."

"Many of the local people are superstitious. It could simply be the color of her eyes." The padre nodded sagely. "But that does not lessen the threat." He stirred his soup, his brow furrowed in thought. "Some of the ranches are a great distance apart. It is possible that word has not reached us as yet. Are you sure the bandit was telling the truth?"

"While I was visiting with the Schmidts, Thomas mentioned a woman being taken by the Indians from the Upper Concho. He didn't elaborate. The news, as you can imagine, upset me and I didn't inquire further."

"Perhaps then Mr. Schmidt would know who the family is. If you could speak with him and find out more, I would be more than willing to contact the family and help with her recovery."

"Is there any way you could speak directly with Mr. Sanchez and convince him to release the girl into your care?"

"My influence on the desperadoes in this area is precarious at best. If they would listen to me, they wouldn't be desperadoes."

Disappointment settled into Ida Mae's stomach. The piece of bread she was preparing to swallow lodged in her throat. She choked and then coughed. Pain exploded in her side and tears streamed down her face. She was unable to breathe. It was a moment before she was able to draw in small gasps of air.

The padre leaned toward her. "My dear, you shouldn't let the plight of this woman distress you so. The cavalry passes through town often. When I see the captain, I shall inform him that the outlaw, Sanchez, has found the girl and is desirous of a reward. In the meantime, I will pray for her safety."

Ida Mae nodded her head, unable to speak. She pushed away from the table and stood. Fanning one hand at the padre, she mumbled her excuses and left the room. She offered up her own little prayer that she would make it back to the cot before another coughing attack gripped her.

Chapter Fourteen

The image of Ida Mae lying on the cot held fast in Jed's mind. It was hard to imagine the tough boss lady injured. He shook his head in disbelief. The woman had just killed a man and was as calm as if she'd killed a chicken for dinner.

He mounted Big Blue and, taking the reins of the mustang in one hand, rode away from the mission. Mixed thoughts whirled in his head. Where were Ida Mae's emotions? Had she sealed them in a lead box after her husband was killed? He reflected on the war and the close skirmishes that were fought with fixed bayonets, bringing death to a much more personal level. He'd seen enough dead and dying men to last ten lifetimes. But it never became easy, and he never buried a man without feeling some type of emotion.

Jed rode up the street to Portello's General Supply Store. After securing the horses, he entered the dimly lit establishment and nodded at the heavyset proprietor.

Pausing a moment to look around, he addressed the man. "I'd like to purchase some clothing."

"Not carrying no credit fer any drifters," the man replied gruffly.

"Didn't ask for any."

The man's brow wrinkled as he stared at Jed. "Didn't I see you come through town earlier this morning?"

"Might of."

"And didn't you ride down toward the mission with the Greeley woman just a while ago?"

"Could of."

"No need to be smart with me, Reb. I just wanted to know if yer working for the Greeley woman."

"Could be."

"Consarn it. I'm trying to be of help here."

Jed frowned. "And how is that?"

"Sold my business. All accounts have to be cleared up. The new owners said for me to tell everyone with outstanding debts that they have a week to pay up. If they're not paid in full by then, a lien will be placed against their land and cattle."

Jed's jaw tightened. "I'm taking it you want me to pass this information on to Mrs. Greeley?"

"Rather she heard it from you than me."

"I see," Jed said quietly. "Now, about the clothes."

After paying for his purchases, Jed led the horses to the livery where a thin white-haired man was cleaning the stalls.

"I would like to stable the two horses for the night," he called to the man.

"Bring 'em right on in, sonny," the man replied.

"Also was wondering if there was a decent place a body could have a bath and shave?"

The older man grinned. "Got a horse trough in the back, and I'm considered a pretty good barber. I'll even throw in supper if you'd care to join me."

"Sounds agreeable to me," Jed responded.

The older man introduced himself as Isaac Winslow and not only proved to be a good barber, but also an excellent cook. The combination of the cool water, fresh shave, and clean clothes left Jed in a pleasant mood. Isaac was a talkative fellow and was especially interested in Big Blue's bloodlines.

After several hours of arguing the merits of different breeds of horses, Jed muffled a yawn. "Mind if I bed down in your stable for the night?"

"Not at all. In fact, I've a tarp and blanket you can use," Isaac answered, still in a talkative mood.

"I thank you for your hospitality, Mr. Winslow. I do believe your skills are wasted on horses though. You should open a hotel."

The older man smiled sadly. "That's what my wife and I had planned on doing as soon as we got to California. We got this far when my Bessie took sick. She's buried in the mission's graveyard. Didn't have the heart to go off and leave her here, so I stayed."

"I'm sorry to hear that." Jed looked away uneasily. Too many people were getting this far and dying. "I understand the supply store is changing hands," he remarked casually, hoping to change the subject.

Isaac scratched an ear and contemplated the grounds in his coffee cup. "Heard that," he said, his voice turning quiet.

Jed sensed a reserve in the man's tone. "You don't sound too happy to have new neighbors."

Isaac frowned. "I'm not caring much fer the idea."

"For the new owners, or for the fact that all the debts are being called in under the threat of taking the people's land and cattle?"

"You might say both."

"Who are the new owners?"

"Portello won't say, but I got my suspicions."

Jed stood and gathered up the tarp and blanket. "I'd say a lot of chicanery is going on in these parts. Bandits, cattle rustlers, Indian raids. Why, a man was safer in the war. At least you knew in what direction to point your rifle."

"Oh, I know which way to aim my gun," Isaac said.

"You got a name in mind?"

"Let's just say some of the cattle ranchers in these parts are getting too big fer their britches. You mark my word. There's gonna be a range war, and the good people like Mrs. Greeley are the ones who'll be the losers."

Jed pushed open the door and stepped out onto the porch. He turned back to Isaac. "The Circle-M and Cradle's Peak, are they the only large ranches here about?"

"The Triple-X lies east of the Greeley ranch. But they got plenty of grazing out their way. No, it's the Greeley ranch that has the best grazing hereabouts. Dan Greeley knew what he was doing when he laid claim on that piece of land next to the river."

"This Worley from Circle-M, is he the owner?" Jed asked.

"Nah, just the foreman. Bunch of land investors from around Memphis are the owners."

Jed stepped off the porch and walked to the stable. If it were land investors who owned the Circle-M, then more than likely they were the ones who had bought out Portello. He twisted his shoulders, trying to relieve the tension gripping him. With Cotton's cursing keeping him awake the night before and the emotional strain of today's events, he needed a quiet corner to get some rest. He didn't want the pain to return.

After climbing to the hayloft, Jed moved to a place near the loft's open window. This location would provide him with plenty of fresh air and also enable him to hear if anyone entered the barn. He settled down and drew the blanket over him. His mind returned to Ida Mae and the image of her lying by the wagon, gripping her gun—defiant, yet vulnerable.

The gray shadows of early dawn still clung to the ground when Jed shook himself free from the warm blanket. He was at the trough washing up when he heard Isaac call to him.

"Got some hot vittles, son, if you care to join me."

"I'll do that, my friend," Jed answered. "But I insist on paying you for it."

"Suit yourself. I ain't got nothing against money."

The breakfast was indeed hot, and Jed enjoyed the continued conversation with Isaac. After settling up with the talkative stable owner, Jed saddled both horses, thanked Isaac for his hospitality, and then rode to the mission.

When he arrived, he saw Ida Mae sitting on a bench in a side courtyard. He stepped down from his horse and approached her quietly. She was watching several children play with sticks and a rag ball. The morning sun caught highlights of the reddish-gold in her hair. Her face was quiet and serene. A half-smile played at the corners of her mouth as she watched the youngsters bat the ball to and fro, rolling it across the cleanly swept ground. The hardness in her face was gone, and she was clearly caught up in the children's playful spirit.

Jed paused, taking in the scene. Ida Mae's beauty was apparent, her face and thoughts blissfully absorbed with the children. Gone was the tough facade of cattle rancher, determined to make it in a man's world regardless of cost.

The children's laughter also made Jed pause. He too found himself smiling at their antics. A sense of things being right with the world passed over him. Then he frowned. Nothing would be right until he found Kate. Until she was located, he wouldn't allow himself to think of someone like Ida Mae, or of children of his own who would make him smile.

Jed's thoughts were interrupted when he saw Ida Mae turn her head and glance toward him. She placed her hat on her head and pushed herself up from the bench.

Jed hurried to her side. "Here, let me help you, ma'am," he said.

Ida Mae shook her head. Her face was once again a mask of determination. "I can manage, thank you. Do you have the horses ready?"

"Saddled and ready to go."

"Good. Then let's be on our way."

Jed was careful how he helped Ida Mae into the saddle this time. He found it difficult to touch her and not feel his pulse quicken. He cursed himself for being attracted to her and reminded himself that she was a hard woman.

They had been on the trail for over an hour when Ida Mae spoke to him. "I see you've acquired some new clothes. And where on earth did you find a barber?"

Jed smiled. So, she had noticed. "Fellow by the name of Isaac Winslow. He runs the stable. Let me spend the night in his hayloft and even provided supper and breakfast. I enjoyed talking with him."

Ida Mae laughed softly. "Yes, Isaac. It's a wonder you have a leg to stand on this morning. I don't believe the man ever runs down."

"I reckon you know the fellow all right." Jed paused a moment. "Did you know that Portello's has been sold?"

Ida Mae's brow wrinkled. "Who bought it?"

"Portello wouldn't say. Just said to tell you that the new owner was calling in all the outstanding debts. If the debts aren't paid within a week, they would be placing liens against the debtor's land and cattle."

"They can't do that, can they?" Ida Mae frowned and shifted in the saddle as her gaze searched his face.

Jed shrugged. "You wouldn't think the government could take your property and sell it for back taxes while you were away fighting a war, but they did. All legal-like and tied with a blue ribbon." His eyes met her gaze. "Out here, without any law to speak of, I reckon they might do most anything."

Ida Mae lifted her chin. "Well, they better not come looking to take my land. I told Portello that I would pay him, and I have every intention of doing so."

"I don't think it's him that you will be dealing with," Jed answered quietly.

"Then who?"

"Isaac said that he thought it was one of the bigger spreads who bought it. His theory is that they're trying to control all the grazing land and that a range war might be in the making."

Ida Mae took a shaky breath. "It's not enough that we have to battle the elements, now we're going to start killing each other. Did he say which big ranch?"

"My take on the matter is that it has to be the owners of the Circle-M. Isaac said they were investors from Memphis. They'd be the ones who would have the money to pull off a land grab."

"I don't believe that," Ida Mae said. "Cliff Worley would never work for anyone who's dishonest."

"Then that leaves Cradle's Peak." Jed cut a quick glance at her to catch her reaction.

Her shoulders stiffened, and she turned her gaze toward him. "That's even more ridiculous. Besides, just because Isaac

Winslow thinks it's one of the ranch owners doesn't mean it is. It could be anyone."

Jed nodded. "I reckon you could be right."

They were within sight of the ranch buildings, and Jed heard Butch's bark as the dog alerted everyone of their arrival. The adobe ranch house looked secure, and the horses in the corral nickered as they raced around, stirring up dust. He could see Cotton, standing at the edge of the bunkhouse, shading his eyes against the sun as he tried to determine who they were. It wasn't rightfully home, Jed thought, but it felt good to be back.

Chapter Fifteen

Ida Mae felt embarrassed by the fact that she noticed how strong and warm Jed's hands were as he helped her down from Big Blue.

"I can manage now," she said, turning to him.

He looked at her for a moment, his eyes intense, then touched his hat and turned his attention to the horses.

With one hand she brushed strands of hair from her face. The nearness of him flustered her, and she wished he wouldn't look at her like that. It brought up feelings that were best left buried.

She saw Cotton limping across the yard toward them as she spoke quietly to Jed. "Thank you for your help and for coming to my aid. I'm glad you were able to retrieve some of what was taken from you."

Jed gathered up the reins. A hint of a smile played on his face as he looked at her. "Thanks, ma'am. Just glad to see you back safely."

She watched him walk toward Cotton. The two men paused as they exchanged a few words, then Jed continued on to the barn. She waited until Cotton was near enough to hear her without raising her voice. "Looks like you're able to get around now."

The scowl on Cotton's face didn't bode well. She knew why he had walked up to see her and why the scowl.

He came to a shuffling halt in front of her. "McCabe said yer team bolted, broke the wagon tongue, and left you stranded. Said you're hurt, maybe a busted rib or somethin', and that you

115

shot and killed a man. Now how in blue blazes did that happen?"

Ida Mae waited a few seconds before answering. "Right now I need a drink," she said.

Cotton followed her up the steps and into the house. He pulled out a straight-back chair and sat near the door. Ida Mae watched his slow, deliberate actions from the corner of her eye as she slipped out of her boots and made her way to the pantry. Cotton had done this before, sitting in that same chair, declining offers to sit elsewhere and stubbornly refusing to remove his boots. He was mad all right. Mad about the wranglers. Well, that might be so, but with McCabe retrieving his gun and one of his horses, more than likely they would be short a hand come morning.

Ida Mae retrieved a bottle of brandy and two glasses from the pantry. After pouring a generous portion in each glass, she walked gingerly back to where Cotton was seated and handed one to him.

Cotton swirled the amber liquid around the glass several times before tipping it up and draining its contents in one thirsty swallow. He let out a sigh and raised one bushy eyebrow at her.

She also knew that look. She took a sip of the brandy and, turning, selected a soft leather chair to sit in. After lowering herself into its contours, she settled back. It would be a long conversation.

Briefly Ida Mae told Cotton of her visit with Schmidt and his offer to buy the ranch. She could see Cotton's face turn a dark color and marveled at his ability to keep his comments to himself. "Of course I turned him down," she added quickly, and then skipped to her visit with Worley at the Circle-M Ranch and then on to the encounter with Gonzales and his partner.

"I suppose I shouldn't have left the Circle-M in such a hurry," Ida Mae reflected. "But when the rider said it was Apache that were attacking, everything came back to me. I wanted my rifle and the safety of this house. I was pushing the horses hard and maybe that's why the tongue broke." She took another sip of

the brandy and studied Cotton's face. "When those two bandits came upon me, I thought at first they were the wranglers
Thomas insisted on sending."

The color in Cotton's features deepened and his lower lip
pursed outward. "Those two saddle tramps that are passin'
themselves off as cowhands need to go," he said, his voice surly.
"I told them to get themselves gone, but they said McCabe told
them to stick around until you got back. Now I wanna know
somethin'. Am I still straw boss here, or not?"

"Look at us, Cotton. You have a nasty leg wound, and I have
bruised or cracked ribs. In a couple of weeks we'll need to
start pushing cattle north if we're going to attempt a trail drive
on our own. We need help. I don't know if Jed told you, but
that dark-colored horse I was riding is his. He also took back
his gun from the other bandit. The only reason McCabe was
working here was to buy time until he recovered those items. I
wouldn't be surprised if he's not gone come morning."

Cotton chewed on the edge of his mustache and frowned. "I
think you have that feller figured completely wrong."

There was shortness in Ida Mae's breath and it wasn't because of her ribs. "How so?"

"I think he was actually worried 'bout you, even though I
told him you could take care of yerself."

Ida Mae fought the urge to smile. "I'm not sure how the
standoff with the other bandit would have turned out, but I did
appreciate McCabe showing up when he did."

"Why would Gonzales try to kidnap you?" Cotton asked,
his voice puzzled. "That bunch of thieves knows yer not exactly rollin' in money."

"It wasn't my people Gonzales wanted money from. For
some reason he thought Sanchez would've been willing to
pay him for information of my whereabouts so he could play
the hero and rescue me."

Ida Mae shook her head and took a sip of her drink. "The
pity of it all is that he also told me that Sanchez found a white
woman who had escaped from the Indians, wandering lost in
the desert." Ida Mae was quiet for a moment as she tried to

recall exactly what Gonzales had said. "I got the impression that the woman is a bit of a spitfire. Sanchez thinks he should have a reward from her family for her return."

Cotton puffed out his chest. "It's one thing to hold some nester's woman, but it's another when they think they can take one of us."

Heat rushed to Ida Mae's cheeks. "It doesn't matter if it's a cattleman's wife or a homesteader's wife, a sister or a daughter. It's not right." Ida Mae's hand trembled and her glass shook visibly.

"If I wasn't injured," she continued, "I would ride into Sanchez's place and take her out of there myself."

"None too smart to go barging in on a den full of thieves. That's what the soldiers at Fort Chadwick are for."

Ida Mae rubbed her cheek thoughtfully. "When I was at Cradle's Peak, Thomas mentioned something about a woman being taken by the Indians. Father De La Cruz suggested I contact Thomas and try to learn more about her family. The best I can do is write a letter asking Thomas to notify the captain at the fort." She shifted position in the chair and looked at Cotton. "One of Schmidt's hands can take it right away."

"Only one? Why not send both of 'em? By thunder, even Butch doesn't like 'em. He growls every time one gets near him."

"Cotton, as much as I appreciate Butch's judgment on character, those two riders will have to stay. When we get all the cattle brought in, then I'll make a decision on whether I let those men go or not."

Cotton pushed himself to his feet. "You said somethin' about Worley corrallin' the team and fixin' the wagon. When I see Worley, I'll have a talk with him. I think a deal can be worked out for you to put yer cattle in with the Circle-M's. Kyle and I can ride along with his crew to help. We don't need to be beholden to Schmidt or anyone else."

Ida Mae was quiet as Cotton replaced the chair in its original position and then shambled toward the door. "Oh," she said. "I just remembered. Gerta sent some herbs to make a poultice for your wound. I'll prepare it, and you can apply it tonight."

"When ducks grow ears, I might," Cotton growled, turning toward her. "I'm not about to plaster myself with her potions."

"Now, Cotton," Ida Mae said, her voice reproachful. "You know very well that Gerta is an herbalist."

"You mean sorceress."

"Cotton . . ."

"Same thing," Cotton retorted, cutting her off. "I know what she's up to. She wants to put me under a spell, maybe even kill me. Then that lowlife brother of hers can have a clear shot at you."

Ida Mae shook her head. "Did you ever take into consideration that Gerta might care about you?"

Cotton turned to her, his eyes widening, "Good gol-almighty, that's even scarier."

Ida Mae rubbed one temple. "Tell one of Schmidt's hands to come up to the house," she called after him. "And I mean only one. I'll have the letter ready and lay it on the bench outside."

It had been difficult to sleep on the narrow cot at the mission. Without room to adjust to the pain in her side, she had stared at the wall most of the night. Now the warm brandy relaxed her, and she could feel the tension in her body beginning to ease.

She concluded that Cotton was being impossible. If the wound appeared not to be healing, she would suggest the poultice again. Right now, she needed to lie down. But first, the letter.

Her large bed with its goose-down comforter was like an oasis beckoning to her. It had taken longer to write the letter than she'd anticipated. It was difficult to explain what transpired and not alarm Schmidt to the point he felt he needed to come and check on her. If only she had asked Thomas more about the woman. She could have made it a personal plea and sent the letter directly to the fort. She would make it her business to find these things out. Frustrated and tired, she sealed the letter and placed it outside on the bench.

Undressing was a slow and painful process. The flannel gown she selected slipped over her bare shoulders and brushed against her ankles. Its soft texture immediately spread warmth throughout her body. She pushed the coverlets back and eased into bed. Her last thought before sleep overcame her was Cotton's words: *I think he was actually worried about you.*

Chapter Sixteen

Butch sniffed at Big Blue's heels as he followed Jed and the horses to the barn. When Jed heard Butch growl, he glanced up and saw the two cowhands from Cradle's Peak riding up to the corrals. Jed unsaddled the horses while keeping an eye on the approaching riders.

"How's everything been going here?" he asked as the two men dismounted and let their horses nuzzle in at the watering trough.

The one called Laredo slouched against the corral poles while Joe ambled slowly toward Jed. "Cattle sure are scarce. I don't think there's much more out there to get," he said.

"Where's Kyle?" Jed asked, pulling the silver-studded saddle from Big Blue.

Joe's gaze shifted between the saddle and Jed. "I'm not rightly sure," he answered slowly. "That the boss lady's horse?" he asked.

Jed started toward the tack room. "I suppose in a way it is," he answered without looking at him.

Laredo pushed away from the corral fence. "Mighty fine trappings fer a lady to be using. You right sure 'bout that? She was driving a buckboard when she spent the night with Schmidt."

Jed's shoulders tightened and he stopped. "What did you say?" he said, turning toward the short, smirking cowboy.

"He meant the night she visited with Miss Gerta," Joe quickly put in. "Laredo here, he don't put a whole lot of thought into what he says. He didn't mean anything."

121

Jed stood for a moment, gripping the saddle. "How many times has he had his jaw busted for not thinking?"

Laredo squared his shoulders and shifted his hand toward his gun.

Joe quickly sidestepped in front of the bantamlike cowpuncher. A lazy grin slid across his mouth and his eyes were hard. "He ain't worth it, McCabe. Let it go."

"Where I come from we don't insult ladies." Jed shifted the saddle to his left hand and rubbed his open palm against his thigh. "And we're especially careful around one who's just killed a man."

The two cowhands remained quiet as they stared at Jed. Joe turned and looked at Laredo and then back at Jed. "That's Gonzales' saddle. I'd recognize it anywhere, but I ain't never seen that horse before. You trying to tell us she killed Gonzales, and he was riding that horse?"

Jed gave them a tight smile. "You're smarter than you look. I wonder if you're smart enough to mount up now and go look for Kyle."

Laredo moved his hand away from his gun and stepped from behind Joe. "We ain't had anything to eat all day. That old buzzard in the bunkhouse won't give us any vittles. Nobody told us we had to bring our own grub. The least you could do is give us some pulled beef to chew on. Why, we can't even find a rattlesnake to kill and eat."

"I'll see what's in the bunkhouse." Every nerve in Jed's body tingled as he turned and walked into the tack room. Men who didn't think before they spoke or acted were the most dangerous kind. He was thankful he had his gun back and instinctively pulled it from the holster, sliding it back and forth, checking its resistance against the leather. It moved freely. He didn't consider himself a gunfighter, but his quick reflexes had saved his and Johnny's lives more than once. He glanced toward the two men who were now standing by their horses. He didn't trust either one, but it wasn't his call to send them packing.

Jed was spooning reheated beans onto cold sourdough biscuits when Cotton pushed his way into the bunkhouse.

"What are those two doin' standin' out there like a couple of women on a Sunday picnic? Why aren't they out helpin' Kyle?"

Jed picked up the two tin plates and started for the door. "They said they were hungry. I was fixing them something to eat before sending them out to help Kyle." Jed paused and looked back at Cotton. "Do you know where the boy is?"

"He left this mornin' to ride to Bitter Creek," Cotton said. "Ain't seen him since. Those two yahoos bring any cattle in?"

Jed shook his head. "They said the cattle were mighty scarce."

Cotton eased himself down onto a chair and grunted. "About as scarce as fleas on Butch's behind. They're probably herdin' them all back to Schmidt's spread."

Jed turned to go when Cotton stopped him. "Ida Mae wants one of those riders to take a letter to Schmidt. She said she'd leave it outside on a bench by the door. As far as I'm concerned the other one can go too. And neither one of 'em needs to come back."

Taking a step, Jed hesitated. "One of those fellows is gunning for a fight, and the other one is a little too smart for his own good. Which of the two do you want to send?"

Cotton lifted one eyebrow and squinted at Jed. "Send the smart one. The ones full of bull aren't so brave when their backup is gone."

Jed didn't rightly agree with Cotton. He would rather see Laredo leave. He looked at the two riders as he approached them with their food. Laredo was the kind of fellow you didn't want to turn your back on, he concluded.

"The boss lady wants one of you to take a letter to Cradle's Peak," Jed said as he handed the plates to the men. "Joe, when you're finished eating, go up to the house. The letter will be by the door."

Joe dropped down on his heels and rested the plate of food

on one knee. "What's so important that I have to leave this late in the day?"

"Didn't ask," Jed replied.

"Well, I ain't gonna ride all the way over there today. I'll stay the night in town and ride the rest of the way in the morning."

Jed shrugged. "Suit yourself. Just make sure the letter is delivered, and you're back by tomorrow night." He turned to the younger rider. "You and me, we're going out to find Kyle."

Laredo continued to eat, his eyes sullen as he glanced up at Jed. "Whatever you say, boss."

Jed didn't particularly desire Laredo's company, but wanted to keep the young rider out of Cotton's hair.

After rubbing down both horses, Jed fed them and turned them out into the corral. Catching Star, he saddled her and mounted.

"You ready to go?" he called to Laredo.

The wiry cowhand didn't answer as he turned to his horse and swung into the saddle.

Jed's hands gripped his reins. Laredo's actions reminded Jed of a Yankee Johnny had taken prisoner in the brush country near Chickasaw Bayou. He had been quiet, keeping his face downcast. Johnny had searched him and then tried to be friendly by offering him tobacco. Johnny turned his back for only a second when the man lunged at him, a knife hidden within his clothes now clutched in his hand. Jed had drawn and fired without even realizing he had done so, and the man fell dead at Johnny's heels.

Jed made sure that Laredo never dropped behind as they rode eastward toward Bitter Creek. The lack of cattle in the area surprised Jed. He had been in this area when he tracked Cotton's assailant. There were plenty of yearling calves and brood cows then. Where were they?

When they arrived at the mouth of Bitter Creek draw, Jed spotted Kyle working his horse down among some rocks. A small stream trickled intermittently along the bottom of the ravine. He pulled his horse up.

"There he is," Jed remarked.

"I don't see why you needed me along," Laredo answered. "Doesn't look to me like he was lost."

"Maybe I wanted you to earn your pay."

"Ain't you who's paying me."

"Then earn it from the man who is," Jed said quietly.

A sour look twisted Laredo's face, and he shifted his weight to one side of the saddle.

Kyle lifted his head when he saw them. With one hand he motioned for them to come up the draw to meet him.

"Come on. I think he has something he wants to show us," Jed said.

Laredo made no move to follow. "Nothing up there that's gonna interest me."

"All right," Jed said, his voice even. "Then stay here. If I see you even lift your reins, I'll blow you out of the saddle."

Laredo jerked upright. "No call for you to talk to me like that. I ain't done nothing to you."

"And you dang well better not try," Jed said as he urged Star up the wash.

A frown furrowed Kyle's brow as Jed drew near. "Did I hear you say you were going to blow that little banty rooster out of the saddle?"

"You did."

"What's going on?" Kyle asked. "Is Ida Mae all right?"

"She'll be fine. She had an accident with the wagon and one of Sanchez's men tried to take her hostage. We can talk about that later. Now, what have you found that's kept you here all day?"

"Ten head of cattle. All dead. There's a watering hole up the draw some. Looks as though they went up there to drink, then didn't make it very far before they went down." Kyle pushed his hat back and scratched his head. "One died not too long ago," he continued. "The slobbers and foam were still wet around the mouth. I think the water might be poisoned."

Jed glanced down at the water trickling along the bottom of the wash. "Is this Bitter Creek?" he asked.

"Yeah, part of it. It goes underground for a ways, then resurfaces about here." Kyle studied the small stream. "This part should be all right. It's where the water is pooled in the draw that I'm thinking is bad."

Jed looked up the narrow canyon and then scanned the sides. "I rode this area yesterday. I found one dead cow, but I figured it got caught in the rocks and drowned during the storm."

Kyle shook his head. "These cows all died either last night or early today."

"Ever have any trouble with this creek before?"

"Nope. At least not to my knowledge," Kyle added.

"Maybe it's called Bitter Creek for a reason," Jed speculated. "We did have a heavy rain. Maybe it washed or leached some type of poison from the soil."

Long shadows filled the wash, and Jed glanced at Laredo. Did the man already know about the dead cattle? Was that why he didn't want to ride with them? He should have gone along with Cotton's advice and sent him back with his partner.

"We best string some rope across this wash to keep any more cattle from going in," Jed said. "We'll let Cotton know what happened and see if he wants us to build a permanent barricade around the watering hole tomorrow."

The sun had slid below the horizon and darkness was laying claim on the land by the time the trio began the ride to the bunkhouse. On the way back, Jed relayed the information on Ida Mae's mishap to Kyle. He also advised Laredo to once again bunk in the tack room.

"That's not why that place is called Bitter Creek," Cotton said, shaking his head. "There's nothin' wrong with the water up there. The reason it's called that is because of a standoff with some Comanche sometime back. The cavalry cornered them in there and slaughtered most of them. The Indians have called it Bitter Creek ever since."

"Those cattle watered there, and now they're dead," Kyle stated. "Something's wrong with the water in that pool."

"Come mornin' I'll ride up there and have a look," Cotton said. "Could be a varmint got in the water and died."

"You sure you're up to riding that far?" Jed asked.

"Up around Cheyenne I rode forty miles with an arrow stuck in my behind. I'm pretty sure I can ride five miles with a scab on my knee," Cotton retorted.

"Shouldn't we tell Ida Mae about the cattle?" Kyle asked.

"I was up there earlier to check on her and took her some beans and cornbread," Cotton declared. "You're the one who found the cattle. You go up and tell her."

Kyle swiped a shirtsleeve across his forehead and reached for his hat. "You think she'll still be up?" he asked, his voice hesitant.

"I'll go with you." Jed's voice was quiet. "There's a little something I'd like to discuss with her."

Chapter Seventeen

When Cotton brought the food up to Ida Mae, the sound of his voice had jarred her awake. For a moment she felt confused, but as she rolled to her side, the painful events of the past few days sank in. She eased from her bed and slowly pulled her robe around her. Cotton's offering of beans and freshly made corn bread was a welcome treat. Stepping onto the veranda to retrieve milk from the cooler, she noticed that the sun had already set. She inspected the damp, burlap-wrapped structure carefully. On more than one occasion she'd found a snake coiled among the stored items. Fresh milk and gathered eggs, along with a basket of garden beans, rested neatly on the shelves. Kyle had kept busy.

Ida Mae returned to the kitchen with the milk and sat down to enjoy her meal. The thought of Kyle running the ranch in her absence gave her a glow of satisfaction. The boy had grown into a responsible young man, and she couldn't help but feel somewhat proud.

This must be how a mother feels, she thought. She pushed her loosened hair back, cupped her chin in one hand and rested her elbow on the table. She stared at the food. *Kyle and Cotton are the closest things I'll ever have to family.*

The thought saddened her, and she mentally berated herself for lapsing into self-pity. "But for how long?" she said aloud. She picked up a spoon and began to eat. And how long would she be able to count on McCabe? She thought of Jed's search for his sister. Men had passed through the area who had abandoned their families. He was the only one she had met who was searching for one.

On their ride home, Jed had mentioned that he lost his wife and unborn child during the war. What type of woman had she been, and how did she die?

Her thoughts returned to Kyle, only fifteen when she hired him three years ago. She wondered how old Jed's sister was, and if he found her, what his plans would be.

Her mouth tightened. *This is ridiculous*, she thought. *Don't let yourself be attracted to this man. He made it perfectly clear that he only intended to stay until his property was recovered. And now that it has, he probably won't stay around much longer.*

Finished with her meal, Ida Mae stood and carried her dishes to the kitchen's work area. She washed the utensils, and after drying them, placed them carefully back into their appointed places. She held her robe loosely around her midsection, and as she turned toward her bedroom, a sharp knock at the door startled her.

"Yes?" she called, her voice unsure.

"It's me, Kyle."

She walked slowly to the door; after sliding the bolt back, she pulled it open. She was surprised to see both Kyle and Jed standing on the veranda. Kyle stood in his stocking feet, his boots placed by the door. Jed stood behind Kyle, his boots on and his arms crossed.

"We need to talk with you for a few minutes, Ida Mae," Kyle said, removing his hat as he stepped through the doorway.

She stepped aside and watched as Jed moved to just inside the doorway, then removed his hat and leaned against the doorframe.

Self-conscious and a bit apprehensive, she tightened the robe around her.

"Has something happened?" she asked.

Kyle nodded. "Found about ten head of cattle up in Bitter Creek . . . all dead. Looks like the watering hole up there has some kind of poison in it. Foam was around the cattle's mouths. Cotton thinks some critter may have fallen into the watering hole and died."

Ida Mae's face paled. "Ten head?" she whispered. She shook her head. "With the rain, the cattle have other sources for water. They wouldn't drink from a pool that was contaminated with a dead carcass."

"Could the rains have leached something from the soil into the water?" Jed asked. "Or maybe they grazed on some poisonous plants?"

"I suppose anything's possible," Ida Mae said. "But we've never had a problem like this before. There are various weeds that can be harmful, but usually the cattle will show signs of that before they die. How long do you think they've been dead?"

"Looked like most died after the rain," Kyle responded. "But one could have died before. Jed said he found it already bloated when he checked there the morning after the rain. I figure one died not more than an hour before I found it."

Ida Mae walked slowly to a chair and sat. "Someone will have to go back in the morning and take a closer look."

"Cotton said he felt well enough to go," Kyle put in.

"I believe a barricade needs to be built around the watering hole," Jed said. "Could be that someone deliberately poisoned the water."

Ida Mae shivered. That was an unsettling thought. The situation needed to be evaluated, but Cotton shouldn't be on a horse just yet. She took a deep breath and winced. The pain in her side drew her shoulder downward.

"I hate for Cotton to ride up there," Ida Mae said. "He needs to mend as quickly as possible. I'll ride out in the morning and take a look."

Kyle and Jed exchanged glances. "Cotton's dead set on going," Kyle said. "I don't see the need for both of you to go."

Ida Mae rubbed her side thoughtfully. Kyle was right. Cotton could be as stubborn as an Ozark mule when he set his mind to something. Plus, he would be able to read the signs better than she. She thought of their conversation earlier when he had wanted to know if he was "still straw boss." Perhaps Cotton felt his position was being threatened.

"All right," she agreed. "If Cotton thinks he's able to ride, then let him."

Jed pushed away from the doorway. "Another thing, ma'am. That fellow named Laredo, I don't trust—"

"You've been listening to Cotton blowing off at the mouth too much," Ida Mae cut in. "As I told Cotton earlier, we're not in a position to complain about the help that's been sent us. When the cattle are rounded up, that's when I'll decide whether to keep those hands or send them back to Thomas."

"Right you are, ma'am." Jed resettled his hat, turned on his heel, and stepped through the door. He strode across the veranda and continued down the steps and into the yard.

Kyle glanced at Jed's retreating back and then looked at Ida Mae. "We'll let you know what we find out at Bitter Creek," he said as he grabbed his boots and pulled them on. "You have a nice evening."

Ida Mae watched as Kyle closed the door behind him. Jed's abrupt reaction to her comment caught her off guard. She hadn't meant to be critical or sharp with him, but decisions had to be made and now wasn't the time to base those decisions on vague accusations. Surely he realized that.

Besides, she didn't have time to coddle McCabe's prickly personality. First an accounting of all the cattle had to be made. If there weren't enough market cattle to cover the expense of a trail drive, she would be forced to accept Thomas' offer. But how much of Thomas' offer was she willing to accept?

Marriage was out of the question. That would put Thomas in control of the ranch, and Cotton and Kyle would leave. No, regardless of how caviling she could be at times, she would never forsake them.

If she accepted only his offer to pay her after the cattle were sold, it wouldn't be in time to prevent a lien against the ranch and seizure of her cattle.

Cotton said he would talk with Worley. But what if McCabe

was right and it was the Circle-M owners who were behind all the troubles? Cotton and Kyle could be in danger if they rode with them on the trail drive.

The only other way was to drive the cattle to the market themselves, but they couldn't do that without more riders. And with her abrupt response to Jed's concern regarding Laredo, she wouldn't be surprised if she had one less hand come morning.

A decision would have to be made soon, and whoever bought out Portello would simply have to wait.

Chapter Eighteen

Jed's gait was stiff as he strode toward the bunkhouse. What was he wasting his time here for? He could hear Kyle stumbling down the veranda's steps behind him, attempting to push his boots on and catch up at the same time. Kyle needn't bother. The boss lady had made it plenty clear she didn't give a tinker's tap about his opinion. Any excuses Kyle made for her would be wasted. He could take strong-willed women to a point—this one had stepped over it.

Jed pushed open the bunkhouse door and silently walked to his bunk. His gaze settled on his saddlebag stuffed with the few belongings he had left. It was a pitiful showing for a man of his age. He took a deep breath and sat on the edge of the bunk. He had his horse and gun back. He needed to move on.

Cotton rubbed one thumb across his lower lip and looked at Jed from under bushy eyebrows. "You look like a young pup who's grabbed a snappin' turtle by the tail."

"I sure as heck don't feel like a young pup," Jed answered quietly. "But you've got the snapping part right."

Kyle hobbled into the bunkhouse and shook his head at Cotton. "What in all the blue blazes did you say to Ida Mae to get her so defensive about those hands from Cradle's Peak? She dang near took our heads off when Jed mentioned he didn't trust that Laredo fellow."

Cotton's eyebrows shot up, and he fixed his faded-blue eyes on Jed. "That a fact, now?"

Jed scowled. "Doesn't matter. She's the boss. If she wants to send mush letters to Schmidt and put up with one of his hired killers, that's her business. Mine's just about settled here."

"You have a mighty thin hide, boy, if you let that tough-talking redhead get under yer skin," Cotton snorted. "Now, which is aggravatin' you the most, the letter or that polecat in the tack room?"

Jed shifted his gaze to the floor. "The letter is none of my affair. But that poor excuse for a hired wrangler out there tried to push me into a gunfight earlier today. If those are the kind of hands she wants to work here, then it's best for me to clear out before I'm forced to draw on him."

Cotton sat up straighter and grinned. "Now yer talkin', boy. Figured you were the kind of feller that wouldn't put up with a lot of horse apples."

"Why did he try to push you into a gunfight?" Kyle asked. Jed remained quiet for a moment and then shook his head. "Again, it's not any of my business. I guess I overstepped my place when I called him on it."

"Okay, call me dumb," Kyle said. "But what did you call him on?"

Jed shrugged one shoulder. "He said something about the boss lady that I took as insulting. A man doesn't make those kind of remarks about a lady where I come from. So I called him on it. The other fellow, Joe, stepped in and tried to smooth it over. Now it looks like I was wrong, and Laredo had it right."

Cotton pushed himself off his bunk and chuckled as he walked slowly to the stove. Picking up the coffeepot, he poured some into a cup. "Well, McCabe, I think you need to take some time to cool down with a hot cup of coffee." He picked up the cup and handed it to Jed.

Jed glanced up at Cotton's grinning face. He was uncertain what ailed the old man, but took the offered cup. He stared into the steaming black liquid and waited for Cotton to explain what it was that he found so gosh darn funny.

"First of all," Cotton said, as he ambled back to his bunk,

"Ida Mae don't like anyone tellin' her what she should or shouldn't be doin'. Shoot, I haven't had any say around here since the day Dan was killed. So don't get yer britches in a bind jest 'cause she didn't want to hear what you had to say."

Cotton dropped down on his bunk and eased his shoulders against the adobe wall. "The other burr that seems to have gotten under yer saddle is the letter. From what Ida Mae told me, she's all steamed up about some old sodbuster's girl bein' taken by the Indians. Gonzales told her that Sanchez had found her in the desert after she escaped from the Indians. He's keeping her at his compound. Thinks he should have a reward for finding her."

Cotton leaned forward and rested one elbow on his knee. "Ida Mae said that Schmidt had already told her about the missing woman. That's why she sent the letter, so that Schmidt could notify the captain at Fort Chadwick of her location."

"Fair enough," Jed responded, his agitation somewhat subdued. "But that gunslinger in the tack room is bringing trouble, mark my word."

"When that happens, it'll be my pleasure to take care of it—and him," Cotton said.

"Don't underestimate him," Jed said. "His kind will hit you when you least expect it."

Kyle glanced at the door, then picked up a chair and wedged it against the heavy planks. He grinned sheepishly. "I plan on getting a good night's sleep."

Kyle's wedged chair did little to alleviate Jed's restless night. Although he kept his gun within reach, it wasn't from fear. Images of Ida Mae floated through his mind. Her slender frame lying against the wagon wheel, the gun in her hand, never wavering. Riding Big Blue, her back straight and her shoulders square, despite her injuries. The feel of her body in his arms when he lifted her into the wagon, and again when he carried her into the mission. The pale and vulnerable look on her face when Kyle told her of the dead cattle, and her explosive response when he tried to explain his suspicion about Laredo.

An urge to smash the wall with his fist made his jaw ache and his shoulders tense. How had he let himself be completely sucked into these people's lives?

Jed stared into the darkness. It wasn't the letter or the gun-fighter who had gotten under his saddle. It was Ida Mae.

The sudden clank of the coffeepot against the metal stove brought Jed out of his slumber. Lamplight filled the small room. Cotton was up and moving about as he prepared to make breakfast.

Jed rolled out of his bunk and dressed silently. He had come to a decision. He would stay until the cattle were rounded up. After that, any obligation he owed the Greeley woman would be settled and he could get on with his search. The thought of giving up on Little Jesse bothered him, but Kate was out there and he had to find her.

"Get that fool in the tack room up," Cotton said. "Come daylight, we need to be on our way."

Kyle groaned and shook his head. "Somebody dress me and hang me on my saddle horn. I'll wake up later."

"Maybe you should jest wear a breechcloth," Cotton said. "That way you wouldn't have to bother with dressin' and you could water the cactus whenever the urge struck you."

"Now there's a downright intelligent idea," Kyle mumbled. "In fact, I might just do that."

"And I might smack your bony behind with this skillet if you don't roll out of there right quicklike," Cotton snapped.

Kyle lifted up on one elbow. "Dang, you've gone from saucy to sour this morning. What bug crawled in with you last night?"

"Ain't no bug alive that'd have the backbone to crawl inta my bed," Cotton shot back.

"You're right," Kyle said, swinging his feet to the floor. "They'd die from the smell first."

"Well now, since you're so helpful this mornin' with yer

keen observations," Cotton replied, "I'll let you carry these vittles out to that varmint in the tack room."

"Truth has its own rewards," Kyle said solemnly.

Early-morning darkness still obscured most of the ranch's buildings when the four men rode away from the corrals. Cotton had tethered Butch to a fence post to prevent him from following and perhaps getting into whatever was killing the cattle. Lavender clouds lay in quilted softness across the eastern sky. A cool wind caused Jed to hunch his shoulders against the penetrating dampness. No one spoke other than Laredo, who continued to grouse about the breakfast Kyle had brought him.

"Why, I thought you'd mistook me for the hogs," Laredo kept on. "Weren't even fit for them."

Jed held Big Blue to the back of the group. The way Laredo was working the one-sided conversation, Jed expected Cotton to blow at any moment. If he guessed the situation right, that was what the young cowboy was prodding for. Jed had seen his kind before. Bullies during the war if they held rank above you, irritating as hungry mosquitoes when they were of the same rank. Always spoiling for a fight or an argument and never satisfied unless they could rile someone. Their kind seemed to take pleasure in seeing how far they could push a man before he rose up against them. Jed had seen it result in bloodshed more than once.

The sun climbed above the clouds and warmed the air by the time they reached the mouth of the small draw that was Bitter Creek. Single file, they worked their way up the narrow ravine, Jed bringing up the rear. The horses made their way around the remains of a young steer, its belly already bloated in the warm sun. Several more carcasses lay scattered among the rocks lining the bottom of the wash. Disturbed by the approaching horses, turkey vultures lifted from the mounds of torn flesh, making a dark cloud in the sky. A stench filled the air and several coyotes scattered up the ravine, disappearing into the dry brush.

Cotton held up one hand as they approached the watering hole. "We'll leave the horses here," he ordered as he dismounted. "The whole lot of you stay here too. I want to look around before we mess anythin' up."

Cotton handed his reins to Jed and stood quietly, his injured leg slightly askew as he studied the muddy water. He walked carefully around its perimeter, stooping every few steps to examine the ground. Finally he lifted his head and motioned to Jed.

"McCabe, come over here. I want to show you somethin'."

Jed glanced at Kyle. "Keep an eye on my horse," he said. "Don't let him drink any of that water." Jed dismounted and, after handing the reins to Kyle, picked his way through the rocks and to Cotton's side.

Cotton was staring at the ground. He lifted his gaze and searched the sides of the ravine, then turned to Jed. "Take a look around and tell me if you smell or see anythin' that doesn't look right," he said.

"I see a bunch of dead cattle that smell like a week-old battlefield, but I'm fairly sure that's not what you mean."

Cotton's mustache twitched and he shot Jed a hard look. "Look at the ground and smell the water."

The mud surrounding the pool was churned with the cattle's hoofprints. Jed squatted and scooped up a double handful of the brackish-colored water. He held the cupped water to his face and took a deep breath, then looked up at Cotton. "I can't smell anything but the stench coming from those cows."

"Exactly," Cotton said. "If a varmint had drowned in here, its carcass, or at least parts of it, would be floatin' on top, and the water would smell foul. There's none of that." Cotton gestured down the ravine. "Look where the cattle are. The farthest is about three hundred yards from here and the closest about a hundred. Even the one who died late yesterday is already bloated. That tells me some type of poison is in the water. It's affected their stomachs and caused their muscles to stiffen up fairly quick. My guess is that they all died within an hour after drinkin' from here."

Jed backed away from the water's edge and wiped his hands against his pant leg. "I rode this area the day before yesterday. I found one dead cow, but I assumed it was from the storm and the rising water."

"Could've been," Cotton acknowledged. "But if the water had been poisoned before the storm, the runoff would've flushed the water out and sent it on down the ravine and inta the sand. My thinkin' is that the water's been poisoned or repoisoned after the storm, which would've been yesterday mornin'."

Jed took a deep breath, willing himself not to look at Laredo. He studied the muddy imprints of the cattle on the ground and followed their direction of travel. Most had come up the draw to drink and were on their way back when they collapsed. He moved up the side of the ravine to study the upper part of the canyon.

"I didn't ride all the way up when I was here before," Jed said. "Does it have a way out, or is it a dead end?"

"You can get out if yer crawlin' on your hands and knees and hangin' on to rocks and sagebrush, but horses or cattle would have a hard time. That's why some of the Comanche were able to escape and live to tell about the killin's."

"So anyone coming in here would have to come in from below," Jed remarked. He began stepping carefully around the pool. If poison was deliberately put in the water, it would have been introduced where the small stream trickled into the pool. He worked his way to the upper end of the pool and studied the ground carefully. He could make out the hoofprints of a horse. Not unusual, he thought, since wild mustangs ranged in this area, but this horse was shod. What caught his eye was the deep imprint of a single boot. The depth of the print indicated that the weight being placed on it was from a man dismounting from a horse. A couple of partial boot prints were still discernible among the churned mud. The rest, obliterated. He bent and examined one of the prints. Something was squished in the mud to the side of it. Jed reached out and plucked a leaf from a nearby chaparral bush. Using the oval-shaped leaf as a spoon, he scooped up the specimen and placed it carefully in the front pocket of his shirt. He straightened and turned to Cotton.

"I think those lariats we strung across that narrow place in the draw last night will prevent any more cattle from coming up here for a while," Jed called to him.

Cotton nodded. "We need to push some more rock and brush in alongside of the rope to make sure." He turned to Kyle and Laredo. "Take yer horses back down and get to movin' brush and rock against that rope fence," he ordered.

After Kyle and Laredo started down the wash, Cotton turned to Jed. "Did you see the horse and boot prints?" Cotton asked.

"Yes," Jed said quietly. "Made sometime yesterday. Think they could've been Kyle's?"

"Nope. No way. That pointy-toed print belongs to a small man. Kyle's boots are twice that size and round as a plow horse's hoof at the toe." Cotton hitched his weight to his good leg. "Saw you pick up somethin'. What'd I miss?"

Jed waited a moment as he watched Kyle and Laredo disappear around a turn in the wash. Fishing the mud-encrusted leaf from his pocket, he held it out to Cotton. "It was the color that caught my eye," he said. "It looked the wrong shade to come from any of the shrubs hereabouts."

They both looked at the smidgen of crushed leaves imbedded in the mud.

"I think you've found the source of the problem, McCabe," Cotton said. "It might be best if we don't leave Kyle alone with that killer fer very long."

"Unless we yank one of his boots off and compare it to the print, there's no way to prove it was him who poisoned the water," Jed pointed out. "And for that matter, we can't even say that this *is* what poisoned the water."

Cotton's heavy eyebrows knitted together. "Gimme that leaf," he said.

Jed handed the mud-encrusted leaf to Cotton and watched as he wrapped it carefully in a large bandanna. Tucking it into his own shirt pocket, Cotton tipped his head at Jed.

"I've got me an idea," he said. "But the first thing we need to do is get down there and help get this place sealed off."

Using boulders and the existing brush, the men were able to construct an impassable barricade across a narrow part of the ravine. "That'll do for now," Cotton declared. "Best we head in."

Kyle was the first to mount, with Laredo following. Jed hesitated. He wanted Laredo to stay in front of him. The sun was drifting downward and dusky shadows were forming in the washes. There was no way he was having Laredo ride behind him.

With some effort, Cotton pulled himself up. "You comin', boy?" Cotton said, eyeing Jed's deliberate dawdling.

Jed nodded, noting that Kyle and Laredo had already started down the worn cattle path. He mounted and nudged Big Blue forward. He moved in ahead of Cotton and then pulled his horse up. He studied the beaten path for a moment and looked at the two riders ahead of them.

"What itch you gotta scratch now?" Cotton grumbled as he checked his horse.

"Nothing," Jed said slowly. "Nothing at all."

Chapter Nineteen

Ida Mae rose early and watched from the veranda as the men saddled their horses and rode out into the early dawn. It chafed at her that she wasn't riding with them. The desire to be in the thick of things made her edgy. Methodically, she began cleaning. Wiping away the dust, polishing the globes in the lamps, everything she was able to do. After venturing to her garden and attempting to pull a few weeds, the sharp pain in her side convinced her that the weeds would have to wait for another day. Returning to the house, she filled a pot with dried beans and covered them with water to soak.

The ever-present wind had sifted a layer of silt on the veranda. Ida Mae took particular pride in keeping the porch swept each day, and it irritated her to see footprints in the dust. Retrieving a broom, she began to sweep the wide porch with slow, measured strokes.

Butch's sharp bark from where he was tethered caused her to pause. She turned her gaze in the direction he was looking and saw dust rising along the trail leading into the ranch. Propping the broom against the building, Ida Mae stepped inside and picked up her rifle. After placing a shell into the chamber, she moved to a shuttered window and peered out.

A lone rider approached the house. Ida Mae quickly determined that it wasn't the hand returning from Cradle's Peak but a stranger, dust-covered and hard-faced.

She pushed the shutter open and pointed the rifle at him. "That's far enough," she called.

The man pulled the horse to a stop in front of the gate. He

sat for a moment, seemingly to appraise the situation. "I need to speak with a Mrs. Greeley," he announced.

"I'm Mrs. Greeley."

"I have some papers for you. Is it all right if I step down from my horse?"

"What kind of papers?"

"It's documents concerning your husband's death."

"My husband's been dead for four years. Why would I be receiving something now?"

"Ma'am, if you would be so kind as to let me step down, I'll give the packet to you and you can see for yourself."

Ida Mae moistened her lips with the tip of her tongue. What possible legal matters could Dan have been involved in that she was unaware of? She opened the door and stepped onto the veranda, still holding her rifle.

"You can step down now," she said. "Lay them on the edge of the porch."

The man dismounted and pulled an envelope and a narrow card from his saddlebag. He pushed open the gate and approached Ida Mae, a smile quirking the edge of his thin lips. "I'm sorry, Mrs. Greeley, but I'll need your signature or your mark on this delivery card before I can release the papers to you."

"What kind of nonsense is that?"

"I just deliver, ma'am. I don't get paid unless I have proof that the documents have been delivered to the proper recipients. Your signature or mark will verify that." The man's smile stretched further, showing the edges of narrow, yellowed teeth. "You can write, can't you?"

Ida Mae's fingers tightened on the rifle. The insolent sack of cow dung—who did he think he was talking to? "Of course I can write," she snapped, releasing one hand from the rifle and holding her hand out.

The man quickly stepped forward and thrust the card and pencil into her hand. "If you'll sign on that bottom line, Mrs. Greeley, I'll give you the packet and be on my way quicker than a lamb can bleat for its mama."

Ida Mae moved to the bench by the door and sat. Placing the rifle across her knees, she placed the card on the bench and signed it. Her hand trembled as she returned the card to the man. In turn, the man handed her a narrow, sealed envelope.

The rider touched the brim of his hat with one hand. "Pleasure doing business with you, ma'am," he said, tucking the card in his saddlebag. With the deftness of a seasoned rider, he mounted and wheeled his horse away, urging it into a canter down the wagon track.

Leaning the rifle next to her, Ida Mae sat on the bench. She opened the envelope and read the letter carefully, then closed her eyes.

The man had lied. The letter had nothing to do with Dan's death. Her debt at Portello's store had been placed with a firm in Houston. It stated that litigation proceedings were being initiated and a lien had been placed against her ranch and livestock.

Ida Mae refocused and scanned the pages again. Something wasn't right. The amount that the document stated she owed was incorrect. She stood, picked up her rifle, and walked slowly into the house.

She removed a packet of carefully catalogued sales receipts from her desk and sank down on a round cushioned stool. Picking up a pencil, she began to write figures on a sheet of paper.

Ida Mae stopped her calculations only long enough to place the beans on a low fire and retrieve a few slices of smoked ham from the smokehouse. The day slid by as she stubbornly reworked the figures several times.

"They're not getting away with this," she fumed. She would confront Portello with this absurdity and pay him what she owed, nothing more.

Ranchers were always eager to increase their herd of breeding stock, she reasoned. She would sell some of hers. Selling brood stock wasn't the best financial move a rancher could make, but it was her only option.

When the rider returns from Cradle's Peak, I'll send him

back with another letter to Thomas. Surely Thomas will be
willing to give me cash for several brood cows.

Ida Mae continued to labor over her calculations and, by
late afternoon, was convinced that enough breeding stock would
remain to produce a sufficient calf crop the following year.

But how could she keep from going into debt again? And
how long would Cotton and Kyle be willing to work without
pay and only promises? McCabe was hard to figure. He probably wouldn't stay after the roundup was complete, perhaps
not even that long.

Her grip tightened on the pencil as she thought of how her
emotions had almost betrayed her when he held her against
him, supporting her weight as he helped her down from his
horse. Perhaps it had been best she fainted. She might have
embarrassed herself.

Butch's low growling bark brought Ida Mae to her feet. She
glanced out the window and saw the rider, Joe, returning from
Cradle's Peak. It was too late now to send him back to Thomas
with a note. It would have to wait until morning.

She finished preparing dinner, steaming fresh greens from
the garden and making a pan of sourdough biscuits. The sound
of the horses nickering in the corral signaled the return of the
crew.

Prepared to call out to Kyle, she opened the door and was
surprised to see Cotton limping toward the ranch house. He
was using a broken tree limb for support, and a heavy scowl
lined his face.

Ida Mae's lips tightened. She knew he shouldn't have ridden out this morning. *When will the old fool learn he's not a*
young buck anymore? she fumed. *Now it will take even longer*
for his leg to heal.

Cotton labored up the steps and leaned against a porch pil-
lar. The gathering shadows under the eaves obscured his features, and his breathing was heavy. He tucked his chin in close
and looked at her from underneath craggy eyebrows.

"Guess I may have overdid it today," he wheezed. "My leg
feels like I rode through catclaw. Maybe I'll take that poultice

after all. I can fix it up and use it tonight on my leg. You want to fetch it for me?"

Ida Mae frowned. Cotton's leg would have to be really hurting for him to admit he needed the poultice after his high dramatics of yesterday.

"Perhaps I should take a look at your leg," Ida Mae offered.

"No need fer that. I can tend my own self. Jest give it to me."

"All right," Ida Mae said, her voice hesitant. She retrieved the package that held the comfrey leaves and handed it to him. "You do understand how to prepare it, don't you?"

"I been plasterin' poultices on backsides since I was knee high to a gnat. You don't need to tell me how to prepare a poultice."

Ida Mae smiled. "I wouldn't doubt you for a minute. What did you find at Bitter Creek?"

"Nothin' I can put my finger on. We blocked off the area fer now. Somethin' more permanent will have to be built across it later."

"That's an important watering hole. Can it be cleaned up?"

Cotton glanced down at the small packet Ida Mae had given him. "Depends on what's in it."

"I don't suppose there's any way to find out if it could have leached from the soil like McCabe suggested?" Ida Mae asked.

"If it came from the soil, it would've always been bad."

"Then perhaps a poisonous plant washed into it."

Cotton nodded his head slowly. "That's my thinkin'."

"If that's the case, it will have to be drained and the mud cleaned from the bottom. Right now we don't have time. Go ahead and build a better fence and then finish with the roundup." Ida Mae paused and took a tentative deep breath. "Also, I need several of the brood cows brought in and put in the corral."

Cotton arched one eyebrow as his gaze searched her face.

"Had a visitor today," Ida Mae said, answering his unasked question. "There's a debt that's due before the cattle can be marketed. I'll need to sell some of the brood cows in order to meet that obligation."

"I never heard of—"

Ida Mae waved her hand at him, cutting him off. "Never mind, I'll take care of it. Now, if you'll send Kyle up, I have supper for the hands. I would rather all of you eat at the bunk-house tonight."

"You feelin' all right?" Cotton asked. "Didn't have any trouble with that feller, did you?"

Ida Mae pushed away from the doorframe where she had been leaning. "I'm feeling better, and no, I didn't have any trouble with my visitor."

Cotton nodded, then turned and stepped down from the ve-randa. Ida Mae watched him as he limped slowly back to the bunkhouse. It occurred to her that his gait became stronger the closer he got to the bunkhouse. Cotton was up to some-thing. She would bet her best linen sheets on it.

Chapter Twenty

When Jed and the rest of the riders returned to the ranch's headquarters, the first thing Jed had noticed was Butch. Clearly agitated, the dog was pacing the length of his tether. Joe, the rider from Cradle's Peak, was seated in a chair cocked back against the tack room, just out of Butch's reach.

"With no more than you fellows have to eat around here," he'd remarked, "I was tempted to shoot that fool dog and boil him up for supper."

Jed and Cotton had remained silent as Laredo and Kyle acknowledged Joe's greeting.

"Take care of my horse," Cotton said quietly, handing the reins to Jed. "I'm going to have a little palaver with Ida Mae."

Jed had nodded and begun unsaddling the horses. He wasn't happy to see Joe. This put a new spin on how things would need to be handled. The indication that the pool of water had been poisoned was bad enough, but what he'd discovered on the ride back could lead to deadly consequences.

A fresh hoofprint in the trail had brought Jed to a sudden stop. It matched the one he had followed after Cotton was shot. Laredo's horse was throwing her right front leg, leaving the distinctive print in the soft dirt.

Now he needed time to figure out how he should use this information. If he told Cotton of his suspicion, Cotton might call Laredo on it. The chances of Cotton outdrawing the young gunslinger were pretty slim. With Joe's return, it meant more lives than just Cotton's would be at stake. Jed wanted to keep it from boiling to that point.

If he took the information to Ida Mae, would she listen or brush him aside like she did before? Back home, depending on the color of a man's skin, a hoofprint matching the horse he rode would have been enough to get him hanged. Jed hadn't agreed with that line of thinking, and he didn't agree now.

Jed was still mulling things over in his mind when he saw Cotton returning to the bunkhouse. He was using a walking stick in one hand and in the other he carried a package. Jed couldn't help but smile when Cotton ditched the makeshift cane and climbed the steps into the small adobe building.

"Is Cotton's leg bothering him?" Kyle asked, passing Jed as he carried his saddle into the tack room.

Jed brushed the dust from his clothes. "Not enough to keep him from whatever he's doing."

Laredo jerked his saddle from his horse and threw it over his shoulder. He stood for a moment, directing his gaze at Jed. "I'm reckoning that Joe and me will be bunking in the tack room again, seeing as how we're not fit to bunk under the same roof as the regular hands."

Jed kept his voice even. "I reckon you're right."

"By dang there'd better be some decent grub tonight," Laredo grumbled as he carried his saddle into the tack room.

Jed looked at Kyle and winked. "Let's see what the old man's up to."

When they entered the bunkhouse, Cotton was busy lighting the lamp. He turned and looked at Kyle.

"Ida Mae has supper ready. She wants you to go up and fetch the vittles back here." Cotton sat down on a chair and placed the wrapped poultice on the table. "When you get back," he continued, "don't start jawin' with those two sidewinders out there. I'll fix 'em some plates, and you can take it to 'em."

Kyle hesitated and scratched at one ear. "I know you don't care for those fellows, but . . ."

"Go ahead and do what Cotton asked," Jed cut in quietly. "We need to keep those two busy for a while and the best way to do that is to feed them."

"When you two get through with your plotting," Kyle said, clearly aggravated, "I expect to be let in on what's going on."

Cotton chuckled as he watched Kyle turn and leave. "A body would come nearer catchin' a weasel asleep than to fool that boy."

"So, what *are* you up to?" Jed asked as he stepped closer to the table.

Cotton retrieved the leaf from his shirt pocket. "I'm goin' to compare the leaves in this poultice to what we found."

"Do you think Schmidt's sister would try to poison you?"

"She'd do whatever her brother asked her to do," Cotton said as he untied the package. Opening it carefully, he exposed the crushed leaves. He placed the small specimen they found at Bitter Creek next to the poultice mixture. They were of a different color and texture.

"I'd say that shoots holes in your theory," Jed remarked.

"Maybe, maybe not," Cotton said. "Still doesn't prove that this here poultice isn't poisonous."

"Well, I'll be hanged if I know how you're going to find out," Jed said as he sat on the edge of his bunk.

The door pushed open, and Kyle came in carrying several cloth-covered bowls.

Cotton pulled tin plates from under a shelf and spread them on the table. "Let's feed those two saddlebums out there, then we can relax and enjoy ours." As Cotton spooned food onto plates, Kyle picked up a bar of soap and a towel.

"I feel like I could use a good scrubbing," Kyle said. "I'll eat when I get back."

The thought of a refreshing wash appealed to Jed. He shook out a clean shirt from his saddlebag and turned to Cotton. "I can take those plates out to those men. I want to get a little of this dust off too before I eat."

Cotton handed the plates to Jed. "Tell those two I hope they choke on it."

*   *   *

As they prepared to turn in for the night, Kyle removed his boots and glanced at Jed. "How long you plan to wait before you let me in on what you two discovered up at Bitter Creek?"

Jed looked at Cotton before addressing Kyle. "That it's been poisoned."

"A body doesn't need a book full of smarts to figure that out," Kyle retorted. "I'm talking about what you two saw at the upper end of the watering hole and were palavering about when you decided to send Laredo and me back down the wash."

"We weren't tryin' to keep anythin' from you," Cotton put in. "It's those rowdies out there we can't trust."

"Well, they've already bunked down, so what gives?"

"There was a sign that pointed to one of those riders as being responsible for the poisoning," Jed responded. He was careful not to reveal too much information for fear Cotton would realize he knew more than he was saying.

"Like pointy-toed boot prints that match what that Laredo feller wears," Cotton said. "Ain't nobody around here wears boots like that."

"So how are you gonna prove it was him who poisoned the water?" Kyle asked.

Cotton removed his gun from its holster and laid it by his bunk. "In the mornin' you fellers take those two with you when you ride out. Ida Mae wants some of the brood cows brought in. She said a feller came by and told her she would have to pay a debt she owes right away. I'm thinkin' she's plannin' on sellin' some of her brood stock to Schmidt." Cotton dropped his pants and kicked his legs free. "I aim to prove to her that she can't trust that silver-tongued coyote before she can complete that little transaction."

"Oh," Kyle said softly. "I just remembered, she told me to tell that Joe fellow that she needed him to return to Cradle's Peak again. Now I guess I know why."

"Have you told him yet?" Cotton asked.

Kyle hung his head. "Nah, I forgot. But I can tell him in the morning," he added brightly.

"Nope," Cotton said. "Tomorrow you're gonna conveniently forget again. Then I want you and Jed to take both those cowtenders as far away from here as you can ride. But don't turn your back on them and don't let 'em out of your sight."

Jed stretched out on his bunk and listened to Cotton and Kyle. He had a good idea which debt was being called in. He frowned and glanced at Cotton. "And what are your plans for the day?" he asked.

"I'm ridin' inta town and havin' a confab with the padre. That hoodoo mama, Gerta, isn't the only one hereabouts who knows about roots and herbs. I think Father De La Cruz will at least be able to tell me if I'm on the right track."

Jed wondered what Cotton hoped to gain by proving to Ida Mae that Cradle's Peak was responsible for the poisoned water. It was clear that Laredo was the culprit, but pointing it out wouldn't nullify Ida Mae's debt. If she didn't get the money from Schmidt, who would she get it from? The Circle-M? Jed shut his eyes, willing himself to fall asleep. It wasn't his affair.

The steel-gray light of dawn had already seeped into the bunkhouse when Jed heard Cotton rattling pots on the stove. "Roust those two in the tack room while I fry some fatback and make another pot of coffee," he said, not bothering to look at Jed.

Kyle yawned and stretched in his bunk. He lay silent for a moment, staring at the ceiling. "Dang," he suddenly said. "I just don't feel right about not telling Joe about Ida Mae's orders."

"If it will make you feel any better," Cotton growled, "I'll tell her I'm the one who told you not to."

Jed ran his hand through his tousled hair. Despite his reservations, he addressed Cotton: "If you don't want Ida Mae to sell those brood cows to Schmidt, then where is she going to get the money to pay off her debt?"

"The only debt she owes, that I know of, is to Portello. And he can dang well keep his shirt on 'til we get the herd to Abilene."

"According to Issac Winslow, Portello sold his business." Jed spoke slowly, choosing his words. "It wouldn't be him who's demanding payment."

Cotton worked his mouth as though he'd bitten into something sour. "Did Windbag Winslow say who bought the store?"

"Portello wouldn't tell him." Jed pulled one boot on and reflected a moment. "Winslow did say, though, that he thought it was one of the larger ranches."

"Uh-huh." Cotton nodded. "Schmidt."

Jed pulled on his other boot. "Not necessarily. The Circle-M owners are the ones who would have the money backing them to put the squeeze on the smaller ranchers and then buy them out."

"Nah." Cotton shook his head. "It's not them."

"All I'm saying is, don't let your dislike for this Schmidt fellow cloud your thinking. It's just possible that there's more than one outfit that's pushing for a land grab." Jed finished buttoning his shirt and stepped out of the bunkhouse.

The fresh morning air felt good against his face as he walked to the tack room and rapped on the open door.

Both wranglers were sprawled in their bedrolls, still asleep. Jed banged on the door again and raised his voice. "Coffee's hot." Neither man moved. He stepped inside the small room. Laredo's slight form was curled into a fetal position. His face appeared drawn and his breathing was labored.

Joe was sprawled on his back, his head slanted to the side. A puddle of drool dampened the folded jacket he was using as a pillow.

Jed kicked Joe's outstretched leg. "Hey!"

Joe rolled his head, his eyes fluttering open as he attempted to focus on Jed. "Yeah?"

"Time to roust out," Jed answered. "And see to it your partner gets up too."

Joe nodded, his eyelids drooping downward as though weighted.

Jed shook his head. Something was wrong with the two riders, and he had a pretty good idea what. He returned to the bunkhouse and addressed Cotton. "You'd better make that coffee thick as sorghum molasses. I believe your tack room riders will need it. Seems as though they're having a bit of a problem waking up."

Cotton turned owlish eyes toward him. "Now, you don't say."

"How much of that hashish did you put in their food?"

Cotton grinned. "Just enough to prove a point."

Jed struggled to keep a straight face. "You could have killed them, you know."

"Better them than me."

Kyle rolled out of his bunk and attempted to feed his legs through his trousers. "Hash what?" he asked. "What do you mean?"

"The poultice," Cotton answered. "I knew there was some-thin' wrong with it."

Jed raked a hand across his jaw. "It still could have been what the lady said. It just shouldn't have been eaten. I say we send them back to Schmidt, providing we can get them awake enough to ride a horse."

Cotton eyed the boiling coffeepot, then picked up the coffee can and added more grounds to the mix. "Now that's a fine idea," he said. "They'll probably be mighty glad to get back to the grub at Cradle's Peak."

Picking up two cups and the boiling coffeepot, Jed took a deep breath, walked out of the bunkhouse, and headed toward the tack room. When he entered he saw Laredo had rolled to his stomach and pulled his knees under him. His head still rested against his saddle.

Joe sat on his bedroll, arms resting across his knees. He raised bloodshot eyes and focused on Jed. "What did you pie-holes feed us last night?" His words were thick and measured.

"Maybe the same stuff you put in the watering hole," Jed answered.

Joe shook his head. "I don't know what you're talking about."

"Perhaps your partner does."

Laredo lifted his head, wavering on his knees as he turned

to look at Jed. "I'll kill the lot of you for this." One of his hands wormed its way toward the holstered gun that lay beside him.

Jed poured the hot coffee into one of the cups and watched as Laredo pulled the pistol from its holster. With slow, deliberate motions, Jed tossed the steaming liquid onto Laredo's hand that gripped the gun.

Laredo yelped and the pistol spun across the room. Jed dropped the cup and pulled his Navy, keeping an eye on Joe, who continued to sit, rubbing his forehead.

A movement behind Jed caused him to whirl. Kyle stood quietly, a questioning look on his face. Jed let out his breath. "Take their guns," he directed Kyle, "and check their boots to make sure they're not carrying anything more."

Kyle moved quickly, picking up Laredo's revolver and slipping Joe's from its holster. He felt inside their boots and then lifted their bedrolls, where he discovered carbines under each. Picking up the guns and ammo belts, Kyle walked outside and turned to Jed. "What now?" he asked.

"Put all those firearms in the bunkhouse," he said, "and then come back and saddle their horses for them. I believe their work here is finished and they'll be heading back to Cradle's Peak."

Chapter Twenty-one

Several scraps of paper were crumpled into small wads and stacked neatly at the corner of Ida Mae's writing desk. To ask Thomas if he would be interested in purchasing some of her nurse cows was an open admission of defeat. How would she recover if she were forced to sell her producing stock to stay financially afloat? More importantly, would Thomas think he now had the bargaining edge to force her into accepting his proposal of marriage? She intended to make it clear to him that she had other options, even though she wasn't rightly sure of what those were.

Rising early to draft the letter, and now satisfied with the wording, she moved into the kitchen to fix her breakfast. Horses moving across the yard caught her attention, and she stepped to the window to take a closer look. Both Cradle's Peak hands were leaving the ranch and heading toward the trail that led to town. Ida Mae frowned. Had Kyle forgotten to tell Cotton about her letter? Why was Cotton sending both hands in that direction? Most of the cattle ranged north. She glanced back at the bunkhouse and saw Kyle and Jed standing by the corrals, watching the two riders. Had the hands gotten into an argument with Cotton and quit?

After a quick meal, Ida Mae found that dressing was still difficult and took time. When she left the house the sun was already warming the ground, and Jed and Kyle were nowhere in sight. Ida Mae walked slowly to the barn, where she spotted Cotton saddling his horse in back of the tack room. She approached him quietly.

"Fit enough to ride this morning?"

Cotton's frame jerked, and he twisted toward her. "Dadgum it, woman. Don't go sneakin' up on a body like that."

"Since when did you become so jumpy? Time was when you could straddle a coiled rattler and never bat an eye. Wouldn't have anything to do with the Cradle's Peak hands leaving, would it?"

"No, heck no. Those two puddin' foots quit of their own accord. I was headed up to the house to tell you."

"And you needed to saddle your horse to ride up to the house?"

"I was plannin' on riding on over to the Circle-M and talkin' with Worley after I spoke with you. I thought if the wagon was fixed, I'd bring it back." Cotton finished tightening the cinch and flipped the stirrup down. "I wanted to ask him about throwin' in with them for the trail drive."

"How near are we to having all the cattle pushed together?"

"We've found about all there is left," Cotton said. "I sent Kyle and Jed to check the upper rims. I told them to bring in any brood cows they come across. That way you'll be able to keep a better eye on them while we're gone."

Ida Mae's lips tightened. "You say those two men quit. Why?"

Cotton shrugged. "Those two boys were in one foul mood this mornin'. Complained about the food. Said we were trying to poison them. I told them I didn't know that beans and biscuits caused hangovers. They just saddled up and left after I said that." Cotton scuffed one boot in the dirt and spit. "I'd say good riddance."

Ida Mae crossed her arms and scowled. "Cotton . . ." Butch's barking interrupted her, and she turned to see horses coming up the trail.

Removing the carbine from the scabbard on his saddle, Cotton moved to the edge of the bunkhouse.

"Are you expecting trouble?" Ida Mae asked.

"Bein' cautious is all."

A team and wagon came into view. Ida Mae recognized it

as her own. Worley was driving, and Rooster was following on horseback, leading Worley's horse.

The Circle-M's foreman pulled the team to a stop in front of the corrals, and after the dust cleared, Ida Mae and Cotton walked over to greet them.

Rooster jumped from his horse and swept his hat from his head. "Morning, Miss Ida. Fine day, wouldn't you say?"

"Quit your yammering, Rooster," Worley growled at the grinning cowboy. "Try making yourself useful by unhitching the wagon and tending to the horses."

Worley turned to Ida Mae, removed his hat, and nodded at her. "Morning, ma'am." He turned to Cotton and shook his extended hand. "For a man who's supposed to have been shot and on death's door, I'd say you're looking mighty fit."

"Well, you know what they say about us old cowpunchers. Ain't no lead hard enough to punch a hole in our behinds."

Ida Mae walked to the wagon and inspected the tongue. "I appreciate the work your man did on the wagon, Cliff. I'm surely indebted to him and you."

Worley grinned, his eyes twinkling. "The boys and I always look forward to your pumpkin bread, Miss Ida. That's all the payment we would need."

"Then pumpkin bread it shall be." She walked back to where Cotton and Worley were standing. "I'm wondering about something, Cliff. Who bought out Portello, and why are they demanding immediate payment on the outstanding debts?" Ida Mae fastened her gaze on Worley. "Are the owners of Circle-M the ones who bought the store?"

Worley blinked several times before answering. "No, ma'am. I heard about Portello selling, but I can tell you for a fact that it wasn't the Circle-M owners who bought it. The way I understand it, it was an investment broker out of Houston."

Ida Mae frowned. "Broker? Does that mean the real buyer, or buyers, are hiding behind the broker's name?"

"I'm reckoning you've got it figured about right. Portello always sent my bills straight on to the owners in Memphis.

Our outfit was paid up, but I hear some of the smaller spreads got hit hard. Most don't have the cash right now to settle."

"This whole business is an outrage," Ida Mae said, "and I intend to fight it. But for now, there are other matters more urgent. I hate to impose on you any further, Cliff, but Cotton has suggested that we throw our cattle in with the Circle-M's for the trail drive. That is, if your bosses don't have any objections and it's agreeable with you."

Worley shifted his boots in the dust and glanced at Cotton.

"Me and Kyle would be ridin' along to hep," Cotton quickly interjected. "It was just a thought, since we're down two hands this mornin'."

Worley scratched the back of his neck and grinned. "I met those two fellows on the roadway. They told us they'd been working here. I gathered they weren't too happy with the grub."

Cotton snorted. "Mighty finicky eaters fer cowhands is all I can say."

The lines around Worley's eyes crinkled, and he turned to Ida Mae. "I don't see a problem with throwing the herds together. Having Cotton along will be like old times. Is the new fellow, McCabe, going to stay here and help you with the place?"

"I haven't discussed my plans with McCabe," Ida Mae said. Her words sounded defensive even to her. She straightened her shoulders and lifted her chin. "In fact," she continued, "I'm not sure if he plans on staying on after the roundup."

Ida Mae noticed Worley's eyebrows rising and a quick sidelong glance in Cotton's direction.

"Miss Ida, I don't think it would be a good idea for you to stay at the ranch alone," Worley said. "When we spent the night in town last night, we crossed paths with a company of horse soldiers. The captain said they were tracking some renegade Indians who had taken a white woman from a ranch on the Upper Concho." Worley shook his head as he continued. "I don't think it's safe for you to stay here with the Indians on the prowl."

"I'm aware of the story, Cliff, but the woman escaped. Sanchez found her and now thinks he should have a reward for her return." Ida Mae took a measured breath. "Word needs to be gotten to the captain of her whereabouts as soon as possible."

Worley shook his head. "That's going to be hard to do. After I told them about our little skirmish at the Circle-M, they wanted to know in what direction they had gone. No telling where they might be by now."

Ida Mae's voice rose with exasperation. "Then word needs to be sent to the fort. Surely there are more soldiers than just the one company."

Taking a step back, Worley's Adam's apple bobbed noticeably. "I understand your concern, Miss Ida. But if Sanchez wants a reward, he most likely has notified her family."

"My concern," Ida Mae responded sharply, "is for her safety. Sanchez may be treating her like found treasure—I don't know. But according to Gonzales, the other outlaws regard her as something of a witch."

Cotton rubbed his chin thoughtfully. "Why would they think that?"

"According to Gonzales, it's her eyes. He said she had the eyes of a cat."

Cotton took a deep breath and shook his head. "I can't hep but feel you're gettin' yerself all worked up over somethin' that's not that bad. If Sanchez expects a reward, he won't let anythin' happen to her. I'd say quit worryin' 'bout it."

"I can't believe this," Ida Mae stormed. "You're both impossible." She turned and walked toward the house, clenching her fists. *That poor woman, how frightened she must be.*

Ida Mae stepped inside the darkened interior of her home and eased down into a soft leather chair. Her thoughts turned to the roundup and the meager supplies she had on hand. There wouldn't be enough to outfit her share of the trail drive. She would have to come up with the money to purchase more from somewhere.

Tomorrow I'll take the buckboard into town, she thought.

While I'm there, I'll talk with Father De La Cruz. Perhaps he's already spoken with the captain. If not, when I speak with Thomas about the brood cows, maybe I can persuade him and some of his men to go into Sanchez's camp and negotiate her release.

A knock at the door interrupted her thoughts. "Yes?" she called.

Cotton pushed the door open and poked his head in. "I'm gonna ride inta town with Worley. I'm in need of some chew. Also need another lariat and some leather to repair some tack before we leave on the trail ride."

"That will be all right," she said quietly. "And Cotton, limit the amount of time you spend in the cantina. I expect you back here tonight."

Cotton didn't answer, and Ida Mae heard the door shut with a hard thump. She wondered how much whiskey he'd be able to drink with Cliff and still make it back before morning.

Chapter Twenty-two

That Laredo fellow was mad enough to eat cactus thorns," Kyle remarked. "I hope he doesn't come back and try to take his anger out on us."

Jed pulled his horse up. "His kind will. That's why I took their guns. I'm hoping he'll cool off some before he gets his hands on another one."

"What if he doesn't?"

Jed's gaze drifted across the rims of nearby washes and arroyos. "Then he'll have to be dealt with," he said quietly.

"Dang," Kyle swore. "I was getting used to keeping an eye out for Indians. Now it's going to make me all itchy having to watch out for someone intent on picking me off."

Jed glanced at the boy. "Try having thirty thousand men armed with everything from bayonets to cannons trying to pick you off. You'll get used to it."

Kyle shook his head and nudged his horse forward. "I see some cattle over on that far rim. If you'll go 'round behind them, I'll stay here and keep the ones that are range sour from circling back."

Before deciding to saddle Big Blue earlier, Jed had hesitated. He wanted the feeling of having his own mount under him again, but now he saw it was a mistake. Big Blue proved totally inadequate in herding or stopping cattle that were brush savvy and rattlesnake quick. The rogue steers blew past Big Blue like flies through an open doorway. He would have to bring Star back to help round up those mavericks. The rest of the small herd was easier to handle once they were separated from the leaders.

"Go ahead and take those in!" Kyle yelled at Jed. "I'll round those ornery ones up and bring them along."

Jed raised his hand to acknowledge Kyle's instructions. To leave Kyle out here alone wouldn't put him in any immediate danger for now. It would be him and Cotton who would have to remain watchful.

Jed herded a couple of brood cows and several steers he gathered in with the main herd and then rode up to the bunk-house. Kate weighed heavily on his mind this morning, and he was anxious to move on. The Navy in his holster felt comfortable, and Big Blue was in good shape. The thieves hadn't mistreated him. And if he understood Cotton correctly, the cattle were mostly gathered. He had mentioned there was still some branding and doctoring, but that shouldn't take long.

The returned team and wagon caught Jed's attention. He looked for Cotton's horse. It was gone. The Circle-M fellows must have returned the team, Jed surmised, and Cotton rode back to town with them.

After dismounting, Jed allowed Big Blue a drink of water while loosening the cinch. He glanced toward the ranch house. Ida Mae was nowhere in sight. Maybe he should check on her. It would give him a chance to let her know of his plans to leave.

He heard Ida Mae's soft answer when he knocked on the door and saw a flit of a shadow at the window when she glanced out. The bolt slid back, and the heavy door swung partially open.

Jed removed his hat and nodded. "Just checking on you, ma'am. Everything all right?"

"Yes, I'm fine, and no, everything's not all right." She leveled her dark hazel eyes at him.

Jed's body tensed as his gaze searched the room behind her. "In what way do you mean?" he asked.

"Come in," she said, moving aside.

The interior of the house was dark and cool; the scent of spices and prepared food filled the room. Jed stepped inside and closed the door. He remained where he was and watched as Ida Mae walked to a large leather chair and slowly sat. The dimness of the room softened her features but did little to diminish the worried frown creasing her forehead.

She rested her head against the chair's high backrest and again fixed her gaze on his face. "Now, Mr. McCabe, would you please tell me what happened last night to cause the two hands from Cradle's Peak to quit?"

"You sure you want to hear?"

"I'm asking, aren't I?"

"You didn't want to hear before when I tried to tell you about them."

Ida Mae was silent for a moment. "I suppose I deserve that," she said. "But I'm listening now."

"All right. Cotton and I have a strong belief that the fellow called Laredo was behind the poisoning at Bitter Creek."

"Is this a belief, or a fact?"

Jed frowned and tightened the grip on his hat. "It's a fact, ma'am. The watering hole was intentionally poisoned. A boot print matching Laredo's was found at the edge of the pool and some crushed, dried leaves smashed into the imprint. The horse he's riding has the same print and throws its right foreleg as the one I followed when I trailed the rider who shot Cotton."

Ida Mae leaned forward in her chair. Her eyes grew wide, and he heard her catch her breath. "Did Cotton confront him?" she asked.

"No, I'm the one who sent them packing. I didn't tell Cotton about the hoofprint. I figured he wouldn't stand a chance if Laredo drew on him."

Ida Mae placed a hand against her mouth. "That was probably a wise decision." She took a quick breath and looked directly at him. "The other thing I want to know is, why did they complain about the food?"

Jed shifted his position, his gaze still holding hers. "Cotton seasoned their food with some of the poultice you gave him."

A surprised expression washed over Ida Mae's features. An involuntary laugh escaped from her lips, and she quickly clamped her fingers over her mouth.

Jed wasn't sure if she was surprised by her spontaneous mirth or the audacity of Cotton's actions.

"I should have known," she said, shaking her head. "I knew Cotton didn't want that poultice for the reason he gave. That fool, he could have killed them. But then, if what you say is true . . . But why? Why would they try to kill Cotton and poison the cattle?"

She stood abruptly, wincing at her sudden move. "This . . . this changes everything. I can't believe Thomas would do this. It doesn't make sense."

She turned to him, her eyes seeming to implore him to offer some type of explanation. Jed gripped his hat brim and buried the urge to put his arms around her and tell her everything would be all right. He wasn't that big of a fool.

She walked closer to him and tilted her head back. "And what about you, McCabe?" she asked softly. "Now that you have your horse and gun, will you also be turning your back on us?"

The abruptness of the question took Jed by surprise. He stepped back, his shoulders pressing against the wall. This wasn't going how he planned. The way she thrust the words at him made him out as a deserter. "My plans have always been to move on and continue the search for my sister," he said, his voice stony. "But I've never quit on a job until it's finished. I see mine as finished when the cattle are ready to move out to market."

"Mr. McCabe, if I asked you to stay for a while longer, would you?"

"Depends, ma'am."

"Depends? On what?"

"If my help is needed, or even appreciated."

Ida Mae's eyes narrowed, and she remained silent as she continued to focus on his face.

Jed set his jaw and drew in a deep breath. The scent of her, so close, made it hard to concentrate.

Ida Mae shifted her gaze to the floor and nodded. Her voice was quiet as she lifted her chin and looked at him. "I'm sorry if you find me harsh, Mr. McCabe. But when you've had your heart ripped out and served back on a hard plank and seasoned with sorrow, you have a tendency to protect yourself." She paused a moment before continuing. "If I'm not mistaken, you're suffering from the same affliction."

Jed's mouth felt dry. It wasn't his nature to speak of his feelings, and he wasn't about to start now.

"I reckon we've all had our share of sorrows, ma'am. It goes with the times."

She turned slowly from him. "Another week will be all I need. I spoke with Worley this morning. I can throw my cattle in with the Circle-M's for the trail drive. Cotton insists he's able to ride along, and with Kyle's help, they should have enough hands. If you could stay until then"—she turned to him and smiled—"I would be most appreciative."

Jed's throat tightened, and he found it difficult to swallow. "I suppose I could oblige you that much," he finally managed.

A slight frown creased her brow as she continued. "It seems Worley thinks I might be in some danger if I stayed here alone at the ranch, but I'm not afraid. He said he ran into some soldiers in town that told him about the woman that the Indians took captive. But Gonzales told me she had escaped from them and that Sanchez found her. Now he wants a reward."

Ida Mae paced a few steps. "I'm at a loss now of what I should do. I had planned to ride over to Cradle's Peak and speak with Thomas about selling him a few of my brood cows in order to pay off the lien against the cattle. While I was there, I intended to persuade him to send some of his men into Sanchez's camp and negotiate the release of the woman. But taking into consideration what you've said . . ." Ida Mae stopped her pacing and looked at Jed. "There's something about the woman's eyes that make the desperadoes think she's evil. I'm worried for her safety."

Jed's body jerked as though a fist had slammed into him. "Do you know anything about this woman?" he demanded, almost choking on the words.

She shook her head. "Thomas was the first to tell me of her when I was there. Then Gonzales told me of Sanchez finding her."

"Did they say how old she was, and where she was taken from?"

A puzzled look pinched at Ida Mae's face. "Thomas said she was young and had been taken from the Upper Concho area. Why? Do you think this woman might be your sister?"

"She could be. She has yellowish-green eyes that sometimes change colors. Some people call them cat eyes."

Ida Mae took a quick breath. "That's what Gonzales called them. But McCabe, I wouldn't jump to conclusions. The chances of this woman being your sister would be slim."

"You said Schmidt mentioned she was young. How many young girls with catlike eyes would be in this area?"

Ida Mae wet her lips and nodded. "You have a point. How old is your sister?"

Jed steadied himself, trying to control his breathing and still think clearly. "She would be about seventeen now."

"I still think it's only a remote chance," Ida Mae said.

"I'll need some time off, ma'am," he said abruptly. "I'll also need directions to Sanchez's place."

Chapter Twenty-three

Ida Mae paced the length of the room. She had tried to persuade Jed to wait for Cotton or Kyle's return so that one of them could accompany him. He refused, brushing away her warnings about the dangers he faced in trying to penetrate Sanchez's stronghold alone. When he asked for directions to Sanchez's place, she was vague but not dishonest. She wasn't sure of the route herself.

Now she twisted her fingers together as she watched him walk back to the bunkhouse. Her chest felt constricted, her muscles tense. She was unsure if it was simply concern for his safety or something more. It hadn't been easy, asking him to stay. Now the big lunkhead was going to get killed.

Ida Mae turned and walked to her bedroom, where she retrieved the Springfield rifle and a box of cartridges. Moving to the pantry, she wrapped jerked beef and dried fruit in a cloth. After removing a leather pouch from a nearby peg, she stuffed the food and cartridges inside. Picking up the rifle and pouch, she left the house and walked to the corrals where Jed was preparing to leave.

"Here," she said, thrusting the rifle and pouch at him. "If you won't listen to reason, at least take these."

For a moment Jed's face registered surprise before he shook his head.

"Ma'am, I couldn't take—"

"Take it. It's a converted rifle that's easy to reload. There's cartridges and food in the bag. I have other guns and plenty of ammunition. If . . . if you make it back, you can return the rifle to me."

Jed hesitated for only a moment. Without saying anything, he reached for the rifle, his hand brushing hers as he took the gun and pouch.

Ida Mae pulled her hand back, curling it into a fist. It burned as though she had touched an open flame, and she was painfully aware that her cheeks were also flaming.

The subtle strength Jed displayed as he checked the rifle, opening the breechblock and checking the firing mechanism, showed his deep familiarity with firearms.

She shifted her gaze away and retreated to the edge of the corral. A rail gave her support as she watched him finish tying on his bedroll and slicker.

Jed picked up the reins and looked at her. He stood for a moment, staring silently, and then walked closer before stopping a few feet away. His mouth was a hard line when he spoke.

"If for some reason I don't make it back, I'd like for you to know that I appreciated your hiring me and giving me a place to stay." Jed shrugged one shoulder. "If this girl is my sister, she'll require more help than I can give her. I'd be more than willing to help with the trail drive, if you could help my sister."

Ida Mae was quiet for a moment. Her mind raced. The young woman would certainly need help, but was she capable of caring for her? She was unsure of her nursing or mothering skills. She supposed if she found the task overwhelming, she could recruit Señora Gomez from the mission.

"Of course," she answered. "But Jed, don't get your hopes up."

"I have to take that chance. If she's not her, then I've rescued someone else's sister."

Ida Mae took a step closer to him and placed her hand lightly on his arm. "Jed, I want to come with you. I know Sanchez. He'll listen to me. I can persuade him to release her to us."

Jed shook his head. "That's mighty generous of you, but it's out of the question. You're in no shape to ride that far, and you don't owe me for anything."

"I haven't paid you yet," she said, smiling ruefully.

A smile flitted across Jed's lips. "If it hadn't been for you, I wouldn't have gotten Big Blue and my gun back. I think we're even."

"One last bit of advice," she said. "Regardless of what you think of Sanchez, I've always found him to be a reasonable man. Try explaining to him who the woman is. Even if she isn't your sister, convince him she is. Tell him you work for me and that I'll make sure he receives a reward."

Jed glanced down to where her hand rested on his arm. He lifted his gaze and met her eyes. "Are you sure Sanchez will appreciate the fact that you killed his partner?"

Ida Mae smiled. "Remind him I did him a favor. And Jed, I expect you back. Both you and the girl. I know things come out of my mouth at times that might make you think I haven't appreciated your help, but I have."

Jed was quiet as he continued to gaze at her. He smiled slightly and appeared to be on the verge of saying something.

Ida Mae saw his eyes soften. It transformed his features, bringing a gentle look to his face. She felt something inside of her crumble, and she fought to maintain her composure.

A cross between a smile and a grimace twisted Jed's mouth. "I have to go, Ida Mae." With one hand he touched his fingers to her cheek. "Take care of yourself," he said softly.

Not trusting her voice, Ida Mae only nodded. She watched as Jed mounted and rode away, and for the first time since Dan's death, she felt tears well in her eyes. Turning from the corrals, Ida Mae walked toward the ranch house. It had been her belief that she would never again experience the love she and Dan had shared. She shook her head. The man's mere touch had nearly sent her flat on her fanny.

Chapter Twenty-four

Jed squinted against the sun and settled his hat low on his forehead. He clenched his jaw and willed himself not to look back at Ida Mae. There was no need. Her proud stance and slender figure were etched in his mind.

Riding away from her, a familiar feeling seeped into his bones. It wasn't the same as when he rode away from the farm and Matilda, but yet, it was. He had felt a sense of separation and sadness when he left for the war, but the prospects of adventure and the youthful confidence that he would return shortly had kept him in high spirits. But when cornfields turned into battlefields and the furrows ran full with blood, he knew his world would never be the same.

The feelings coursing through him now were different. The cold ache in the pit of his stomach spread into his chest and arms, causing his heart to race and his chest to tighten. It was a familiar feeling. The one he experienced when he had crouched in the brush, waiting for the order to charge a hill and fight an enemy that had more troops and better positions.

It wasn't Sanchez that brought the cold fear to his stomach. It was the fear of not returning, and he knew he wanted very much to return—return to Ida Mae, the ranch, and even Kyle and Cotton, who seemed to have some hold on him.

When he looked into Ida Mae's eyes and saw the swirling emotions, he knew she felt something too. Her sudden smile had sent his blood coursing through him, and the feeling when their hands brushed together made his insides tremble. It had taken every ounce of self-control to keep from wrapping his arms around her and crushing her to him.

Jed rode west most of the afternoon. As night fell, the dancing flames of a campfire in the distance beckoned him. He approached cautiously, sizing up the situation. They were Circle-M hands, working on bringing in the cattle for the approaching trail drive.

"Light and sup with us," one of the men invited. "We've plenty of grub and are in need of someone new to swap yarns with. These peckerwoods here are completely out of anything new to yammer about."

Jed introduced himself and told the men of his quest to find Sanchez.

The man who welcomed him to the campfire introduced himself as Harry Strom. He shook his head after hearing of Jed's intentions. "You wouldn't want to go into Sanchez's place without a company of horse soldiers backing you. If you did manage to get in, you'd never make it out. My suggestion is that you ride in to Fort Chadwick and have them send in a troop of cavalry. Sanchez won't argue with the Army. He knows what battles he can win and the ones he can't."

"I don't want to wait that long," Jed said. "I'm not wasting any more time. I'm going in. I just need some solid directions."

Strom stood and spit into the fire. "It's your burial. I can give you directions; even tell you how you might get in. But as I said, you ain't gonna make it back out."

"I'll deal with that when the time comes," Jed replied. "Now, about those directions?"

After a warm meal and a couple of hours' sleep, Jed was up and on his way. He considered the chance meeting with the Circle-M cowboys a stroke of luck. The directions Strom gave him were much different and more definite than the generalities Ida Mae had offered. According to Strom, he would have to ride north for most of the day before coming to the Big

Rock country. From there, he was to look for two rocky peaks with a ravine feeding down from the saddle between them.

The glare of the sun and the ensuing mirages made it difficult to judge distances. Jed kept Big Blue at a steady pace across the treeless plains for most of the day. As the sun eased into the western horizon, he could see the craggy peaks jutting into the skyline.

A wash slashed its way across the land, and Jed eased Big Blue down into its narrow and shaded inner space. The depth of the cut afforded cover for a horse or a man, but not a mounted rider. He quickly dismounted and eased up to the edge of the embankment, peering over and studying the area. A sparse stand of cedars covered the base of the pinnacles. Cedars, buckeyes, and mesquite grew in a tangled mass up the steep slopes. The deep cleavage of the ravine that led to the top was marked by darker shadows. This was where the trail that Strom said led to Sanchez's compound was located.

According to Strom, sentries were stationed on both sides of the canyon and could see any approaching rider for miles. Jed figured that in all probability, he had been spotted. His only advantage was the rapidly approaching darkness of night.

While waiting for the cover of nightfall, Jed continued walking along the bottom of the dry wash but in the direction away from the base of the ravine. If he had been seen, the sentries might be expecting him to follow the cut up to the base of the canyon and would be waiting for him.

The moonless night worked to Jed's advantage. Mounting, he eased Big Blue out of the wash and into a mile-eating walk across the high desert. The dark outline of the twin crags against the lighter hue of the star-studded sky was easily visible. Jed continued riding east, away from the mouth of the ravine. When he judged it safe, he circled back and came up along the bottom of the rocky slopes below the bandit's hideout.

Working his way into the fringe of scattered trees, Jed was able to discern a small grassy opening among the thick, resinous shrubbery. He slid from the saddle and dropped the reins to the ground. There was no fear of Big Blue straying. The large horse would only leave the area if he was spooked or called.

Angling up through the junipers and piñon, Jed worked his way toward the ravine. He found an open space with a view of the desert below him. A satisfied smile creased his tense face. On the flatlands and next to the wash, a pinprick of light brightened and then diminished. Another glow, not fifty feet away, pulsed in the clear night air. Both sentries were there, smoking while they waited for him to exit the cut. Would the sentries have left the ravine unguarded? He would have to chance that they did.

The climb was steep, and Jed was careful not to dislodge any rocks or small pebbles. Occasionally he stopped and listened. Hushed rustling on the hillside near him spoke of small animals on the prowl—a good sign that none of the two-legged species were anywhere near.

After following the faintly discernible trail for some distance, Jed became uneasy. A large boulder ahead of him jutted over the pathway. The perfect spot for a sentry. Quietly, he cut away from the trail and worked his way above the rock. He hunkered down next to a small juniper and listened. Something moved to his right. The source of the sound was obscured from his view by an outcropping of rock. Jed unsheathed his bowie knife and waited.

"Anton?"

The hushed whisper directed Jed's attention to a dark shadow slipping toward him from around the edge of the rocks. Jed remained still and forced his breathing to become even and shallow.

The shadow hesitated, crouched, and then continued its movement forward. Jed calculated that the man would pass just below him.

But the man didn't. Jed saw the rifle swing upward just as he sprang at the man, bringing the knife down heavily into the side of the sentry's neck. The rifle fell from the man's hand as he grasped helplessly at the knife. With one hand, Jed grasped the man's throat, quelling any sound that might escape, and held it until the man fell limp at his feet.

Releasing his hold, Jed shoved the fallen rifle under a bush and dropped back down to the main trail. He would have to move quickly now. If the sentries returned and discovered the body, the chance of penetrating the stronghold unchallenged would be impossible.

Jed was surprised that after a short climb he topped out into the small valley that sheltered the bandits' compound. Shaped like a large shallow bowl, the soft glow of lamps emanated from several adobe structures that lay in a semicircle against the eastern edge. A larger structure nestled against the slope of one of the crags. Jed surmised that this would be Sanchez's dwelling. Moving through the scattered junipers lining the edge of the small vale, he skirted the corrals that held the remuda. Horses were as good as watchdogs when it came to something or someone unfamiliar.

He approached the house cautiously, deftly working his way through the jumble of rocks and trees. Laughter and an occasional whoop coming from one of the smaller adjacent huts left little doubt that a rousing game of cards was being played.

Moving with the stealth born from years of sniper warfare, he approached a lamp-lit window. Working his way under it, he raised his head and peered in. A large Mexican woman stood by an open hearth. She was speaking in rapid Spanish and was gesturing toward someone in a far corner. Jed moved slightly and was able to see Sanchez seated at a table. His back was to Jed, and his face turned toward the agitated woman.

Across from Sanchez, another woman was seated at the table. Dingy blond hair hung loosely about her face. From what Jed could see of her, she appeared to be tall and thin. The plain homespun dress she wore hung from her gaunt frame. She looked too old to be Kate, her features taut and worn. But there was something about her that seemed familiar. Her head was held high, her shoulders squared. Her gaze pivoted between the perturbed woman and Sanchez. As her head turned, Jed's heart took a quick bounce. The high cheekbones, the slender nose. It was his mother's face. The woman was Kate.

He eased up on the veranda leading to a back doorway. He could hear the large woman still speaking, her tone scornful, her voice guttural.

Jed pulled his revolver, took a deep breath, and kicked open the door.

The woman at the hearth gasped, clutched at her chest, and backed away from the open fire. Sanchez and Kate didn't move. Jed leveled the revolver at Sanchez and saw his hand slide silently off the table.

Jed shook his head. "Don't do it," he said. "Put your hand back on the table."

Sanchez smiled and held both hands over the table, palms up. "Ah, señor, you enter my home in the most uncivilized way. Surely you must expect me to protect my family."

"I believe there's someone here who isn't part of your family, namely the lady seated across from you."

Sanchez frowned. "If you are her family, there was no need to break into my home in such a manner. I am willing to discuss the reward with you."

"And what kind of reward are you asking for the horses you stole from me?"

Recognition crept into Sanchez's eyes. Slowly he placed his hands on the table, palms down and his face grim. "You are the gringo we should have finished off. A mistake I won't make again."

A movement to his left drew Jed's attention away from Sanchez. The Mexican woman was propelling her large frame toward an open doorway behind Kate. Before Jed could react, Kate quickly stood, grasped the fleeing woman's arm and twisted it, sending her crashing to the floor.

Jed swung his gaze back to Sanchez. The man who made his living from thievery was in the act of pulling a short-nosed revolver from his waistband. Jed rushed him, bringing the barrel of his pistol down on his head while shoving him to the floor. Once more, Jed slammed the revolver against the back of the outlaw's head. Blood spurted from the wound, and the outlaw's pistol spun across the floor.

Gaining his feet, Jed turned to Kate. "Are you all right?"

Visibly shaken, Kate's piercing eyes studied him. "Johnny?"

"No, I'm Jed. We need to get out of here. Now!" He pointed toward the open door he had kicked in. He could hear the Mexican woman scrabbling to her feet. Sanchez moaned and was attempting to pull himself up using the overturned table for leverage. Jed grabbed a long firepoker and raked embers from the hearth onto the floor, scattering them against the overturned table and chairs. As he rushed out the door after Kate, he saw Sanchez stagger toward the pistol that lay against one wall.

Bounding off the veranda, Jed grasped Kate's arm and pulled her after him. "This way," he said, his voice filled with urgency. He could hear the Mexican woman shouting as she crossed the yard toward the smaller structure, where the game of cards was still in high spirits.

Jed ran for the corrals. The horses panicked and began circling in a nervous frenzy. Pushing the poles through their supporting posts, Jed created a gap in the pen. The animals sensed freedom and bolted for the opening. As Jed pulled Kate away from the stampeding horses and pushed her toward the shelter of the trees, shots rang out. Sanchez had made it out of the torched building and was firing randomly into the darkness.

Yells echoed against the hillsides. Another shot rang across the valley floor. Scrambling up the hillside, Jed turned once to see an angry red glow lighting the slope in back of Sanchez's house.

He alternated between pulling and pushing Kate up the hill, angling toward the ravine and the trail that would lead out of the valley. Jed had to give Kate credit. As undernourished as she looked, she was a fighter. She didn't make a sound as she grasped and pulled herself along, struggling to keep up with him.

All stealth was abandoned as more shots rang out. Jed reckoned they were shooting aimlessly, hoping to draw return fire. He pushed Kate deeper into the timber before leading her toward the trail.

The gunshots would alert the sentries at the bottom of the ravine, and Jed figured the chance of confronting them on the trail was going to be a problem. To stay off the trail and make their way down the ravine would take too long. Their only chance to get out and onto the desert floor lay in doing so before any of the bandits were able to catch their horses.

Whereas stealth had gotten him in, Jed counted on swiftness to get them out. He heard Kate's labored breathing and worried that her strength was giving out. He shook off his jacket and placed it in her hands.

"Put this on," he said, "and stay close behind me. The trail is just beyond those trees. When we start down, hold to my belt and keep moving as fast as you can. If I stop, stay quiet. I'll let you know when to move on."

Kate nodded as she pulled the sleeves of his jacket over her thin arms.

"Good. Let's go," he whispered.

The trail was where he had judged, and they began their descent. At various intervals he stopped and felt Kate pressing against him. After listening a moment, he moved on. As they came closer to the boulder where he had ambushed the one sentry, Jed was apprehensive. They hadn't come upon anyone yet and that could only mean the guards were still below them. Charging down the trail was one thing, but abandoning all caution would be a foolish mistake.

Jed tugged at Kate's hand, guiding her off the path. They worked their way up the side of the hill and then quietly skirted the boulder beneath them. The faint starlight illuminated the boulder enough that Jed could see that no one occupied the lookout. He could also see the faint outline of the sentry's body lying partially hidden under some brush.

The two men below surely had heard the shots and couldn't be too far away. The steep sides of the ravine prevented Jed and Kate from moving any farther down the trail without returning to the pathway. Jed waited for a moment, then reached down and picked up a fist-sized rock. He threw the rock across the ravine, angling it so it would hit farther up. The rock struck the other side with a sharp clapping sound and bounced down the side of the gulley, coming to a clattering rest among rocks at the bottom.

Jed remained still while he listened. Gunshots erupted from the trail beneath them, hitting rocks and sending sparks from the area where the rock first landed.

Placing a hand on his sister's shoulder, Jed pushed her down. "Hunker down as close to the ground as you can get," he whispered. An ominous glow was spreading across the skyline above them. Sparks and smoke billowed into the atmosphere. Within minutes he heard huffing as two shadowy figures trotted by, rifles held ready. When the sentries vanished around a turn, Jed pulled Kate up and helped her back onto the main trail. Without speaking, they resumed their hurried pace down the sloping path.

When they reached the bottom Jed stopped suddenly, causing Kate to stumble against him. He turned and caught her shoulders, supporting her. "We're almost out," he said. "Try to hold on a little longer." She stood mute, leaning against him, breathing heavily.

Jed whistled softly. From below he heard a nicker. He whistled once more before continuing their hurried pace downward. The trail leveled off and Big Blue stood quietly to one side, waiting for them.

"Here's our ride," Jed said. "Let me help you up."

"I can make it," Kate said, her voice a murmur in the darkness. With long, thin arms she grasped the pommel and mounted easily. Swinging up behind her, Jed grasped the reins with one hand and steadied her with the other. "Hold on tight," he whispered.

Within minutes they were off the trail and onto the flat-looking desert. Jed gave Big Blue a loose rein and urged him into a slow canter. The level appearance of the darkened landscape they were crossing was misleading, and Jed prayed that the big animal wouldn't step in a badger hole or dump them into a ravine.

At times Jed reined the horse in, allowing him to walk and

ease his breathing. But Big Blue seemed to sense the urgency of the situation and would quickly resume his pace, carrying them across the starlit terrain, flicking his ears and keeping his eyes focused. Once he shied, almost unseating his riders. Another time he changed direction as a cut's dark ribbon sliced before them.

The powerful horse kept the pace until Jed saw the sky turning pink with the approaching dawn. Big Blue was covered with frothy lather and was breathing heavily. Grunts echoed deep within his chest with every setting of his forelegs.

A copse of cottonwood trees lined a wash, and Jed eased Big Blue down and into the shallow ravine. He let the animal walk for a while, allowing his body to cool down slowly. Greenery against a slide in the embankment signaled water was somewhere below the crusted surface. Dismounting, he helped Kate down and led her to the edge of the wash, where she sank down and rested her back against the sandy embankment. Returning to Big Blue, he loosened the cinch and pulled the canteen from the saddle horn. He uncorked the top of the canteen and walked back to Kate, holding it out to her.

"Try to drink some, Kate. It'll help."

He watched as she took the canteen from him and sipped from its contents. Early morning shadows still covered the bottom of the wash, and a chilly wind swept along its corridor.

Jed smiled. "I have some dried fruit in my saddlebag. I'll get some for you as soon as I dig out a watering hole for Big Blue."

"Big Blue." Kate smiled faintly. "I remember now." She lifted her head and stared at him from greenish-gold eyes. "How did you get here, and how on earth did you find me?"

Jed shook his head. "It's a long story, Kate, and one that will have to wait. Sanchez will be on our trail, and we need to keep moving."

Chapter Twenty-five

As Ida Mae walked back to the ranch house, she battled to keep her emotions in check. It was hard to watch Jed ride away. She willed him to look back, but knew he wouldn't. Sadness gripped her, and she tasted the salty tears as they slid down her cheeks and into the corners of her mouth. Entering the quiet house, her mind was a whirl of thoughts.

Glimpsing the passion in Jed's eyes was almost her undoing. The sensations that coursed through her body when he touched her sent her pacing the room. How had she managed to get so emotionally involved with this man?

To shake off the feeling of impending doom, she focused on Jed's news concerning the men from Cradle's Peak. It was hard to imagine that Thomas was behind the poisoning of the water. But why? He had all but asked her outright for her hand in marriage. Was it her he wanted, or control of her land?

She was well aware that her ranch lay on the best rangeland this side of Mission Bridge. Still, there was plenty of open range, and most of the bigger spreads ran their cattle far and wide. Dan had wanted to keep their herd close. He said with the abundance of feed on their own land, he and Cotton could easily take care of them with only seasonal help.

The Circle-M lay adjacent to Cradle's Peak. If Thomas wanted to expand, he would have gone after the Circle-M.

The Triple-X was the largest cattle operation around and ranged northeast of her. Could they be the ones who had paid Laredo to force her out?

She stopped and stared out the window into the empty

barnyard. It was good that Jed hadn't told Cotton of his suspicion that it was Laredo who shot him. With Cotton's temper, he would have taken justice into his own hands. But how much information did Jed give Cotton? Was that the reason he rode into town with Worley, to catch up with Laredo and confront him?

Her thoughts turned to the soldiers and the captain that Worley had mentioned. Would Father De La Cruz have had the chance to tell them of the whereabouts of the girl? If only she knew for sure.

Frustration boiled within her as she prepared the evening meal for her and Kyle. She knew Cotton wouldn't be back in time to eat with them and probably would only make it back sometime before daylight.

When Ida Mae heard Kyle return to the barnyard, she walked out to the corrals and called to him.

She saw apprehension in Kyle's eyes as his gaze darted between her and the bunkhouse.

"Where's Jed and Cotton?" he asked.

Ida Mae gave him a shortened version of what had happened during the day and Jed's revelations concerning the young woman. "He's convinced the girl is his sister," she said. "When you're finished with the chores, come up and eat. I want to talk about this some more."

While speaking to Ida Mae, Kyle turned his mare into the corrals. "I sure wish you hadn't let Jed ride off alone," he said, his voice anxious. "He'll never make it back. He might be quick with that big gun of his, but there's too many of them up there. He'll be a goner for sure."

"Kyle, don't you think I tried?" Her throat clogged with emotion. "I could have roped him and tied him heel to hand, and he still would have found a way to leave."

Ida Mae turned away from Kyle. She didn't want him to see the worry in her face. She returned to the house and waited until Kyle was eating before pursuing the other subject that was bothering her.

"Were you aware that it was Laredo who shot Cotton?" she asked abruptly.

Kyle swallowed a mouthful of food. "No, ma'am. I didn't know that. I knew that Cotton and Jed suspected both those fellers of the poisoning, but they never said anything about the shooting."

"How convinced was Cotton that it was Laredo that poisoned the water?"

Kyle chewed thoughtfully. "I'd say he was downright positive."

"Then it would follow that he would also suspect Laredo or the other one of being the one who shot him, wouldn't you say?"

"He never mentioned it to me," Kyle said, shrugging one shoulder. "The only thing he did say was that he was going to prove to you that it was Cradle's Peak who was behind the poisoning."

"And how was he planning on doing that?"

"He was taking the poultice and the leaf they found at the watering hole in to show Father De La Cruz. Cotton said that the priest knew about herbs and could identify them."

Ida May lay her fork down and leaned back in her chair. "Have I become so hard and unapproachable that Cotton doesn't feel he can discuss the ranch's business with me anymore?"

"Ma'am, if you promise not to get mad, I'll give you an honest answer."

Taking a deep breath, Ida Mae rubbed her forehead. "Go ahead. I promise."

"It seems to me that ever since Jed came here, you've been acting kind of high and mighty, like you're trying to prove something. Now I don't want you to yell at me, but I'd say maybe you've taken a fancy to him."

Ida Mae felt her face grow hot. She shot Kyle an icy glare. "How dare you . . ." She bit her lip and glowered at her plate. She took several deep breaths and smiled.

"You know, Kyle, you might be right."

Kyle grinned. "I'm glad, Ida Mae. I like him too. That's why I think I should ride after him. I might be of some help. I've talked with Sanchez before. I think I can convince him to let the girl go peaceably."

"No, Kyle, I can't let you do that. I need you here to keep an eye on the ranch."

Ida Mae stood and began collecting the empty plates. "Cotton should be back sometime tonight. In the morning I'll have him drive me into town. We need supplies for the trail drive. When I finish in town, I'll have him take me on to the fort. I intend to speak with someone there and insist that they send troops into Sanchez's place and investigate the story of the lost girl. Hopefully, the troops will catch up with Jed before he locates Sanchez's hideout."

Kyle's face clouded, and he shook his head. "Jed will already be at Sanchez's before you're able to convince anyone to go after him."

"I don't think so," Ida Mae said softly. "It will take Jed a couple of days to figure out that I give really lousy directions."

Ida Mae rose early to prepare for what she deemed necessary if the Bar-DI was to survive. A layer of mist lay close to the river, and in the light of early dawn it shimmered above the water. She peered toward the corrals and saw Kyle saddling his horse. Cotton was nowhere around and as near as she could tell, his horse wasn't in the corral. Unable to contain her curiosity any longer, she left the house and walked down to the barn.

"Did Cotton make it back?" she asked as she approached Kyle.

Kyle shook his head. "No, ma'am. You sure he didn't intend to come back later today?"

"I told him he was to be back last night. He knows we need to have the herd ready to go by next week." Ida Mae shook her head and stared at the hill where the cattle were gathered above the ranch house. "Those cattle are starting to drift. There's not enough feed to hold them in that area any longer." She took a deep breath and turned back to Kyle. "Do you think we have most of the herd together?"

"I reckon so. There's a few more, but not many."

"Then go ahead and separate the brood cows out and push them down toward the river. Gather up the cattle that are starting to range and move them over the hill into fresh grazing. We'll be able to hold them there until Worley comes through. The Circle-M herd will pass north of here. We can join up with them at that time."

Ida Mae rested a hand against her hip and stared at the trail leading into town. She frowned and turned to Kyle. "Before you do that, I want you to hitch the buckboard for me. If Cotton's not back within the hour, I'll drive myself into town."

"I hate to see you do that, Ida Mae. Those cattle will hold another day. I can drive you in."

"No. When Cotton makes it in, you'll need to start separating the calves out from the herd and branding them along with any mavericks. It will take both of you to do that."

Ida Mae returned to the house and busied herself making last-minute preparations for what she hoped would be a quick business deal. The team and buckboard was waiting for her when she returned to the corrals. There was still no sign of Cotton, and though she wouldn't voice her concern to Kyle, she was worried. It wasn't like Cotton to ignore her instructions. Had the fool confronted Laredo?

She climbed into the wagon and urged the team up to the ranch house. Carefully, she loaded her cargo and a few supplies. Then, strapping on her revolver, she pulled herself up and onto the wagon seat. Slapping the reins gently against the backs of the horses, she turned the team down the trail.

On the way into town, Ida Mae kept a sharp eye out for any sign of Cotton or his horse. After stopping several times to check signs on the roadway, she urged the team into a faster pace. She couldn't afford to dally anymore. Her plans were to make it to Fort Chadwick before dark. *And if I have to raise enough of a ruckus to wake the dead when I get there*, she thought, *then I shall. I will not sit by and let Jed do this alone.* Emotion tightened her throat. With practiced self-control, she vanquished her feelings concerning Jed and focused on her immediate agenda.

Entering the town square, she judged it was nearing the noon hour. She ran her gaze over the horses that were tethered at the cantina. Cotton's horse wasn't among them.

Isaac Winslow grinned broadly as Ida Mae pulled to a stop in front of his livery.

"Well, sakes alive, Miss Ida. What brings you to town on such a beautiful day?"

"Morning to you, Isaac. If you would be so kind, could you see to my horses? And when you're finished, I have some business to discuss with you."

Winslow's eyebrows arched noticeably. "You betcha, Miss Ida. Make yourself comfortable inside, and I'll be right with you."

Ida Mae paced the small room that made up the main living area of Winslow's modest lean-to. It grated her somewhat to have Winslow tend to her horses. Normally, she would have taken care of them, but she needed the privacy of Winslow's home in which to conduct her business.

She heard Isaac scrape his boots on the steps and turned to see him enter the room.

Isaac removed his hat, rubbed his chin uncomfortably, and smiled. "What business brings you to my fair establishment, Miss Ida?"

"I won't beat around with exchanging pleasantries, Isaac. It's not a well-kept secret that you dabble in guns. In fact, rumor has it that you sell arms to anyone who has the money, including outlaws and Indians."

Isaac winced and stepped back. "Now, Miss Ida—"

"I'm not here to discuss the morality of your dealings, Isaac. I'm here to do business. I have guns. I'm willing to part with some of them if the offer is acceptable. Are you interested?"

"Well now, Miss Ida," Isaac said, backtracking, "I wouldn't

go so far as to say that I trade with outlaws or Indians. Someone could have misrepresented themselves to me on occasion, but I would never intentionally arm a ruthless man."

A condescending smile crept across Ida Mae's lips. "As I said, I'm not judging or accusing you. I'm here to do business."

"Of course you are, Miss Ida. And as you seem to know all about my business, I too have heard of yours, and I know you're in a bind. So where are these guns?"

"In the back of the wagon. Move my team and wagon inside the livery stable and pull the doors shut. I'll join you, and we can continue the discussion there."

After the doors to the stable were safely barred, Ida Mae lifted a few of the rifles and unwrapped them. They gleamed softly in the dim light.

Winslow pursed his lips and nodded. "You've kept the rifles in good condition," he said. "I recognize that Sharps. I sold it to Daniel when you and he first moved out here." He leaned into the wagon and uncovered two revolvers. "Well, I'll be darned," he muttered. "I sold some just like that to a couple of Mexicans not over a year ago. You want to sell them all?"

"Depends on what your offer is."

Isaac's eyelids blinked several times as his mouth worked silently, obviously ciphering figures.

Ida Mae watched him closely. She was well aware that trading in guns was a chancy business. It wouldn't pay for the Army to get wind of Isaac's dealings.

"I'll give you five hundred for the lot," he said.

Ida Mae drew in a quick breath. This was much more than she had anticipated. But she also knew that a satisfied client wasn't likely to raise a fuss. She tilted her head downward and rubbed her temple with one forefinger. Whatever Isaac's motives were, she could wonder about them later. "Cash?" she asked.

"I think I can manage that."

Ida Mae nodded. "I believe we have a deal."

* * *

With the money tucked inside a small satchel, Ida Mae walked to Portello's store, leaving Isaac to unload the guns within the closed livery stable.

Entering the interior of the building, a couple of cowboys turned to stare at her. She approached the young, thin man with slicked-back hair who was standing behind the counter. "You the new owner?" she asked.

"I'm an employee of the Guthrie Company," the man replied. "How may I be of assistance to you?"

"I'm here to settle up on my bill." Ida Mae reached into her satchel and removed a small leather pouch tied with a leather string. Untying the pouch, she removed a small bundle of papers. "These are my receipts for purchases from Portello that I still owe," she said. "Here is the money for them," she continued, laying the papers and money down on the counter.

The young man stood for a moment, staring at the receipts and money. He raised his head and looked at Ida Mae. "Your name, ma'am?"

"Ida Mae Greeley. I own the Bar-DI north of town."

"Ah, I don't think I can accept this payment, Mrs. Greeley. I'm not sure of the actual amount you owe. You'll need to take the matter up with the new owners."

"Oh, and who might the owners be?"

"The Guthrie Company."

"I gathered that. Who are the principal owners of the Guthrie Company?"

"I . . . I'm not rightly sure."

"How about your name? Can you remember that?"

"Yes, ma'am. It's Henry."

"Well, Henry, each of these receipts is a copy of the ones that Portello kept. I signed each of his receipts, and I have a very distinctive handwriting. When you can produce receipts with my signature on them showing that I made more purchases than these receipts show, then I will be happy to pay them. But for now you will write out a receipt, accepting this money as payment in full on my account."

The young man grinned. "Sorry, I can't do that."

Ida Mae shifted her weight and pulled her revolver from its holster. Her eyes glinted with determination as she leveled it across the counter and pointed the barrel at the clerk's lower body. "If your future plans include marrying that lovely little brunet back home and having a family, you will do as I have asked."

Henry straightened his shoulders. "You can't be serious."

"Young man, I'm as serious as death."

Sweat glistened on Henry's forehead. He cast nervous glances at the two cowpunchers who were grinning. His hand trembled as he reached for a writing pad that lay on the counter. Picking up a pencil, he began scribbling across the pad.

Ida Mae reached forward with one hand and ripped the scribbled sheet off the pad. "That won't do," she said, thumbing back the hammer with an ominous click. "You will write carefully, using your best penmanship: *Received from Ida Mae Greeley, owner of the Bar-DI ranch, one hundred and twenty-three dollars and forty cents in American currency. This money constitutes payment in full for any and all debts owed to Portello's General Supply Store and/or Guthrie Company.*

"Date it with today's date and sign it with your signature. Under your signature, add: *Honest and faithful employee of the Guthrie Company.*"

"You'll never get away with this," Henry said as he finished the note. He tore the sheet of paper off and handed it to Ida Mae. "These two men here are my witnesses," he said. "You forced me to write that note."

Ida Mae backed the hammer off and slipped the gun back into the holster. Folding the paper, she placed it in her satchel. As she turned and walked to the door, she glanced at the two cowboys.

"Good to see you again, Rooster, Hovely. Tell Cliff my herd is together, and we're ready to move out whenever you are." Back on the street, Ida Mae allowed herself a tight smile. If the Guthrie Company wanted to proceed with their threat of taking her ranch away or placing a lien against her cattle, let them. She now had ammunition to fight with.

With determined steps she marched toward the mission. There was still the matter of a lost girl and a missing ranch foreman.

Father De La Cruz was somber as he sat behind his narrow writing desk and observed Ida Mae sitting directly across from him.

"Yes, your foreman was here yesterday, Mrs. Greeley. It was about this same time. I did look at the different specimens he presented to me and determined that one of them contained comfrey, an herb used for healing. There was a trace of another substance, possibly a root herb that had been ground and mixed in with it. I assumed it was for binding purposes.

"The other specimen was only a small piece. I wasn't completely certain, but I suspect that it belonged to the hemlock family. Some of the different species can be fatal even in very small amounts."

"What was my foreman's reaction when you told him of your findings?" Ida Mae asked.

"His manner didn't change. He said he suspected as much. He also indicated that a number of your cattle had died as the result of the apparent poisoning of a watering hole."

"I'm afraid so, Father. I'm also concerned that he may have decided to take matters into his own hands and confront the people responsible." Ida Mae paused and leaned forward. "He didn't return to the ranch. Would you happen to know in what direction my foreman went when he left town?"

"No, Mrs. Greeley. The only thing I can attest to is that he did visit the cantina after he left here, as I saw his horse there. At what time he left the establishment, or in what direction he went, I have no knowledge."

Ida Mae leaned back in her chair, her shoulders slumping. "Thank you," she said quietly.

Father De La Cruz looked at Ida Mae, concern deepening the crease on his brow. "Mrs. Greeley, if there is anything I can do to help you with your current difficulties, please let me know."

"There is one other thing, Father. You remember the girl I

told you about that had been taken by the Indians and then the desperado, Sanchez, found her wandering in the desert?"

"Yes. Does this still concern you?"

"Indeed, it does. Did you have a chance to speak with the company of soldiers who came through town a couple of days ago?"

"Unfortunately, no. I was called to the bedside of a seriously ill man whose home was some distance from here. When I returned, I learned of the soldiers passing through. Have you had a chance to speak with Mr. Schmidt yet?"

Ida Mae shook her head. "I haven't had the opportunity. One of my hands is convinced that the girl is his sister. He left yesterday with plans to rescue her. I fear for his safety." Ida Mae stood and paced a few steps. "I plan to travel to Fort Chadwick this afternoon and insist they send troops into Sanchez's compound."

The priest tilted his head sideways and shuffled the papers on his desk. "Mrs. Greeley, I would like to advise you against that type of action."

A furrow etched between Ida Mae's eyes and her chin jutted forward. "I'm sorry, Father, but this matter has been brushed aside for too long. Mr. McCabe is placing himself in great danger in his effort to rescue this woman."

Father De La Cruz held up one hand and smiled. "You didn't let me finish, Mrs. Greeley. Let me assure you that I sympathize with the plight of the girl and her brother's heroic attempt to rescue her. But you are still weak from your accident, and there are better ways of proceeding with your plans."

The padre picked up a pen and a sheet of paper. "I shall write a letter to Captain Marshall at Fort Chadwick and ask him to investigate this matter. The wording will be such as to imply that the girl's life may be in danger, and they must act with utmost speed. The message will be delivered by one of my trusted souls who work for me and should reach the fort by nightfall."

Ida Mae was relieved but also a little angry. "I . . . I can't thank you enough," she said, shaking her head. She didn't want to be ungrateful, but if Father De La Cruz had offered this when she first spoke to him about the girl, Jed wouldn't be risking his life now.

The priest finished writing the letter, then stood and walked around the desk. He placed a hand on Ida Mae's shoulder. "Mrs. Greeley, it's the best I can do. The fate of your hired man, and that of his sister, is in God's hands. Only He will decide their fate. If you wish to offer prayers for their safe return, please feel free to use our chapel. In the meantime, I will see that this letter is sent on its way immediately."

"I'm sorry, Father," Ida Mae said. "I didn't mean to sound irritable. There have been so many things . . ."

"No need to apologize," the priest said. "I understand what you have gone through and the anxiety you must feel concerning this matter and that of your foreman." He smiled, clasping his hands together. "Now, if you will excuse me . . ."

"Of course," Ida Mae said softly. "And Father De La Cruz, thank you."

On her way out, Ida Mae paused at the arched doorway leading into the chapel. Although she left her pistol at the courtyard entrance, she still felt hesitant. The sweet smell of incense permeated the room. A statue of the Virgin Mary stood near the altar, offering solace. She wasn't used to praying in such an environment. Her prayers were often quick thoughts or short messages spoken aloud. Even as a young girl, she hadn't spent as much time on her prayers as her sister had.

Ida Mae walked quietly down the long hall that led into the courtyard. Collecting her gun at the gate, she slipped through the opening and walked back toward the stables. Father De La Cruz said that Jed's fate was in God's hands. She wondered how God would have received her prayers after she'd sold guns that may or may not be used to slay innocent people, and after she herself had held a gun to a man and threatened him. Although it was to make an honest man of him, she wasn't sure God would see it her way.

Ida Mae found Winslow in the stables.

"Are you ready to leave now, Miss Ida?" he asked.

"Not just yet, Isaac. I need to know if you saw or spoke to Cotton yesterday."

"No, I missed that displeasure, but I knew he was in town. Saw him over at the cantina having a few rounds with the Circle-M boys." Isaac shifted his feet uncertainly. "Is there something worrying you?"

"Cotton was due back at the ranch last night. He never made it. I'm trying to determine if he's sleeping off a hangover or if something happened to him."

Winslow scratched at one ear. "I'm not one to spend my money on whiskey, so I didn't join in on their revelry. But a couple of Cradle's Peak riders were here yesterday about noon. They said they'd been working for you and that something had happened to their guns."

Ida Mae was silent a moment. "How many, and what kind of guns did you sell them?"

"Only one. A pistol. The fellow called Laredo was the one who bought it."

"Ammunition?"

"One box of cartridges."

"One bullet would be all that was needed."

Isaac shook his head. "Did Cotton and this Laredo feller have a falling out?"

"You might say that."

"You know, Miss Ida, if I had known, I wouldn't have sold him that pistol."

Ida Mae leaned against her wagon. "I'm sure you wouldn't have, Isaac. But if he hadn't gotten the gun from you, he would have found one elsewhere. The question now is where are they?"

"I'm not sure about Cotton," Winslow said, "but Laredo and his partner left town right after they bought the gun. I took it they were headed back to Cradle's Peak. I saw Worley and his rider leave town later in the day." Isaac rubbed his jaw. "But I could swear that I remember Cotton's horse still being tied in front of the cantina when Worley and Rooster left."

Ida Mae frowned. "Are you sure, Isaac, that you saw Rooster

leave with Worley? I just saw him and another hand, Hovely, at that new Guthrie store. Why would they still be in town if Worley returned to the ranch?"

"Couldn't answer you on that, Miss Ida. But if you want to ask them, I see two Circle-M horses tied in front of the cantina."

Ida Mae had been in the cantina before. Once to fire a drunken hand, and once to drag out an inebriated but jolly Cotton and transport him back to the ranch.

The tension and activities of the day were starting to wear on her. She was tired and her side hurt. She would have to find a place to rest, but first she needed to speak with those cowhands.

Standing at the cantina doors, Ida Mae's gaze swept the dim interior. Only a few patrons were bellied against the bar, and Ida Mae recognized Rooster as one of them. Rooster saw her at about the same time and quickly hurried to the door.

His hat was pushed back, and his face was flushed. "Howdy, Miss Ida," he said, his grin revealing broken and discolored teeth. "You need a drink?" He turned to his drinking partners and began to giggle, tickled at his own wit.

Ida Mae frowned. She had no patience with drunken cowhands. "Straighten up and get out here now," she said, her voice sharp.

The grin slowly faded from Rooster's face and his eyes attempted to focus on her as he swayed slightly. "You mean out there? With you? In the sun?"

"That's exactly what I mean," Ida Mae said, her words clipped.

"Awright," Rooster responded slowly as he pushed his way out of the saloon, shuffling his feet to keep his balance. "You mad at me, Miss Ida? Me and Hovely, we won't say nothing about what happened at the . . . at the," Rooster hiccupped and then continued, "new store." He turned and shouted through the doorway into the cantina. "We, me and Hovely, we're witnesses." He stumbled against the door jam. "Don't you worry,

Miss Ida. We didn't see a thing. Did we, Hovely? We didn't see a thing."

Ida Mae stepped closer to Rooster and grabbed his elbow. Exerting as much pressure as she was able to, she guided the drunken cowhand away from the cantina. Propping him against the side of the building, she fixed him with an icy glare.

"I don't give a red rat's fanny what you witnessed or didn't. What I'm concerned about is my foreman, Cotton, and why you and Hovely are in town and your boss isn't. Now, do you think you can sober up enough to tell me what's going on?"

"Sh . . . sure. I can do that." Rooster pushed away from the wall, reconsidered, then slid down with his back against the adobe and rested on his haunches. "When Worley and me got out of town a ways, we met ol' Hovely. He said he needed some parts for a wagon he was working on and was headed inta town to get 'em. Th . . . that's when Worley tolt me to ride along with Hovely and keep him outa trouble."

Rooster listed sideways and braced his hand against the ground. "I don't think I did a very good job, Miss Ida. Hovely's drunker than six coons in a broken still. Worley's gonna chew my rear end but good when I get back."

"I'm sure you're right about that, Rooster. Now, can you tell me if you've seen Cotton, or know where he may have gone?"

A puzzled look crossed Rooster's face. "Went? He went home. Back to the Bar-DI."

"No, he didn't. He didn't come in last night, and there were no signs of him on the trail or here in town. Did he say anything about riding to Cradle's Peak or anywhere else?"

Rooster stared across the square, his mouth working as he carried on a muted conversation with himself. He licked his lips and focused his faded blue eyes on Ida Mae. "He didn't like them two fellers from Cradle's Peak, you know. Said he didn't trust 'em. Called 'em all kinds of names. Cotton said he was gonna prove something to somebody, and it was gonna be his pleasure to innerduce those two dandies to the rope posse."

"Did you see Cotton leave town?" Ida Mae asked, leaning over and placing herself within Rooster's line of vision.

With one hand, Rooster scratched at the top of his head. "No, nope, didn't see him leave. He was still in the cantina when me and Worley left. But when Hovely and me got back inta town," Rooster added brightly, "he was gone."

"How drunk was Cotton when you and Cliff left?"

Rooster grinned and shrugged one shoulder. "He was singing along with the fat señorita in there. I think it was a love song. Maybe he's in love. Maybe she took him home with her. Heck, I don't know."

Ida Mae straightened and looked back at the cantina. If Cotton had left with the woman, he wouldn't be happy being tracked down. But on the other hand, if he was drunk enough to think he could take on Laredo, he could be in serious trouble.

Ida Mae walked back to the cantina and entered. She waited a moment, letting her eyes adjust to the darkened interior. Conversation came to a standstill, and all eyes focused on her.

"Mrs. Greeley," the man behind the bar greeted her. "Can I help you with something?"

"Yes," Ida Mae said as she approached the bar. "Mr. Garrison, isn't it?"

"Yes, ma'am."

"I'm trying to determine the whereabouts of my foreman, Cotton. I've been told he was in here until late yesterday. Do you have any idea where he might be now?"

"No, I don't, Mrs. Greeley. But you're right, he was here for a while, and then he left."

Ida Mae's eyes narrowed and she leaned forward, resting one arm on the bar. "Mr. Garrison, I was also informed that Cotton may have left with one of your, shall we say, 'ladies' for the evening. I want her name and where she lives."

"Nah, Mrs. Greeley, you don't want to go there."

"And why is that?"

The bartender's eyes shifted to the men lined against the bar, each leaning toward them, listening to the conversation.

He looked back at Ida Mae and shrugged his shoulders. "Cuz he's not there. He left for the Bar-DI late yesterday."

"You're sure of this?"

"As sure as you're standing there, ma'am."

"Then explain to me why there was no sign of him or his horse at the ranch or on the trail when I drove in this morning. It's my understanding that the last place anyone saw him was here, late yesterday, serenading some señorita. Now, unless you personally saw him mount and leave in the direction of my ranch, I want the woman's name and where she lives."

One of the men leaning against the bar pushed away and made his way toward Ida Mae. She recognized him as Hovely, the other hapless rider from the Circle-M.

"Mrs. Greeley," he said, his breath sour with whiskey, "Garrison's right about Cotton. He wasn't here when me and Rooster got inta town. But the señorita you're talking about was. I'm not saying Cotton didn't spend some time with her before he left, but that was all."

"How do you know that?"

"Cuz Rooster and I danced most of the night with her."

Ida Mae was silent for a moment. "Thank you for that bit of news, Hovely," she said quietly. She turned and walked out of the cantina. She paused a moment, letting her gaze take in the square and shook her head slightly. There was only one other place Cotton could have gone.

Chapter Twenty-six

Kate dropped her head against her knees. Her gaunt frame trembled as she took deep, ragged breaths. Jed touched her shoulder gently. "I'm taking you to a ranch where you'll be safe. Just hold on a little longer. Can you do that?"

Nodding, Kate rubbed her eyes with the heels of her hands. "I thought both you and Johnny were dead," she finally said. "Mr. Ramsey told the Mexican man, Sanchez, I wasn't his kin and refused to give him any money. Sanchez was angry and felt he should be rewarded for finding me, so he kept me."

Kate glanced up the ravine and absently sifted some sand through her fingers. "Mr. Sanchez didn't treat me badly. It was the woman who was mean." A faint smile flitted across her lips. "I think I paid her back."

Some of the tension left Jed's body. He was glad to hear Sanchez hadn't harmed her. Standing, he hurried back to his saddlebag. After removing the packages of food Ida Mae sent, he returned to Kate.

"Here's something to eat," he said, placing the wrapped food in her lap. "While I tend to my horse, you try to rest."

Jed turned his attention back to Big Blue. The horse was clearly spent. His sides were sunken, and he stood with his head lowered. Jed knew he had pushed the horse too hard. He would have to walk him and allow him only short drinks of water. Both would take time—time they didn't have.

Jed walked the horse up and down the bottom of the ravine. He fought to keep his sense of urgency to move on under con-

198

trol. It was crucial that Big Blue was rested before he was ridden again.

Satisfied that the horse had cooled down, Jed used a broken limb from one of the cottonwoods to dig into the soft seepage against the bank. Before long, he was scooping out damp soil. After enlarging the excavation, he sat back and watched as trickles of water filtered into the depression. As he waited for enough water to collect, he climbed to the top edge of the ravine. His gaze swept the horizon. Nothing alerted his attention. Hawks wheeled lazily against the early morning sky, and there were no dust plumes to signal approaching riders.

Jed returned to Big Blue and led him to the pool, allowing him only a small drink of water. He would have to ration him for a while.

Returning to where Kate sat, Jed dropped down on one heel. "Are you hurt anywhere, Kate?"

Kate shook her head. A frown creased her forehead.

"Is something wrong?" Jed asked, his voice showing concern.

"I was just wondering," she asked softly. "Where's Johnny?"

Jed ran the palm of his hand across his face. Johnny and Kate had been close. They were alike in so many ways. The pranks, the love of music and dancing. He didn't want to tell her about Johnny now.

"Kate, there's so much we need to talk about, but we haven't the time."

The sun had climbed into the sky, bringing warmth and gnats with it. Big Blue drank several more times, but still showed signs of exhaustion. He wouldn't be able to carry them both, but Kate weighed very little and wouldn't be a burden for the large horse.

After checking the terrain again, Jed concluded that if riders were coming, they were still too far away to be detected. He also knew Sanchez wouldn't let the destruction of his house go without retaliation of some kind. And since he hadn't made an effort to cover their trail, it was only a matter of time before Sanchez caught up with them.

He turned to Kate. "Are you up to traveling?" he asked. "We're going to have to keep moving. Big Blue's not able to carry the both of us just yet. But if we stay here, Sanchez will be on us before nightfall."

Kate nodded and pushed herself upright. "You don't need to worry about me, Jed. I got away from a passel of Indians and sooner or later I would have done in that blackhearted woman and walked away from Sanchez and his bunch."

"I don't doubt you for a moment, Kate. But Sanchez has his pride, and letting me get away would put a big dent in it."

After helping Kate onto Big Blue, Jed gathered the reins in one hand and led them up the wash. If the horse had been in better shape, he would have laid down some false trails, but he didn't dare waste Big Blue's strength. He needed to find high ground and cover.

One of the positions he had been assigned in the war was covering their platoon's rear when they were in retreat. Using a run-and-wait maneuver, Yankee soldiers pursuing them were picked off randomly. His expert marksmanship had earned him the respect of his company commander, the wariness of the Northern troops, and the reputation of being a backwoods sniper.

Before long, the wash played out. Jed was able to see the surrounding plains clearly. He also saw something else that put a knot in his stomach—a thin cloud of dust rising in the distance. There was no doubt that it was Sanchez and his men.

A jumble of rocks with a sparse stand of junipers and mesquite clinging in among them signaled the end of the wash. Jed led Big Blue in behind one of the larger rock formations. He helped Kate down and removed his revolver from its holster. He handed it to Kate along with a handful of shells.

"Take my pistol, Kate," he said. "Stay here with Big Blue. I'm going to take cover a little higher in the rocks and see if I can persuade some of those outlaws to give it up."

He reached out and patted her cheek. "Get down behind those rocks. If you think I've been hit, or I tell you, hop on Big Blue and head due east." Jed gestured in the direction of the

Greeley ranch. "If you come across anyone, ask where the Bar-DI is. A lady by the name of Ida Mae Greeley runs it. She'll take care of you. You understand?"

Kate raised her eyes and looked at Jed. "Why don't we both go now?"

"They're too close, Kate, and Big Blue is still spent. He wouldn't be able to outrun them. We would be caught in the open without cover. Our only chance is here. If I can take out Sanchez and a few of his men, the rest may turn and run."

Kate was silent a moment. "If I was up higher, I could help," she said quietly.

"No, I don't want to worry about you being in the line of fire. I can do it, Kate. It's what I've been doing for the last five years. Now hurry up and take cover. Keep ol' Blue close to you and do what I said."

Jed pulled Ida Mae's rifle from its scabbard and removed the box of cartridges from his saddlebag. He turned and made his way up through the rocks until he had a good vantage point. Struggling with a few of the heavier boulders, he maneuvered them into a makeshift barricade around him.

He turned to check on the dust cloud and tensed when he saw riders hovering over the edge of the wash where he and Kate had first stopped. He watched as two of the riders crossed the wash. Four riders remained in the main group. In tandem, each group rode along the sides of the ravine, heading toward them.

Jed nodded. The riders were doing exactly what he figured they would. They could follow Blue's prints in the bottom of the gulley, but not be trapped in the wash in case he and Kate had dug a bunker into one of the sides.

All he had to do was wait. Jed was surprised at how quickly the riders covered the distance he and Kate had walked. He couldn't let them get any closer to Kate. He would have to start shooting before they discovered her hiding place.

Jed cursed softly. The outlaws pulled their horses up. They undoubtedly had seen the rocks and brush and realized that that's where he and Kate would be.

One rider, who Jed guessed was Sanchez, made a gesturing motion with his arm. A rider from each group split off and rode away from the cut, circling around the rock formation in order to come in behind him. Soon they would be out of his line of vision. He had to act fast. Taking a deep breath, Jed pulled the rifle to his shoulder. He calculated the distance and the pace of the horse, adjusted his aim, and fired. He didn't wait to see if he had hit his target; he knew he had. In one sweeping motion, he threw open the breechblock, ejected the empty shell, and shoved in another one as he swung the rifle to his right.

The other rider had heard the shot and wheeled his horse, sending the animal into a wild gallop away from the rocks. Jed squeezed off another shot and saw the man slump forward. In that instant he felt a stinging sensation against his face and knew that Sanchez had spotted him and was firing at him. The bullets hit the nearby rocks and sent splintered fragments into the air. He ducked down and pushed another cartridge in.

The riders at the edge of the ravine had dismounted and were scattering like squirrels into the rocks below Kate. For a long while was an uncertain silence. The outlaws' horses, spooked by the sudden gunplay, turned and ran down the edge of the wash. He could easily shoot the horses, but that would be a waste of precious ammunition.

A shot pierced the air and hit just above Jed. He was pinned down. He needed to move, but there was no way to do that without becoming an easy target.

The sun was dropping low in the western horizon. Before long, it would be dark. Under the cover of darkness, Sanchez would send men in behind him. Kate needed to get out before then.

Jed eased his body into a prone position, lifted his head, and squinted down among the rocks. One of the men was scrambling between the scattered boulders, trying to work his way up the draw. It was an easy shot. The man didn't make a sound when he went down. Immediately, several guns roared to life, spraying Jed's position with bullets and flying rock. The outlaws would take advantage of the full-scale assault to improve their positions.

Jed quickly scrambled to the far end of his bunker and lifted himself up, rifle ready. A scurrying figure and a quick shot brought a yelp, and Jed knew he had only wounded the bandit. He ducked down and placed in another shell. He could hear men's voices and the plaintive wail of the injured man. Jed chanced another look. He didn't see any movements among the rocks, but what he did see brought a chill to his body.

Another dust spiral was rising in the distance. More riders were approaching. More of Sanchez's men. He estimated the riders would arrive at their position in less than half an hour. Kate needed to leave now. He didn't have enough ammunition to take care of more outlaws.

He lay out the remaining cartridges within easy reach. "Kate," he called softly. "Count to ten and then get on Blue and ride like the wind."

Jed counted slowly to eight, rose to one knee, and fired into the rocks below. As fast as he was able to reload, he fired several more times. Kate didn't leave. His gaze darted to where she was hidden. He could see Big Blue, switching his tail and stamping his hooves. Then he saw Kate. She was aiming the pistol at someone. The pistol jerked upward with an explosion of noise, and Jed saw a body slide down from behind a rock just below her.

A hot, searing sensation sliced through Jed's upper shoulder. Twisting with its force, he fell, sprawling across the rocks. "Kate, go!" he shouted.

He heard her pistol bark once more, and then a short scream. He was unsure if it was Kate who had screamed or her intended target. His shoulder felt on fire as he rolled to his knees and pulled the gunstock against the bloodied flesh. By his estimation, there shouldn't be more than a couple of outlaws and Sanchez left. If he could make it down to where Kate was, he'd convince her to leave. He might be able to hold off the approaching riders long enough for her to get a fair start.

Their horses would be winded, and Big Blue should outdistance them.

Jed rolled over the top of his barricade and slid down among the rocks to where Kate was. He stopped cold. Kate was standing, her body bent at an odd angle. It only took a second for Jed to see why. Sanchez was standing behind her, twisting her arm up, his pistol pointed at her head.

Chapter Twenty-seven

Ida Mae spent a restless night at the mission. The worry concerning Jed's safety and the whereabouts of Cotton kept her tossing most of the night.

While sharing the morning meal with Father De La Cruz, he informed her that the rider he'd sent to the fort the previous day had returned with disappointing news: Most of the troops were out on patrol and weren't expected back for several days.

Anguish and despair at the news overwhelmed her. With her hands shaking, she excused herself and retreated to her room. Her mind raced as she gathered her few belongings. If she rode to the Circle-M, could she persuade Worley to send men after Jed? Judging from his reaction to her outburst at the ranch, he might be reluctant. She'd have to raise enough of a fuss to convince him. Even so, would they reach Jed in time?

Father De La Cruz stood outside Ida Mae's door, his voice interrupting her anxious thoughts. "Mrs. Greeley, I'm sorry that the news upset you. If you would care to join me in the chapel, perhaps you may find comfort there."

Ida Mae threw a quick glance at the priest. "You don't understand, Father. There's no time. I have to ride out to the Circle-M. They have enough spare wranglers that they can send help for Jed. I will insist."

"Mrs. Greeley, you are asking men to do things that are unnecessary. The rider I sent to the fort left my message at the post. The lieutenant in charge assured my rider that he would send several men to the field with the letter." The priest walked into the room and gently laid his hand on Ida Mae's arm. "Now, please join me in the chapel."

"But I have to do something, Father. I . . . this man . . . Jed. I've come to care about him. I must help him."

The priest smiled and patted her arm. "While I commend you for wishing to help God with his work, please don't get in His way. As I've told you, this man's fate, and that of his sister, is in the hands of the Lord. Only He controls the outcome. You must step aside and place your trust in God."

Ida Mae sat on the cot and buried her face in her hands. She had trusted once, and Dan had been taken from her. Only by maintaining control of the events around her was she able to assure herself of her own safety and that of those she cared about. Was it possible for her to do as the priest asked and place her trust in the Lord?

She lifted her head and looked at Father De La Cruz. "All right, Father, I'll go to the chapel with you."

It was well past noon when Ida Mae arrived at Cradle's Peak. It hadn't been easy to set aside her emotions and follow Father De La Cruz's advice. As she knelt with the priest in the chapel, she had sensed the calmness of the room and the peace it offered. She struggled to place her trust in God. In the back of her mind, she still negotiated. She would trust God to take care of Jed and his sister, but she would continue her search for Cotton.

"This is a very unsettling story you tell me." Gerta's brow was wrinkled in apparent disbelief as she finished pouring Ida Mae a cup of tea. "It is a shame my brother is away on his business. He would be most concerned." Taking a cupful for herself, Gerta settled into her chair with a rustle of silk.

In the soft glow of the afternoon sun, Ida Mae felt her body relax as she tasted the hot tea and related her well-rehearsed story. She'd chosen her words carefully. She didn't want Gerta to know that she suspected Thomas of being the one behind the poisoning of the watering hole. After all, Cotton had been wrong about the poultice. Gerta was only trying to help.

"There seemed to be some disagreement between Cotton and the two men Thomas sent, over the food they were given. I know Cotton can be hot-tempered," Ida Mae said, her voice condescending. "But with some whiskey under his belt, I'm afraid he may have followed your wranglers and confronted them."

"But you saw no trace of your foreman or the two ranch hands on your way here?" Gerta asked.

"No. But if Laredo and Joe have returned here, I would like to speak with them."

Gerta shook her head. "They have not returned."

Ida Mae frowned. "Are you sure? Perhaps your foreman sent them straight out to the roundup."

"It is possible," Gerta replied, raising her eyebrows slightly. "I don't always have such knowledge of the workings of the ranch."

"Could you summon your housekeeper and ask her if the two men did indeed return?"

Gerta remained quiet as she blew on the hot tea in her cup. Ida Mae thought she saw a slight look of irritation flicker across the older woman's face.

"I know it's an imposition," Ida Mae added apologetically, "but this is of utmost importance to me. I have to locate my foreman."

Gerta nodded slowly. "But of course. I will have Carmen go to the adobes and ask." She rose slowly, carrying the cup with her, and disappeared down the center hallway.

Ida Mae sipped gingerly at the tea. It was slightly bitter and the warmth of the liquid spread through her body. She didn't realize how tired she was. For a moment she allowed her eyes to close.

What would she do if the men hadn't returned? Her plan seemed absurd now. There had been no sign of Cotton or his horse along the roadway. Even if she spoke with the men, would they tell her the truth?

She was indebted to Cotton for his loyal support after Dan's death. He had become like a father to her. Admittedly a contentious one, but a relationship built on true fondness for one another. In her impatient desire to find him, had she made a foolish decision? Perhaps it would be best if she returned to the ranch.

Ida Mae took a shaky breath and forced her eyes open. She raised the cup of tea to her lips. The bitter taste caught against the roof of her mouth. Like a bolt of lighting, it hit her. There was something wrong with the tea!

With great care, she placed the cup on the table near her. Her body felt lax, and she wondered if she would be able to make it back to the mission. Nightfall would be on her before she could reach town, but she would have to try. Father De La Cruz was the only one who could help her.

Ida Mae pushed herself up from her chair. For a moment the room spun. Placing one hand on the table, she attempted to steady herself. She was only dimly aware of someone entering the room.

"Are you not feeling well?" Gerta's voice seemed to be coming from a great distance.

Ida Mae tried to focus on the older woman's face. "I, I'm . . . fine," Ida Mae responded slowly.

"Perhaps you need rest," Gerta said. "I will have Carmen prepare the room for you."

"No. No. I'm . . . I'm going to return to my ranch."

"Of course you are," Gerta said smoothly. "First light to-morrow I shall see your team is ready for you."

"Not tomorrow, today," Ida Mae managed.

Gerta's grasp on her arm felt rough, and she could hear her chortle. "You will return to your ranch, *mein* dear, but not in the manner you wish. Help is here now. We will assist you to your room."

"No!" Ida Mae managed to jerk her arm away from Gerta's grasp.

"Such a fool," Gerta snickered. "Did you really think I would let Thomas displace me here?"

"Displace?" Ida Mae's voice was faint.

"My idiot brother thinks to send me back to the old country

and bring you in to be his wife. You! You are not worthy to polish his boots."

Ida Mae felt her body sway as she attempted to shake her head. "Not . . . what I . . . wanted," she finally got out.

"No matter. I will not be pushed aside, not after all I have done for him. He needs me. Without me he is nothing. I will show him for the weakling he is. All of this land is for the taking. The strong shall become rich. The weak will slink away like dogs, their tails between their legs. I, only me, know how to take this land. Thanks to your sloppy ranching, already I have for myself a sizable herd. Soon I shall have the biggest cattle ranch around. My silly brother will kiss my hand and beg for my forgiveness."

Ida Mae took small shuffling steps as she walked in a circular pattern. She grasped the arm of the chair. "The tea. What did you put in the tea?"

Gerta paused in her rant, and then addressed her. "Only a little something to help you sleep," she said darkly. "This time you will feel nothing when your wagon crashes. Your skinny little neck will already be broken."

Leaning against the chair, Ida Mae shook her head, trying to clear her mind. "What . . . do you mean?"

"Your wagon. I had it fixed to break. It was unfortunate that it didn't finish with the business. It would have saved so much trouble."

Holding on to the chair's arm, Ida Mae turned her body and sank into the cushions. A shadowy curtain obscured the images that swirled about her. She could hear another voice. A man's voice. "Thomas?" Her words came out a mere whisper.

Gerta's cackle cut across the growing chasm between clear reality and Ida Mae's ever darkening world.

"Oh yes, my lovestruck brother. Him and his land investment cohorts, they play parlor games. Scaring the little people by having men dress as the Indians. Buying the local store and demanding payments on the debts. Their minds work like children!

"And your silly note about the woman. When the idiot hand

return with it, I laugh. Phu! I knew what you were up to. As if I should give Thomas such a brazen attempt at flirtation."

Ida Mae saw the blurred image of a man approach her and then Gerta's voice: "Get her out before Carmen returns."

Rough hands grabbed Ida Mae around her waist, picking her up. She twisted her body, pushing at the man, trying to break his grip. She reached for her gun, but the holster was empty. When had that happened? Where was it?

"Where do you want her?" Ida Mae heard the man ask.

"The cellar for the roots," Gerta answered. "And Laredo, don't bother to search her. I have already taken her gun."

Laredo. Did Gerta say Laredo? Ida Mae struggled to see the man's face.

"Dang it, Gerta. You've taken away all my fun," Laredo said.

"This is no time for fun." Gerta's voice was sharp. "After you lock her away, go back to the stables and hide her wagon and team. Thomas is due back soon. I don't want him to see them."

Ida Mae could hear Laredo huffing as he carried her through the house. Murky images crowded into Ida Mae's thoughts. She felt her arm bang against a narrow doorjamb and then a sense of being carried down a long hallway. Cool air bathed her face before her body dropped onto a packed earthen floor. Her limbs were like sodden clay. She struggled to lift her head and move her arms, but nothing responded to her efforts. The smell of rotting vegetables and damp earth stung her nostrils as black oblivion engulfed her.

Chapter Twenty-eight

The sound of pounding hooves grew closer. They rumbled like thunder across the open plains. Sweat trickled down Jed's face as he stood stiffly, staring at Kate and the outlaw, Sanchez.

Kate's features contorted in pain as Sanchez twisted her arm more tightly and pulled her in front of him, the pistol pressing into her temple.

"So, gringo, how brave are you now?" Sanchez said. "I hear my men coming. They have rounded up their horses and are arriving in time to see me finish you. Next time you will be more careful of whose home you destroy." Sanchez laughed. "*Lo siento*. I don't believe there will be a next time."

Jed frowned, straining to see in the fading light. He still held his rifle, but Sanchez had placed Kate in front of him, creating an effective shield. It would be foolish to attempt a shot at this close range and in the shadow-filled rocks. He had one chance left.

"How much?"

Sanchez frowned. *"¿Qué?"*

"You wanted a reward. How much money for the girl's release?"

Sanchez whistled through his teeth. "You don't understand. You have nothing to bargain with. Everything you carry is mine to take."

"I don't have the money on me. Someone is holding it for me. I can retrieve it. Two thousand dollars. That should be enough to rebuild your home."

Dust drifted down into the gulch. Horses danced and milled

about as the riders came to a sliding halt. Rifle bolts clicked as ammunition was rammed into firing cylinders.

"You think I am *estúpido*?" Sanchez sneered. "The dinero is nothing. No one comes into my home and destroys it." He pulled the pistol away from Kate's head and pointed it at Jed.

"Drop it, Sanchez!" A voice ordered from the rim of the wash.

Sanchez whirled, a startled look on his face as he glanced toward the men lining the top of the ravine.

Jed seized on the chance and jerked up his rifle.

"You too, cowboy! Drop the rifle."

Jed hesitated and turned to identify the men standing above him.

The voice was menacing. "Now!"

Suddenly Jed realized that the men wore uniforms. They were soldiers. A feeling of relief flooded through him and he lowered his rifle, still hesitant to let go of it.

Sanchez's gaze darted between the soldiers and Jed. A cautious smile flitted across Sanchez's face, and releasing Kate, he stepped back. "Ah, *capitán,* you arrive in time. This coyote, he burns my home and kills my muchachos. I was about to deliver the justice he deserves."

"I said drop your gun, Sanchez." The captain's voice was threatening. "You too, partner!"

Still smiling, Sanchez dropped his revolver on the rocks.

Kate stumbled toward Jed as Sanchez released her. "Are you all right?" Jed asked, taking her arm and laying his rifle on the ground.

Kate nodded and stepped in close to him. Jed put a protective arm around her as he watched the captain and soldiers dismount and work their way down into the wash, their guns drawn. Another rider maneuvered his horse closer to the ravine and dismounted. He walked to the edge of the embankment.

"What in all tarnation are you doing here, Jed?"

It took a few seconds for Jed to recognize Cotton's querulous voice.

"What . . . how . . . ?" For a moment Jed was at a loss for words.

"The 'what' of the matter," Cotton retorted, "is that in the fit of a whiskey rush I decided if Ida Mae was so het-up 'bout that gal Sanchez was holding, I'd see to it her mind was put at ease. So I rode out to the fort and persuaded Captain Marshall here to ride inta Sanchez's place and rescue her."

Cotton paused and spit to the side, wiping his mouth with his shirtsleeve. "Now, the 'how' of the matter is a bit more tricky. With all the gunshots rollin' 'cross the prairie, it sounded like a war was bein' fought. The captain figured he'd best check it out to see if some homesteaders were in trouble afore we went on to Sanchez's place." Cotton's grin grew wider. "Looks like it was a good thing he did. Now, you want to tell me why you're here?"

Jed glanced down at Kate and then toward Cotton. "This is my sister, Kate."

Captain Marshall had paused and was talking with Sanchez. He turned and walked toward Jed. Nodding at Kate, he said, "Did I hear you say that this woman is your sister?"

"Yes, sir."

"Is this the same woman the Apaches took from the Upper Concho?"

Jed looked at Kate. "Is that where the Indians took you from?"

Kate's face was taut. "Yes, I believe that's what the area was called."

"How did you end up with this Sanchez fellow?" Captain Marshall asked.

"I was able to escape from the Apaches when they encountered another group of Indians and began fighting. I think they were enemies. I hid among some rocks for several days before trying to find my way back. Mr. Sanchez found me and took me to his place."

The captain nodded slowly, and easing his hat back with one thumb, he peered at Jed's shoulder. "Looks like you took a bullet. I've an assistant surgeon with me. He can dress that for you. Your sister, does she need any medical help?"

Jed grimaced. He wasn't sure what Kate needed.

"I understand English, Captain," Kate cut in. "I'm perfectly capable of speaking for myself. And no, I don't need any medical help."

Kate's proud posture and piercing eyes sent the captain's eyebrows skyward. "That's good to know, ma'am."

"I think it would be best if we could return to the Greeley ranch as soon as possible," Jed said. "Mrs. Greeley has agreed to take my sister in and care for her."

Captain Marshall grinned. "I don't think there will be much 'caring for' needed."

After glancing back at Sanchez, Captain Marshall returned his gaze to Jed. "Señor Sanchez has claimed that you burned down his house. He wants compensation for his loss."

"Señor Sanchez can sit in the devil's lap for eternity before that happens. He stole two horses and my guns from me. I recovered one horse and a gun. He still has one of my horses and the rest of my guns. I think we're about even."

The captain looked around the area, appraising the situation. "Is it your intention to return to the Greeley ranch tonight?"

"Yes, sir."

"All right. As soon as your wound is dressed, you're free to leave."

"There's one more thing, Captain." Jed sidestepped around Kate and approached Sanchez. "Your pockets, señor. Empty them."

Sanchez scowled at him. *"¿Qué?"*

"The watch. I want my watch back."

"Oh, I don't think so," Sanchez said, his mustache curling up on one corner of his mouth.

Before Jed could process the thought, he felt his fist slam into Sanchez's face.

The outlaw reeled back, stumbling over rocks and falling to the ground.

Jed stood over him, his fist still clenched. "The watch," he said between gritted teeth.

Sanchez struggled to a sitting position, rubbed his jaw with one hand, and reached into his pocket with the other. Pulling the watch from his pocket, he flung it at Jed.

Jed stooped and picked it up. He glanced back at Sanchez. "Now the hombre is even."

He turned and walked back to the captain. "What happens with Sanchez?" Jed asked.

"Probably not much. He didn't initially kidnap the girl, and you've just said you were even. It looks as though you were defending yourself and your sister in the gun battle here." The captain cast a wary look at Sanchez. "He says he meant the girl no harm. He only wanted compensation for her care. For whatever their reasons are, most ranchers hereabouts don't complain about him. But if you want to file charges, we can take him and what's left of his bunch back to Fort Chadwick."

Jed shook his head and offered his hand. "Kate's safe now. That's all I care about. But I want to thank you and your soldiers for your well-timed arrival."

Captain Marshall took Jed's proffered hand and shook it. "The thanks should go to your friend. He argues a good case. The man should be in politics, and you should be a lawman. The West needs men like you."

Jed smiled and glanced up at Cotton. "Thanks," he said quietly.

"Just dumb luck and a lot of whiskey," Cotton replied, his grin now radiating over his entire face.

Dawn was breaking when Jed, Kate, and Cotton rode up to the Bar-DI corrals. Butch's welcoming bark brought Kyle to the doorway of the bunkhouse, cradling a shotgun.

"Hold yer fire, Kyle," Cotton yelled at him. "It's only the conquerin' heroes returnin'."

Jed winced as he slid down from Big Blue. He was glad Cotton was still in high spirits. His spirits had faded as the pain in his arm increased. The doctor had assured him that the wound was clean. The bullet sliced open the fleshy part of his shoulder with only minimal muscle damage.

Kate dismounted, and they both turned and walked toward the bunkhouse.

Kyle set his shotgun aside and approached them. "Is this your sister?" he asked, his voice doubtful.

"Yes," Jed nodded. "This is Kate."

Kyle inched closer. "Kate, do you remember me? Kyle Landry, from the wagon train?"

Kate brushed a hand across her brow and frowned. "I don't know. . . . Yes, yes, I remember. You were Trudy's brother. I'm sorry. It seems so long ago."

Cotton's voice carried from the edge of the corral. "You got any grub fixed, boy? I'm hungry as a newly weaned pup, and I'm reckonin' this little lady could use a good hepin' of beans and corn bread herself."

Kyle turned to Cotton with a flustered look. "I can heat up the beans, but it will take a while to get some corn bread on."

"Then get at it," Cotton yelled back. "Show this little gal what a catch you are."

Even in the early morning light, Jed could see Kyle's face turn a bright pink. Jed grinned and looked toward the ranch house. "Do you think Ida Mae is up?"

Kyle stopped in his retreat to the bunkhouse and turned to him. "She's not home. She left for town day before yesterday and hasn't come back. I figure she's staying at the mission."

An uneasy feeling crept into Jed's stomach. "Why did she go into town?"

"She said she had business to take care of. I think she was also worried about Cotton." Kyle rubbed one ear. "I expected her back last night, but she never showed up."

Cotton walked up slowly as he listened to Kyle.

Jed's gaze shifted between Kyle and Cotton. "I talked to her before I left. She said she'd be here to look after Kate."

Cotton turned his head and spit, hitched up his pants, and frowned. "That cussed Portello. That's why she went inta town. She took some of Dan's guns inta Windbag Winslow and sold 'em. She told me she would take care of that debt, and sure as wooley-heck and I'm standing here, that's how she did it. But Kyle's right, she should've been back afore now."

Jed fastened his gaze on Kyle. "What did she say about Cotton before she left?"

"That it was Laredo who shot Cotton and that she figured Cotton might have gone after him to call him out."

A choking sound came from deep within Cotton's throat. "What! Where'd that come from?"

Jed set his jaw. This was what he was afraid of. "I told her that I suspected Laredo of being the one who shot you," Jed said, his voice quiet.

"Why didn't you say somethin' to me?" Cotton's face turned dark, and his eyebrows bristled.

"Because you would've gotten yourself killed."

"Are you sayin' I couldn't outgun that . . . that," he glanced toward Kate, "that polecat!"

Jed forced his voice to remain calm. "My reason for suspecting Laredo hinged on a hoofprint that I followed the day after you were shot. I linked it to Laredo's horse. That's not proof he was the one who shot you. Only that his horse was in the vicinity of where you were shot. Do you think that's enough evidence to get anyone killed?"

"With everythin' else we know, dang straight!" Cotton's eyes blazed as he glared at Jed.

Jed took several deep breaths and nodded in silent agreement. "First, we'll have something to eat," he said. "Then I'll get Kate settled in the house. Let's give Ida Mae a few more hours. If she doesn't show by midmorning, we'll ride out."

Kate's fingers tugged at Jed's shirt. "If this Mrs. Greeley isn't home, I wouldn't feel comfortable being in her house."

Jed turned to her. "Everything will be all right, Kate. Ida Mae can be testy at times, but it's really okay."

Jed spoke to Kyle. "Go ahead and fix the corn bread. I'll take her on up."

Walking with Kate toward the house, Jed brushed a rough hand over her tangled hair. "I'll tell Kyle to haul up some water so you can take a bath, maybe wash your hair. When Mrs. Greeley gets back, I'd like her to see how pretty my sister is."

Jed awoke with a start. Sunlight filtered through the shuttered window of the ranch house. Kate stood over him, her golden-green eyes studying his countenance.

"Good heavens, you scared me," Jed muttered, quickly adjusting his mind to his surroundings. He hadn't meant to fall asleep, but after they ate the food Kyle brought from the bunkhouse, he had relaxed in the soft leather chair and closed his eyes for what he thought would be only a moment.

A fleeting smile crossed Kate's lips. "This house, it's beautiful." She walked in a small circle, taking in the spacious room and heavy furniture. "Are you sure it's all right that we're in here?"

"If it's not, we'll find out real quick. Ida Mae isn't one to hold back on what she thinks."

Kate sank down on a chair. "This Ida Mae," she asked softly, "how do you know her?"

Jed rubbed the stubble on his jaw. Haltingly, he told Kate of his and Johnny's search for her, Johnny's death, his brush with Sanchez, and how he came to be working at the ranch.

Kate's eyes filled with tears, and she lowered her head when he related how Johnny was killed and where he was buried.

When he finished, Kate wiped her eyes and looked at him. "I'd like to visit his grave someday."

"We can do that," Jed assured her.

"Do you like this Mrs. Greeley?" she asked.

Jed felt his chest tighten. "Kate, it's been a long time. I wasn't with Matilda when she died. I have so many questions I want to ask you. I always thought if I'd been there, maybe I could have done something . . ."

Kate shook her head. "It was an accident, Jed. She was milking. The cow turned sharp and caught her in the side with a horn."

"I . . . I thought she died in childbirth."

"I was the one who found her," Kate continued, her voice

strained. "Mother and I, we helped get her to the house, but she had lost too much blood. Just before she died, she begged Mother to cut the baby from her."

"Cut . . . ?" Jed choked. "Did she?"

Kate nodded. "Yes. He's a beautiful child, Jed."

"He? You said . . . is . . ."

"Yes. Mother bought a nanny goat from the Wilsons. She made up a nurse bottle to feed him. He was so sickly, though, Mother was convinced he wouldn't live." Kate took a deep breath. "That's why she sent word to you that Matilda and her baby had died during childbirth. She said she didn't want you to be worrying about the baby with all you were facing."

Jed stood, his fists clenched. "When she knew the baby would live, why didn't she let me know then?"

Kate averted her eyes and shook her head. "When little Josh—that's what Matilda wanted to name him if the baby was a boy—was about four months old, Mother took sick. She ran a terrible fever and a cough. She couldn't seem to shake it. She was sick most of two months. One morning she didn't get up. I went to her room and found her in bed. She must have died in her sleep. I tried to take care of the baby, but the Ramseys said I wasn't old enough. They took Josh and me to live with them. But I still took care of the baby, along with all of their young'uns."

Kate stood and walked closer to Jed. "When the Ramseys told me that both you and Johnny were killed in some battle, I didn't think I had any choice but to go with them."

Jed reached out and grasped Kate's hand. He tried to control his voice. "My son. What happened to my son? Where is he?"

"As far as I know, he's safe. I was the only one who was taken."

Jed's body trembled, and he closed his eyes for a moment. After he composed himself, he asked softly, "Kate, how was it that the Indians were able to take you captive?"

"The Ramsey children and I were out hoeing in the corn. Little Josh was up by the house playing in the yard. I saw the

Indians just before they set their horses on us. I told the children to run for the house. I stayed and tried to fight them off with my hoe. They grabbed me . . . I don't remember too much after that, other than riding for days. When the Indians that had taken me happened upon another band of Indians, they started fighting. I slid off the horse and ran. When I couldn't run anymore, I found a jumble of rocks and hid. They chased and fought each other until I lost sight of them. After that, they either forgot about me, or there weren't enough of them left to care."

A knock sounded on the door and Cotton pushed his way into the kitchen area. Kyle followed close behind.

"We'd better ride," Cotton said. "Ida Mae's had enough time to come in from town. I don't think she's there."

Jed took a halting breath. "Kyle, could you saddle Star for me? And when you finish, I wonder if you might see to it that Kate has some more fresh water to use."

"I'll get right on it, Jed. But are you sure you're up to riding out? I can go with Cotton."

Jed shook his head. "This is something Cotton and I have to do."

Chapter Twenty-nine

*F*ight it, fight it. Ida Mae kept repeating the words to herself. Despite her gritty determination to stay conscious, she kept drifting into a sea of blackness. She had no recollection of how long she floated in the dark abyss until the dank surroundings, the odor of decaying vegetables, and the sweet, earthy scent of untilled soil made her realize she wasn't in her home, lying in her bed.

She opened her eyes. The darkness caused her heart to pound. Her mind grappled with the details of what had brought her to this unholy place. A faint light came into focus and, with some effort, she rolled onto her stomach and crawled toward it. It was coming from a small space beneath a door. It came back to her now. The root cellar. Her fingers scraped at the packed dirt. The sunlight had progressed into night and the muted glow coming through the narrow slit would be from starlight.

Pushing herself up, she rose to her feet and placed her weight against the door. The resistance of the heavy timbers against the latch confirmed it was locked from the outside. She sank down to her knees. Using her hands, she clawed and scraped at the dirt underneath the door, and before long her fingers were raw and bleeding. In desperation, she stood and felt along the walls, searching for something to dig or pry with.

The light coming from the small opening from underneath the door was becoming brighter. Daylight was fast approaching. If Gerta planned to have Laredo carry out her wishes, he would be returning soon. Ida Mae's hands curled around the handle of some type of tool.

Objects were taking shape in the murky darkness, and she was able to see that it was a small-pronged spade. She returned to the door and placed the prongs under it, prying upward. The wood, decayed from wicked moisture from the ground, crumbled away. Ida Mae worked feverishly, alternating between prying at the timbers and digging away the dirt underneath. The soreness in her side forced her to rest periodically. At last she felt the opening was large enough for her to wriggle through. She dropped to her stomach and squirmed her way under, scraping and skinning her arms and back as she dug her toes into the dirt floor, leveraging her body through the opening. Early dawn was already stealing across the landscape. Ida Mae pulled her knees under her, preparing to stand.

Someone grasped her elbow and yanked her to her feet. Yelping in surprise, she fought to break free. A rough hand covered her mouth, and she felt arms encircle her and pin her against a hard muscular body. She recognized Laredo's voice, his breath hot against the side of her face.

"Don't make me kill you just yet, sweet lady. It messes up my plans. Too bad Schmidt returned a little early. Now we have to change things."

Panic gripped her, and she kicked viciously against his legs.

"Take it easy," Laredo said, his voice gruff. "I can break your neck now, and it will look the same as if it was broken in the crash of your wagon. It's up to you how long you want to live."

Ida Mae's mind raced and rationality set in. The longer she lived, the more chances there would be for escape. She willed her body to relax.

"That's more like it," he said, pulling her back into the cellar.

"Such an idiot!" Gerta's peevish voice followed them into the darkened room. "I told you last night to get rid of her.

Now Thomas is up and looking for you. I won't have her spoiling my plans. Kill her!"

Ida Mae began to struggle. She bit at Laredo's hand and attempted to scream.

Laredo's hands were rough as he flipped her facedown on the ground, his knee pressing into her back and one hand gripping her neck. "For someone who's supposed to have been busted up in a wagon crash and dosed with sleeping powders, she sure can put up a fight."

Ida Mae twisted her head in order to breathe and heard Gerta utter a swearword. "Thomas calls me. I will shut the cellar door and go see what he wants. Finish with that woman and put her body behind the potato bin. Cover it so Carmen doesn't see. Then go to the adobes and come to the house from that direction."

The door closed with a thump, and Ida Mae was painfully aware that she was now alone with Laredo. She felt herself tremble and cursed her weakness.

Laredo's voice was patronizing. "No need to be afraid, Mrs. Greeley. I've been known not to follow orders very well, and you may be worth more alive than dead."

Ida Mae felt Laredo release the pressure on the back of her neck. She took a deep breath, wondering just what Laredo meant. Pain exploded against the side of her head. The darkness returned.

The length of time she was unconscious was lost to Ida Mae. Again, her sense of smell was the first to return, then the awareness that her hands and feet were bound. It was difficult to breathe, and she realized she was covered with a heavy tarpaulin.

Her head throbbed and she lay for a moment, attempting to place her thoughts in order. Laredo must have struck her with his fist. She didn't think she was severely wounded, and if she tried, perhaps she'd still be able to escape.

Her thoughts were fragmented as she explored her options. Gerta's tirade had revealed that Thomas hadn't been in on the plot to poison the watering hole. Although he was in back of the scheme to buy out Portello's in order to put pressure on the small ranchers, the plan didn't involve killing livestock or murder. If she could alert Thomas to her presence, would he come to her aid?

The sound of the cellar door being opened froze Ida Mae's thoughts. Instinctively, she twisted her hands and kicked her legs, trying to free them.

Fresh air wafted over her face as the tarpaulin was yanked back. A quizzical face with large brown eyes stared down at her. In her confusion, it took Ida Mae a second before she realized it was Carlos, Gerta's houseboy.

"Dios mio!" the boy exclaimed. "Mrs. Greeley?"

"Yes, Carlos. Please untie me. I must speak with Mr. Schmidt immediately."

Carlos stood still, uncertain, as his gaze searched the room. He glanced over his shoulder at the doorway, and then turned his frightened countenance back to Ida Mae.

She choked back swearwords and focused on remaining calm. "Carlos, listen to me. Miss Gerta has told the man, Laredo, to kill me. You must help me. Untie me. Quick!"

Carlos continued to hesitate. He backed away from her and turned uncertainly, his gaze shifting around the small room.

"Cuss it all, Carlos. I said untie me!" Ida Mae shouted.

Carlos' eyes grew wide. Tentatively, he approached her and pulled on the rope that bound her hands.

As soon as Ida Mae felt her hands freed, she pushed herself into a sitting position and scrabbled at the thongs binding her legs. Kicking free of the restraints, she looked at Carlos.

"Where are Miss Gerta and Laredo?" she asked.

"La casa," he said, pointing.

"And Mr. Schmidt, where is he?"

Carlos nodded. *"La casa,"* he repeated and pointed again.

Ida Mae stood and then felt herself sink down on one knee. A wave of blackness swept in front of her eyes. She grasped the edge of a wooden crate and waited for a moment. Slowly, she attempted to stand again. Still unsteady, she knew she had to get out of the cellar as quickly as possible.

Taking small steps, Ida Mae made her way to the doorway and leaned against the frame. The yard was bathed in late-afternoon sunlight. The area between the root cellar and the house was filled with hanging laundry. Perhaps that was why Laredo hadn't returned.

Carmen and two young women were busy pinning up the clothing when they noticed her. Dropping the laundry into baskets, they huddled together and stared.

Ida Mae placed her fingertips gently to the side of her head. She felt a large, protruding lump. The intense throbbing made her dizzy. Should she ask Carlos to retrieve her team and wagon and attempt to ride out, or would it be best to alert Thomas to her presence in hopes he would help her?

She felt Carlos brush against her as he slid between her and the doorframe. He quickly ran across the yard and joined the women. Rapid words were exchanged in Spanish, and Ida Mae watched as they all moved hastily toward the adobes. This left her with only the latter option.

A fresh soap smell permeated the air as Ida Mae made her way through the narrow passages between the hanging lines of laundry. She wasn't sure what her next move would be, but her gun was somewhere in the house. If she could find it, someone was going to answer for the ordeal she had been put through. If Thomas was still inside, she would alert him to his sister's intentions. But first she needed her gun. If Thomas showed any indication that he would go along with Gerta's plan, she would deal with him as harshly as she would the others.

As she stood between the lines of flapping sheets, Ida Mae studied the exterior of the house. A small patio led to a side door. Ida Mae remembered that it led into the guest room, where she had once been a happy visitor. Taking a deep breath, she hurried across the patio and tried the door. The handle turned in her hand, and she eased the door open. The room was empty, and Ida Mae stepped inside. She knew that Gerta would more than likely have hidden the gun in her room.

Walking softly across the bare floor, Ida Mae listened at the interior door. Gently pushing it open, she heard voices. They were coming from the front of the house. She stepped into the hallway and saw the large entrance door standing open. Thomas was standing on the wide veranda, speaking to someone in the yard.

Placing her body against the wall, Ida Mae inched her way down the hallway toward Gerta's room. As she neared the entry, Cotton's raspy voice echoed inside the house.

"You know dadburn well what I'm talkin' about," his voice was loud and demanding.

"But I don't," Schmidt replied. "I have not seen Mrs. Greeley since she was here over a week ago. And your accusations against my men are nothing more than whiskey-induced fabrications."

Relief flooded through Ida Mae, and she braced herself against the wall. Another voice spoke, and Ida Mae's heart jumped into her throat. It was Jed's. Jed was here!

"They're not fabrications. Mrs. Greeley's horses are in your corral, and her wagon is parked behind the shed next to it. Now, you have about one minute left to tell us where Mrs. Greeley is." Jed's voice was low, his words measured.

Ida Mae took a deep breath and rushed through the doorway and onto the porch behind Schmidt.

Thomas whirled, a startled expression on his face. "What . . . where did you come from, and what has happened to you?"

Ida Mae ignored Thomas and stumbled across the veranda toward where Jed and Cotton were in the yard. Blackness again threatened her, and she caught her balance against the porch railing.

She turned back to Schmidt. "Gerta told me everything," she wheezed. "She ordered her accomplice, Laredo, to kill me."

"Kill you . . . ? And what do you mean, everything?" he asked, taking a step back.

"About what you've been doing."

"No, no, she's wrong," Schmidt said. "I didn't intend for your Dan to be killed."

Ida Mae stood for a moment, not sure she heard him right.

Then, like a tumbler in a lock, things fell into place. "The Indian raid," she gasped. "It was your men. You killed Dan!"
Her body began to tremble, and she swayed.

Thomas shook his head and held up one hand. "I tried to
make it up to you," he said, his voice pleading. "If only you
had agreed to marry me, I could have made everything right."

"You miserable cur!" Ida Mae shouted.

"Please, Frau Greeley, you must believe me." A small derringer appeared in Thomas' hand and he waved the short-
nosed barrel at her.

An explosion ripped the air. Ida Mae froze as Thomas staggered back, a dark circle spreading across his upper chest.

Ida Mae whirled and saw Jed standing by his horse, placing
another shell into the still-smoking Springfield. A pistol shot
rang out and Cotton, who was still mounted, slumped in his
saddle.

She turned quickly and saw Laredo standing in the yard by
the corner of the porch, his body half-hidden and the pistol
now pointed at Jed. Laredo ducked as Jed swung his rifle toward him and fired. Laredo spun away from the house and
landed face down in the dry alkali dirt.

A high-pitched wail erupted from the open doorway. Gerta
was running across the porch, her fingers pulling at her hair.
She dropped to her knees next to Thomas and continued to sob.
Slowly, like a giant oak crumbling to earth, she fell across his
prone body, gathering him into her arms.

"For you I did it," she cried. "We could have had so much.
I wanted to help. Why did you wish to send me away?"

Ida Mae turned and looked at Cotton, who was lying
across the pommel of his saddle, his face buried against the
neck of his agitated horse, his fingers clutching its mane as
the horse danced nervously. She started toward him when
her gaze shifted to Jed, and she gasped. Joe was standing behind Jed.

Jed's eyes narrowed at Ida Mae's expression. He threw
the empty rifle aside while twisting his body sideways and

drawing his pistol. Dropping to one knee, he leveled it at the nervous wrangler.

"Don't shoot," Joe yelled, raising his hands. "I don't have a gun."

"Keep your hands up," Jed ordered from his crouched position.

"Thundering blazes," Joe stammered, "are you going to kill us all?"

"Only if I have to," Jed replied.

"Ida Mae," Jed called over his shoulder. "Take Cotton's reins and get on my horse. Lead his horse and follow me."

Jed rose from his position and approached Joe. "Now, you're going to walk us out of here. I'll be right behind you with my gun pointed at your head. If any of the vaqueros make a move to stop us, or I see anything I think is suspicious, your head will explode like a melon. So I advise you to tell them to let us pass freely." Jed paused for a moment. "Do you understand me?" he demanded when Joe didn't respond.

"Sh . . . sure," Joe quickly said.

"Good."

Ida Mae started down the steps when she heard Jed shout.

"Get down!"

Before Ida Mae could react, a gunshot reverberated against her eardrums. She lurched down the remaining steps and turned to look back.

Gerta was standing next to Thomas' prone body, clutching his small derringer in both hands and pointing it directly at Ida Mae. "You . . . you are the one to blame for all this." Her voice gurgled as she slowly sank to her knees. The derringer dropped from her hand, and she fell forward across the porch.

"I sure hated to do that," Cotton said, his pistol gripped in his bloody hand. He leaned forward, clutching at his side. "Now, will you quit yer palaverin', boy, and get us the heck home?"

"I'm on it, boss," Jed answered, swinging his pistol back at Joe.

Ida Mae ran to Star and quickly mounted. She urged the mare next to Cotton's horse and grabbed the reins. Glancing back at the porch, she saw Thomas struggling to sit upright. His face was a mask of confusion. A wave of nausea hit her. All this time she'd thought they were her friends.

Her hand shook as she held it out to Cotton. "Give me your gun," she said, wresting the pistol from him. "I've lost mine somewhere, and Jed needs his back covered."

Ida Mae kept a sharp eye toward the adobes as they moved past them. The women and children who normally bustled about were nowhere to be seen. A furtive movement alongside one of the adobes proved to be a young boy, scurrying for safety.

They continued their march for another mile beyond the vaqueros' small homes. Jed's voice sounded weary when he instructed Joe to stop.

"You can go back now," he said to Joe. "But I warn you, don't come after us. There's nothing in it for you but more of what's lying back there."

Joe turned to face him. His eyes were filled with apprehension. "Are they all dead?" he asked.

"Thomas could use your help," Ida Mae answered. "I'm not sure about Gerta or Laredo. I'm hoping they're past help," she added quietly.

"I still don't know what caused all that back there," Joe said. "No one told me anything."

"Somehow I find that hard to believe," Jed answered.

Ida Mae watched as Joe started walking back toward Cradle's Peak and then turned to Jed. "Will you help Cotton down? I should look at his wound before we go any farther."

"Nobody's gotta hep me do nothin'," Cotton growled. Grunts and wheezes ground from his lips as he slid from his horse.

Jed took Cotton's elbow and guided him to a shaded boulder.

Kneeling next to Cotton, Ida Mae pulled up his shirt. "He's still bleeding," she said. "We need something to bind it with."

Jed shook off his jacket. "Use my shirt," he said and began removing it.

Ida Mae flinched when she saw the blood-soaked bandage covering his shoulder. "Your shoulder . . . shoulder . . . ," she whispered.

Jed shook his head. "We'll have plenty of time to talk later."

Chapter Thirty

Doubling up on Star, Jed rode behind Ida Mae. He kept one arm around her waist while keeping an eye on Cotton. He wasn't sure if Ida Mae needed the support, but his arm felt good resting there and she didn't object.

"Don't need to fret about me none," Cotton would respond when Jed inquired on how he was holding up. "Been in worse shape and in worse places."

It was well after nightfall before the three riders reached Mission Bridge. Father De La Cruz ushered them inside and directed his housekeeper to bring hot water, medicines, and bandages. Jed and Ida Mae waited anxiously by the door while Father De La Cruz and his housekeeper worked on Cotton. At last the priest turned to them.

"Your foreman is in serious condition. The blood loss he suffered is significant. However, the bullet was lodged in muscle tissue just under the skin, and Señora Gomez was able to remove it."

The priest paused, wiping his hands diligently on a white cloth. "Unless unforeseen complications set in," he continued, "and with the grace of God, he should make a full recovery." Father De La Cruz glanced up at Ida Mae. "I believe it would be prudent to leave him here in the care of my housekeeper for a while. We also have enough space here for the both of you to lodge with us overnight."

"Thank you, Father," Ida Mae answered.

Jed felt Ida Mae's hand slip into his, tugging gently as she led him into the darkened courtyard.

She turned to him and touched the bandaged shoulder. "We've plenty of time to talk now. Tell me what happened."

Jed's fingers tightened around her hand. It felt warm, firm, and intimate. "You go first. My story will take a bit longer."

In the darkness he felt her move next to him, her body touching his, the side of her face resting lightly against his chest.

Jed felt his pulse quicken and, releasing her hand, he placed his arms around her, holding her close.

"You and Cotton were right," Ida Mae said, her voice almost a whisper. "Thomas was in cahoots with some investors in Houston. They were the ones who wanted to control the grazing and take over the rangeland. It was Gerta who wanted me dead. I think she envisioned herself as some kind of cattle baroness. It wouldn't have mattered who Thomas wanted to marry; Gerta would've stopped at nothing to prevent it."

Ida Mae's body trembled next to him, and he felt her hands slide around his waist, clutching him tightly. He bent and kissed her gently on the forehead.

Her face lifted, and his lips met hers, savoring the eagerness he sensed in them.

Aware of their surroundings, Jed slowly released his embrace and kissed her again, letting his lips linger gently. He drew back and gazed at her for a moment.

"I found out something this morning," he said, his voice quiet. "I have a son."

"The woman. She was your sister?" Ida Mae pulled away and peered at his face.

"Yes. It was Kate. I left her at the ranch with Kyle. But before I left, she said my wife gave birth just before she died."

"And your son, where is he?"

"He's still with the people where Kate was before she was taken. After I see you to the ranch, I'm going after him."

Ida Mae's fingers dug into Jed's arms, and he flinched. "Ouch!" he said. "Why'd you do that?"

"Not without me, you won't. I don't want to ever have to stand and watch you ride away from me again."

Jed laughed softly. "Why, ma'am, I do believe you're proposing to me."

She reached up and placed her hands behind his head, pulling his face close to hers. "That's right, McCabe, and you don't even have to pull off your boots to accept."